A Sam & Friends Mystery

Book Four

Witches' Brew

MARY LABATT • **JO RIOUX**

KIDS CAN PRESS

7 |1¹
16 ⁹⁵

Kids Can Press acknowledges the financial support of the Government of Ontario, through
the Ontario Media Development Corporation's Ontario Book Initiative; the Ontario Arts
Council; the Canada Council for the Arts; and the Government of Canada, through the
BPIDP, for our publishing activity.

Published in Canada by
Kids Can Press Ltd.
25 Dockside Drive
Toronto, ON M5A 0B5

Published in the U.S. by
Kids Can Press Ltd.
2250 Military Road
Tonawanda, NY 14150

www.kidscanpress.com

Based on the book *Strange Neighbors* by Mary Labatt

Edited by Karen Li
Designed by Kathleen Gray and Rachel Di Salle

CM 11 0 9 8 7 6 5 4 3 2 1
CM PA 11 0 9 8 7 6 5 4 3 2 1

The hardcover edition of this book is smyth sewn casebound.
The paperback edition of this book is limp sewn with a drawn-on cover.
Manufactured in Buji, Shenzhen, China, in 10/2010 by WKT Company

Library and Archives Canada Cataloguing in Publication

Labatt, Mary, 1944–
Witches' brew / written by Mary Labatt ; illustrated by Jo Rioux.

(A Sam & friends mystery ; bk. 4)
ISBN 978-1-55453-472-2 (bound). ISBN 978-1-55453-473-9 (pbk.)

I. Rioux, Jo-Anne II. Title. III. Series: Labatt, Mary, 1944– . Sam & friends mystery ; bk. 4.

PS8573.A135W57 2011   jC813'.54   C2010-904764-8

Kids Can Press is a CORUS™ Entertainment company

To my family — M.L.

To all my friends — J.R.

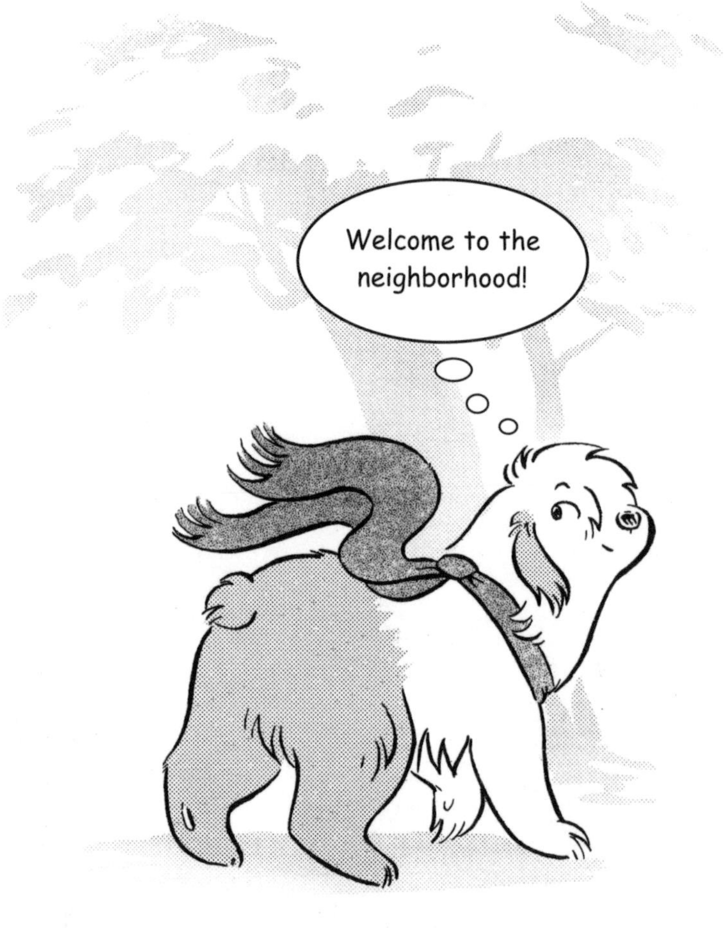
Welcome to the
neighborhood!

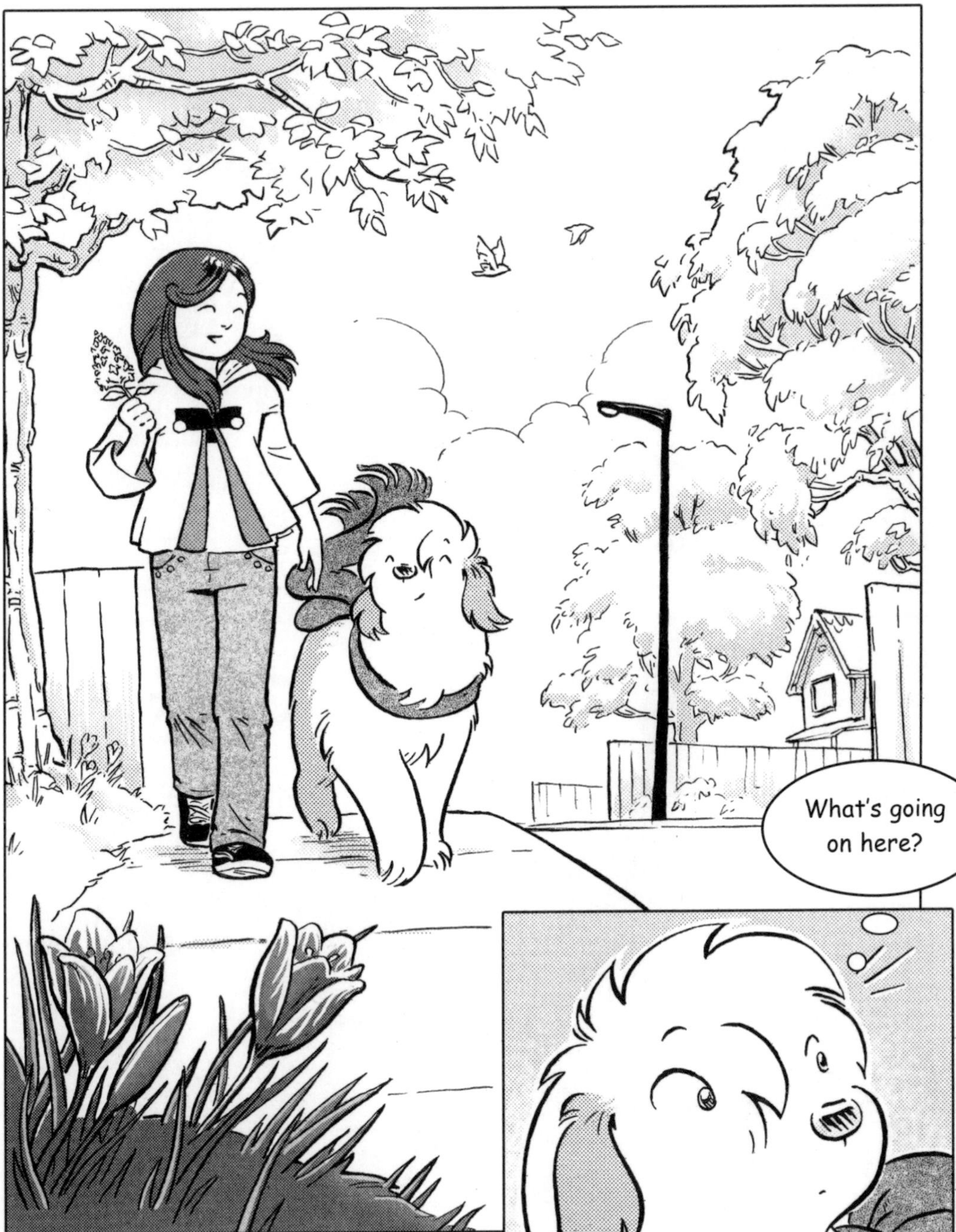
What's going on here?

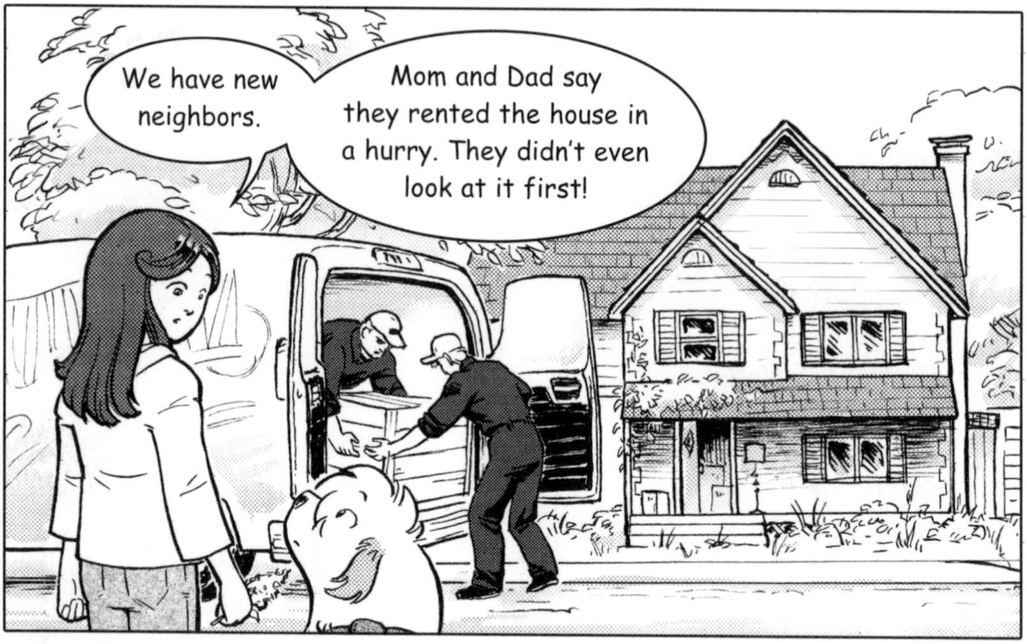
We have new neighbors.
Mom and Dad say they rented the house in a hurry. They didn't even look at it first!

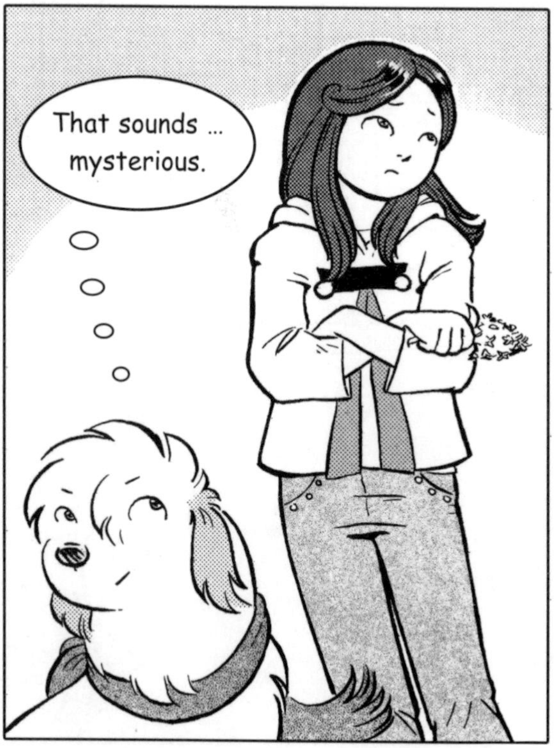
That sounds ... mysterious.

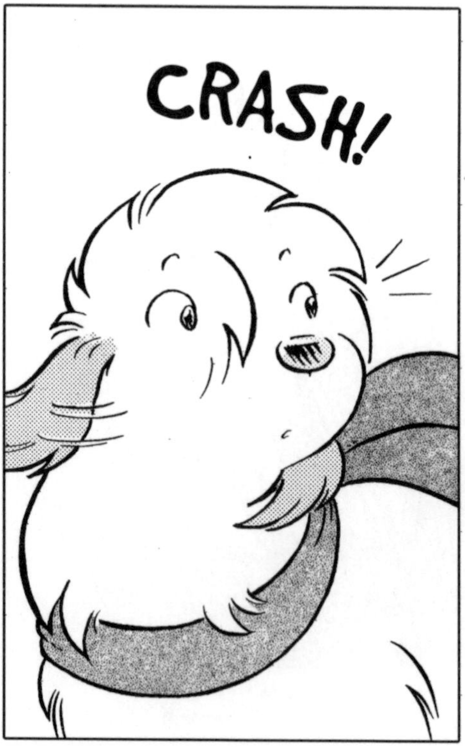
CRASH!

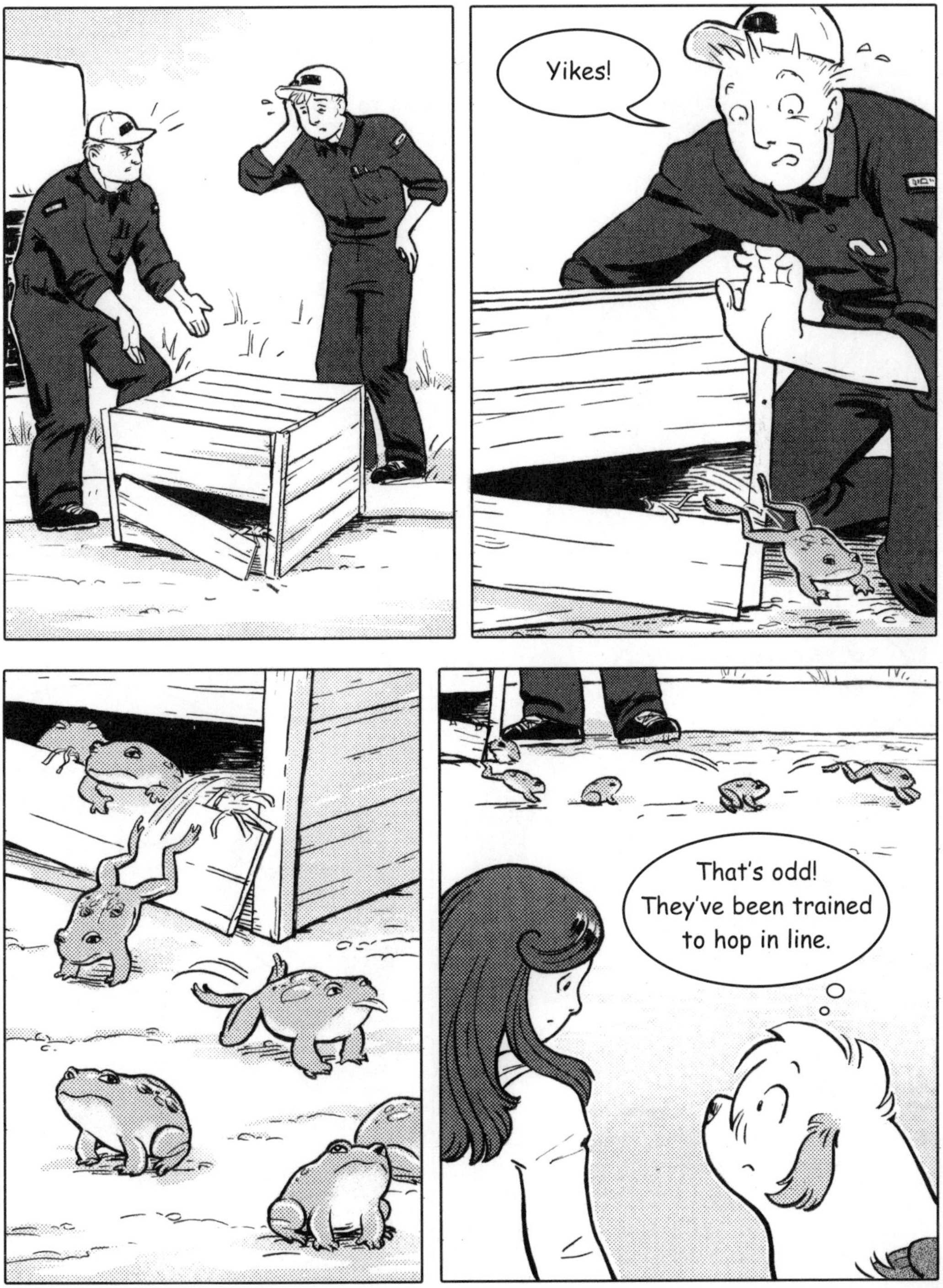
Yikes!
That's odd! They've been trained to hop in line.

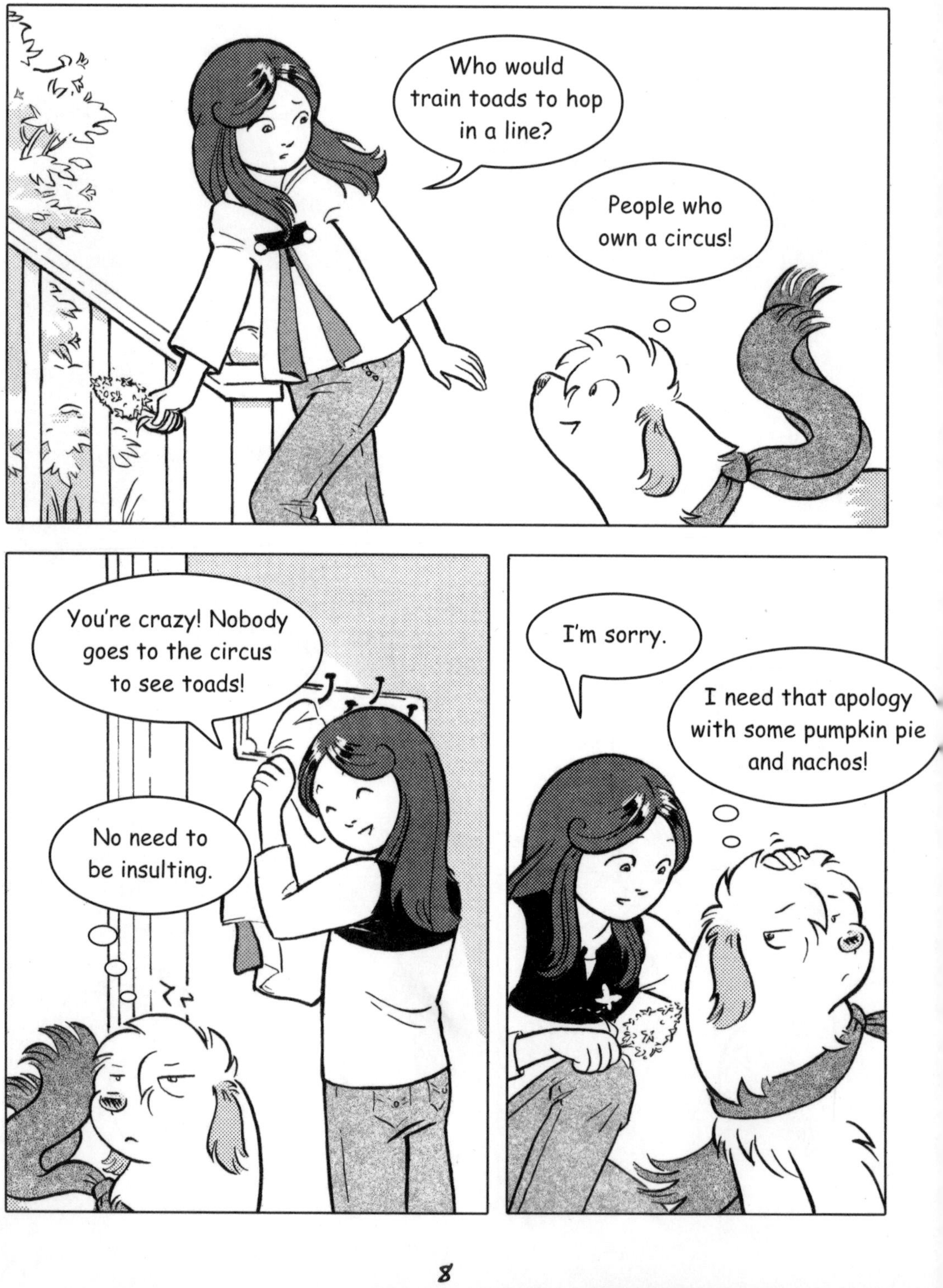
Who would train toads to hop in a line?
People who own a circus!
You're crazy! Nobody goes to the circus to see toads!
No need to be insulting.
I'm sorry.
I need that apology with some pumpkin pie and nachos!

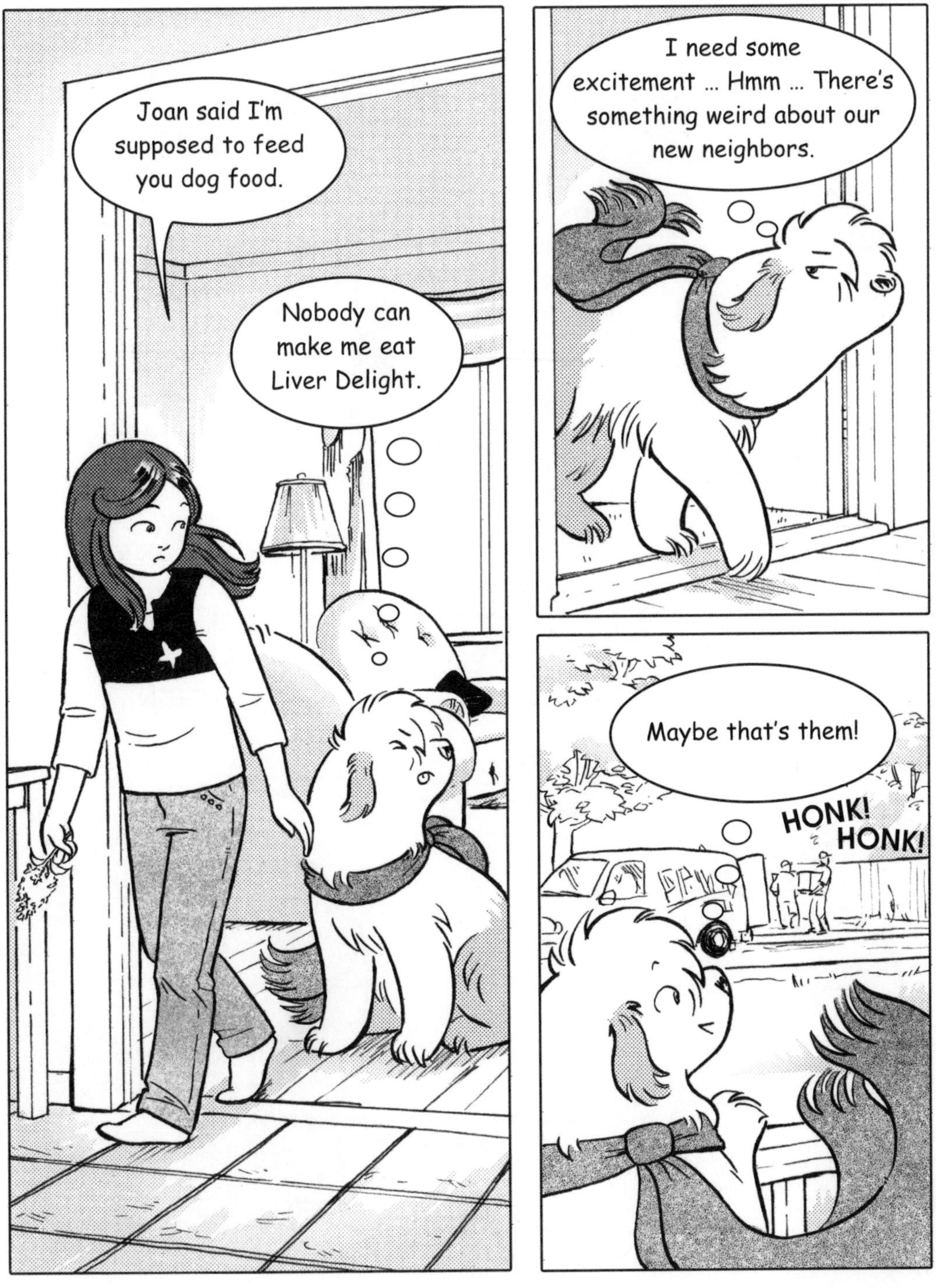
Joan said I'm supposed to feed you dog food.
Nobody can make me eat Liver Delight.
I need some excitement ... Hmm ... There's something weird about our new neighbors.
Maybe that's them!
HONK! HONK!

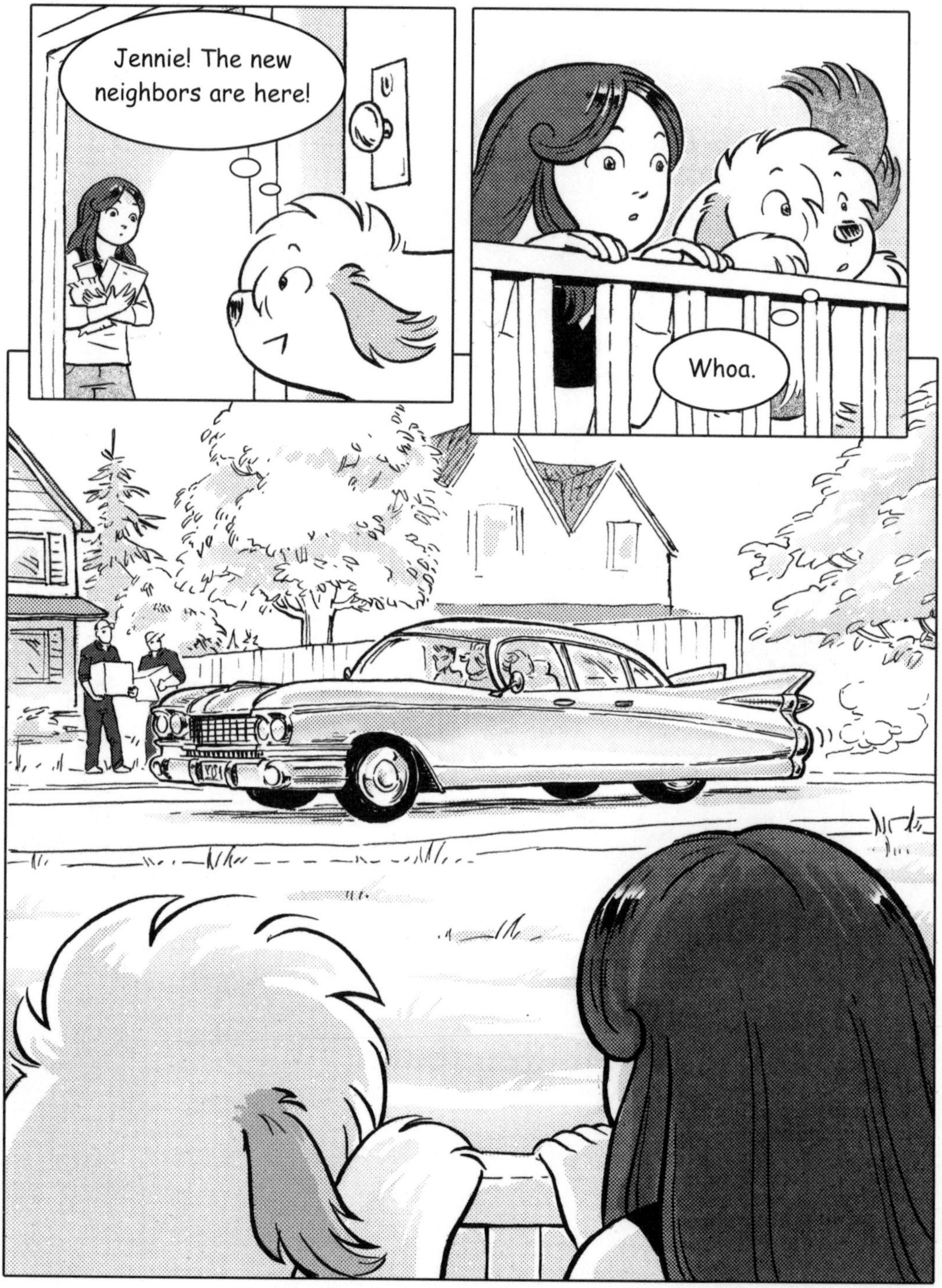
Jennie! The new neighbors are here!
Whoa.

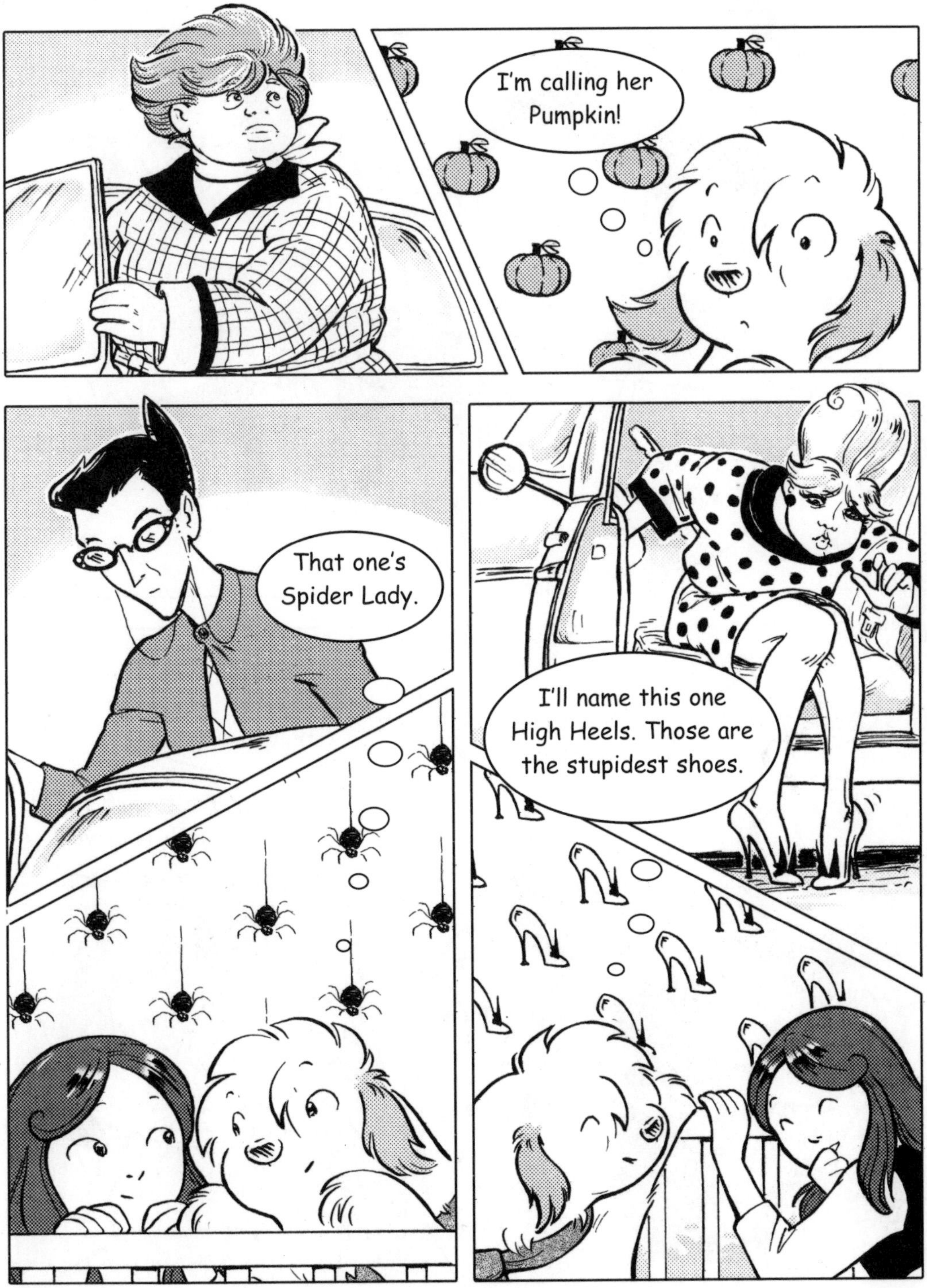
I'm calling her Pumpkin!
That one's Spider Lady.
I'll name this one High Heels. Those are the stupidest shoes.

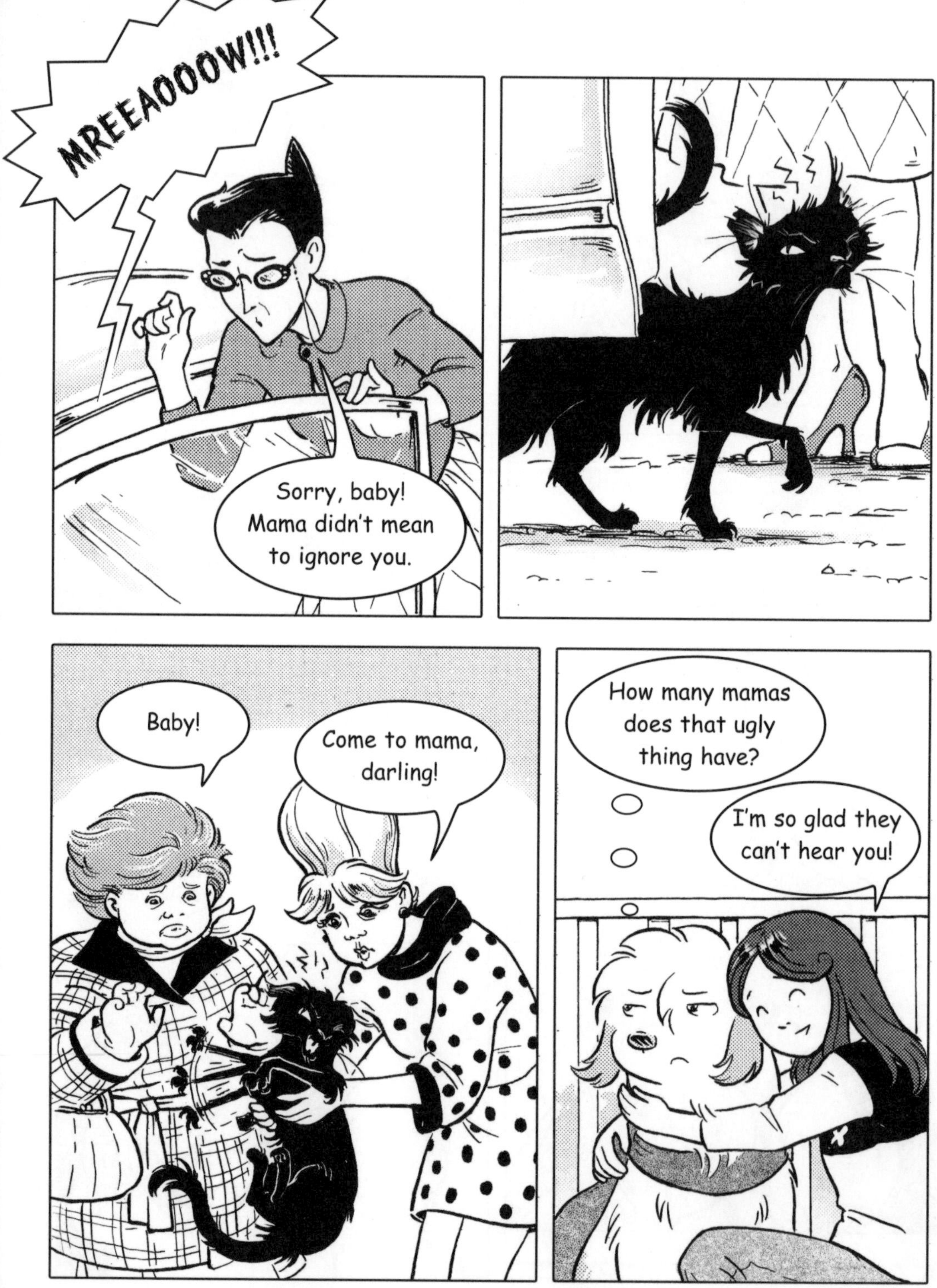

MREEAOOOW!!!
Sorry, baby! Mama didn't mean to ignore you.
Baby!
Come to mama, darling!
How many mamas does that ugly thing have?
I'm so glad they can't hear you!

The next day ...

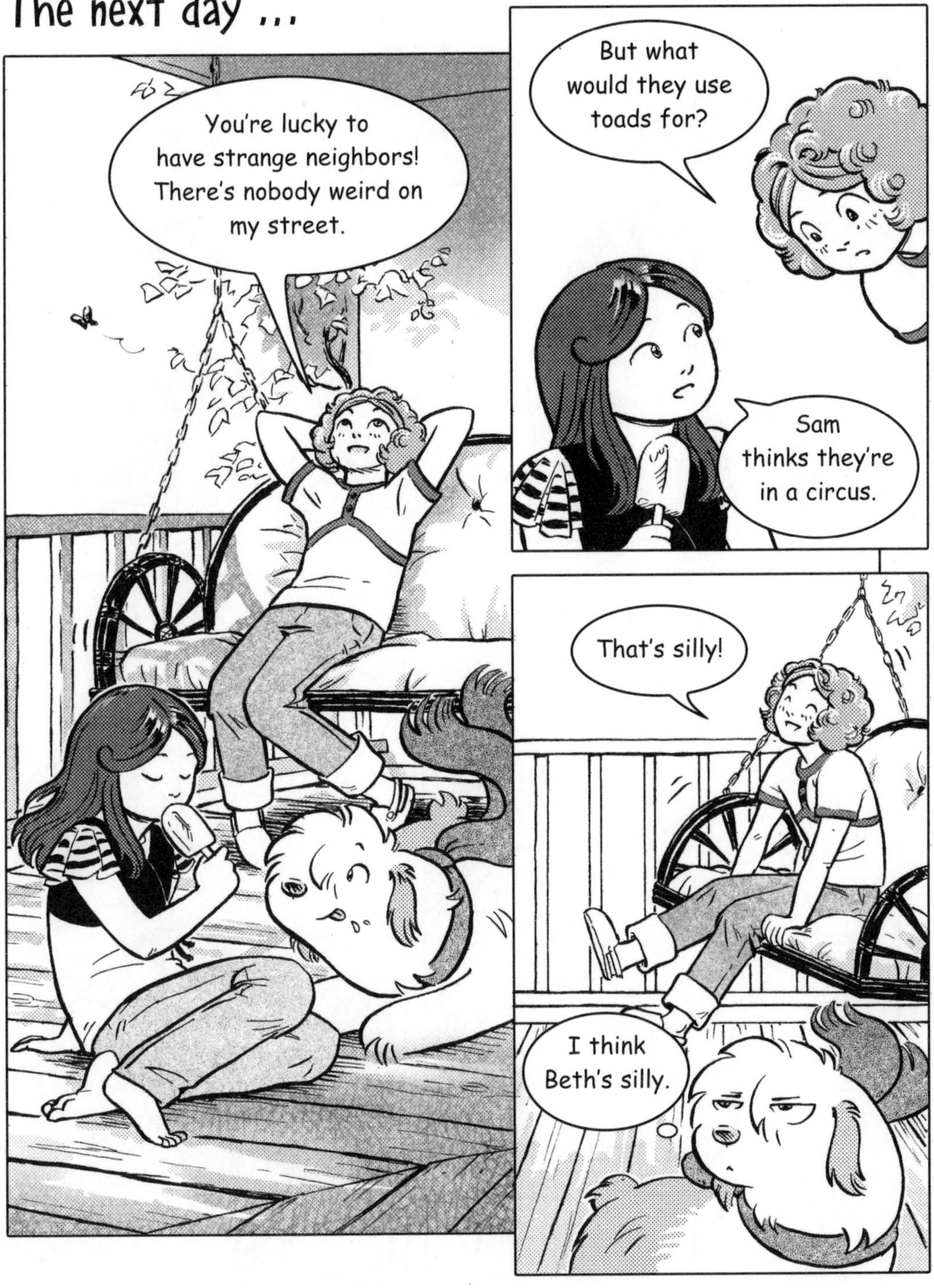
You're lucky to have strange neighbors! There's nobody weird on my street.
But what would they use toads for?
Sam thinks they're in a circus.
That's silly!
I think Beth's silly.

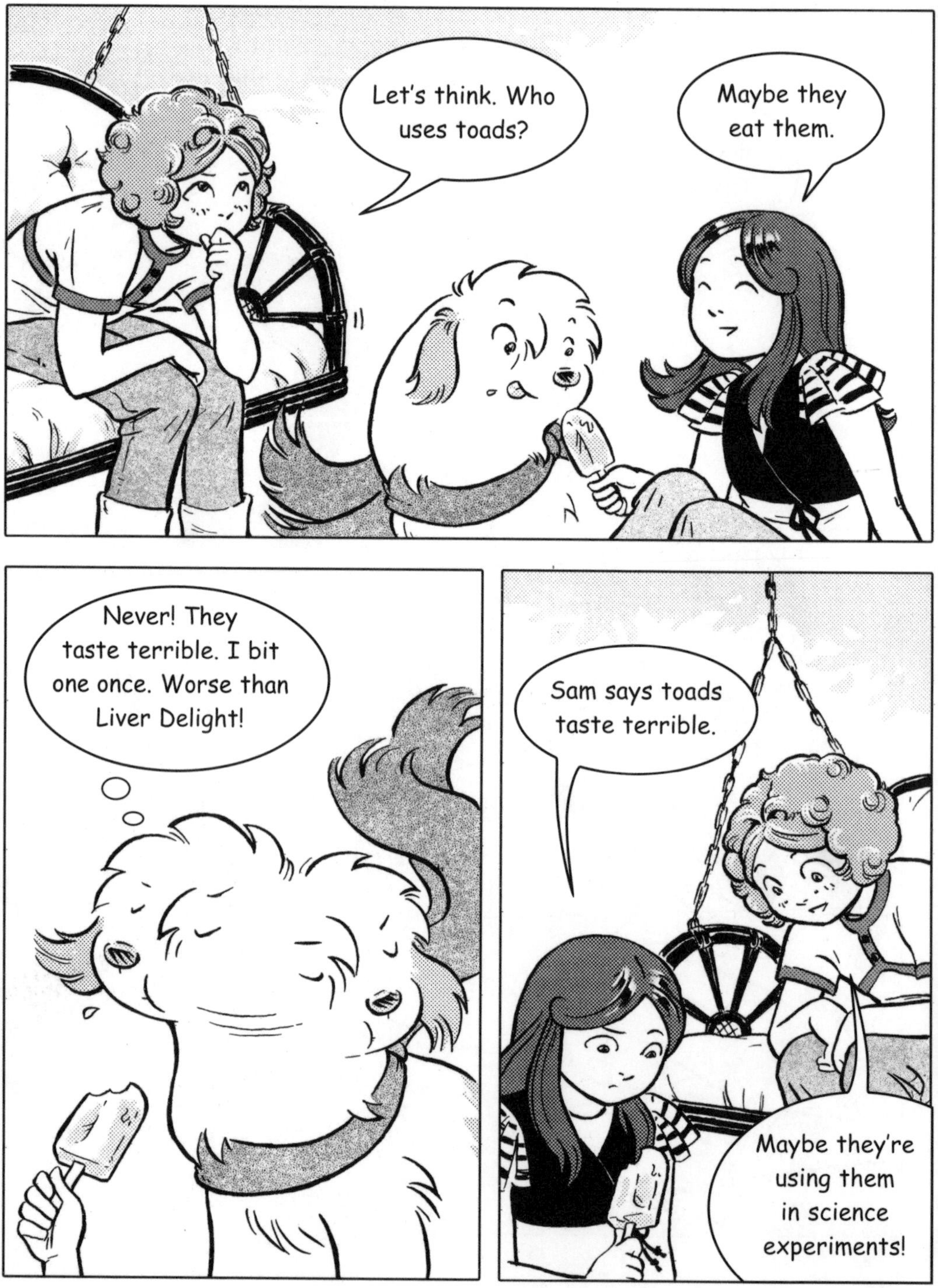
Let's think. Who uses toads?
Maybe they eat them.
Never! They taste terrible. I bit one once. Worse than Liver Delight!
Sam says toads taste terrible.
Maybe they're using them in science experiments!

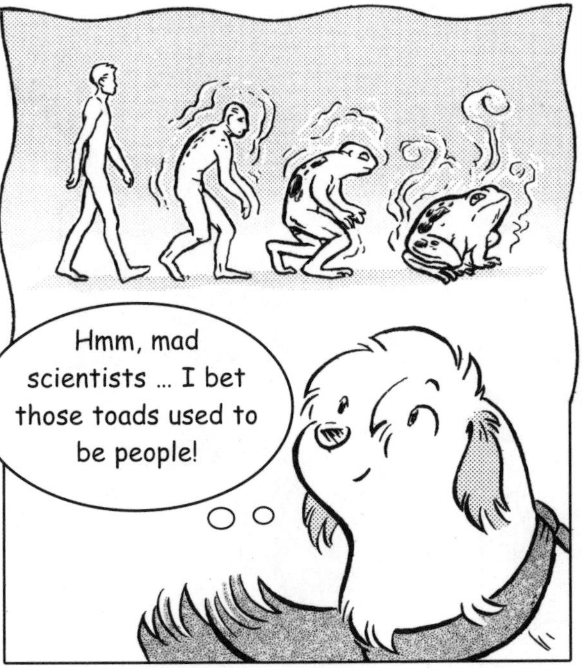
Hmm, mad scientists ... I bet those toads used to be people!

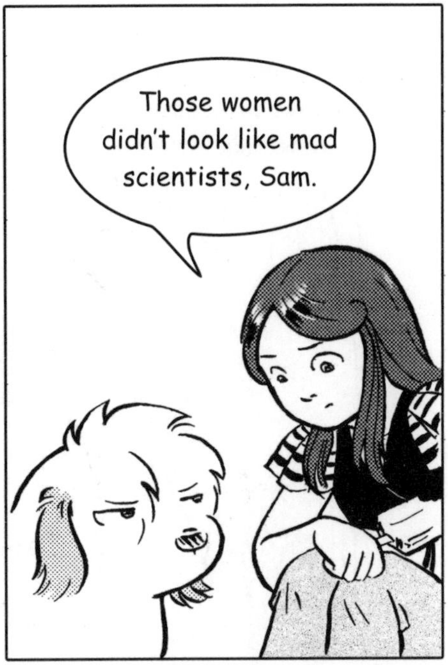
Those women didn't look like mad scientists, Sam.

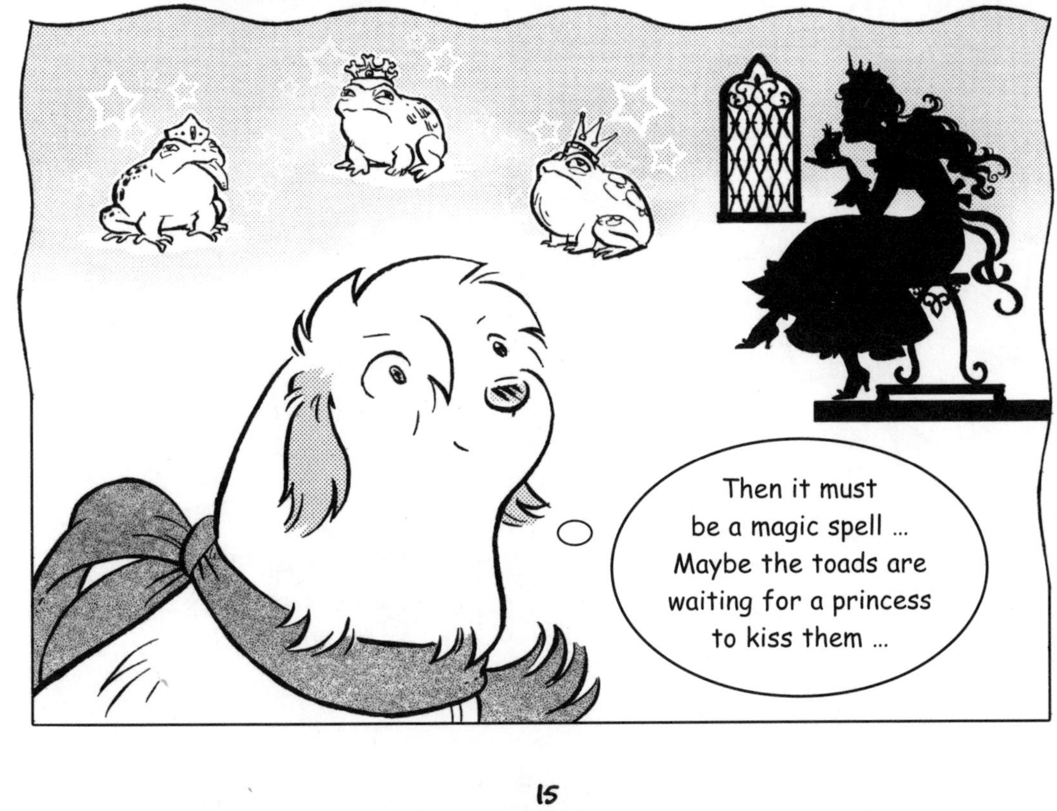
Then it must be a magic spell ... Maybe the toads are waiting for a princess to kiss them ...

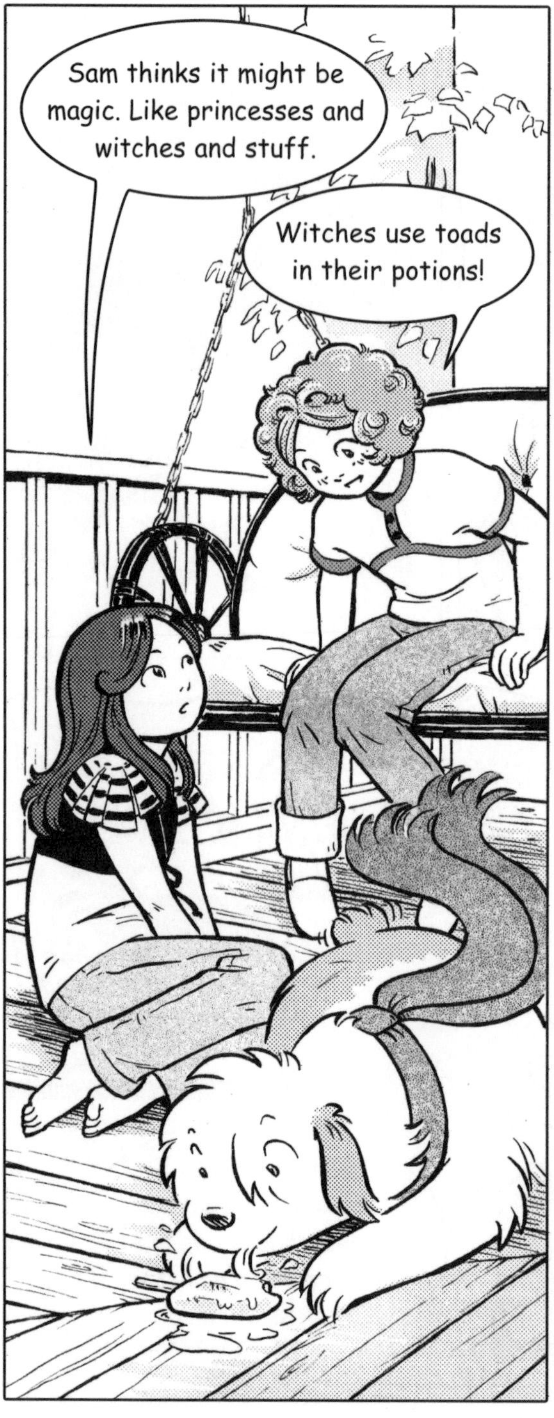
Sam thinks it might be magic. Like princesses and witches and stuff.
Witches use toads in their potions!
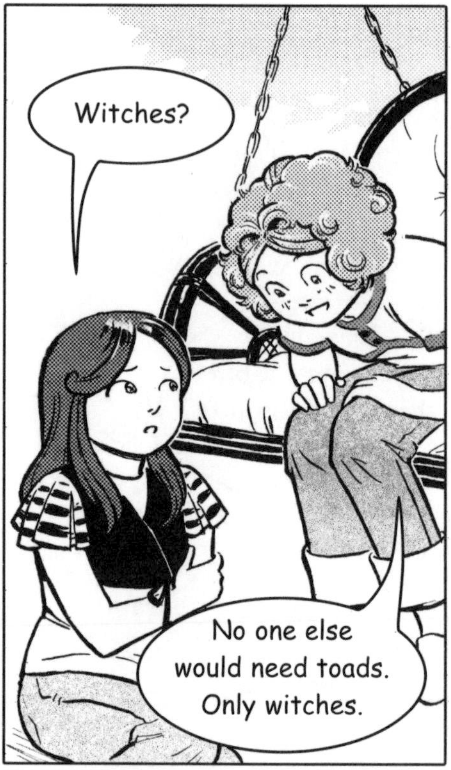
Witches?
No one else would need toads. Only witches.
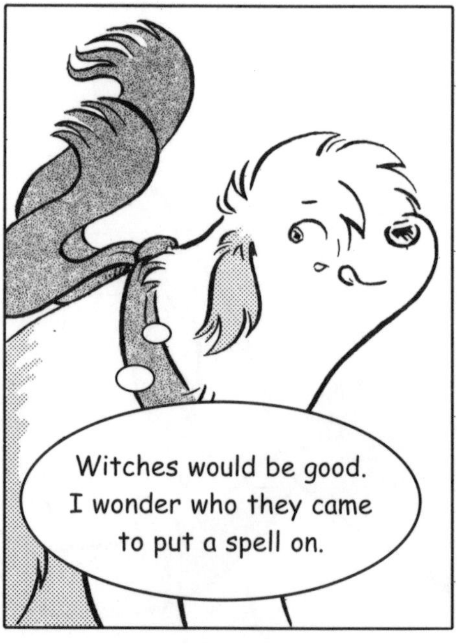
Witches would be good. I wonder who they came to put a spell on.

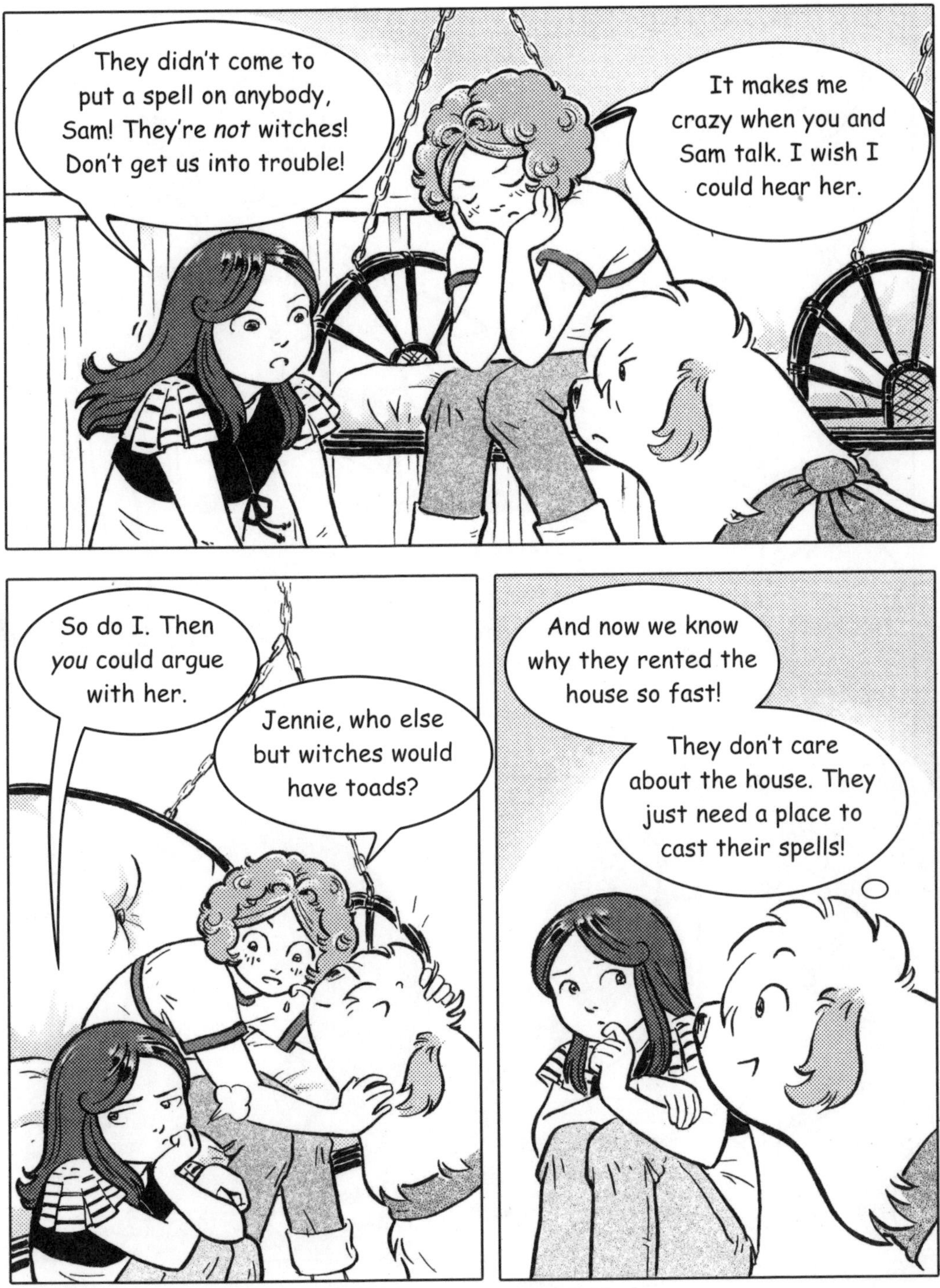
They didn't come to put a spell on anybody, Sam! They're *not* witches! Don't get us into trouble!
It makes me crazy when you and Sam talk. I wish I could hear her.
So do I. Then *you* could argue with her.
Jennie, who else but witches would have toads?
And now we know why they rented the house so fast!
They don't care about the house. They just need a place to cast their spells!

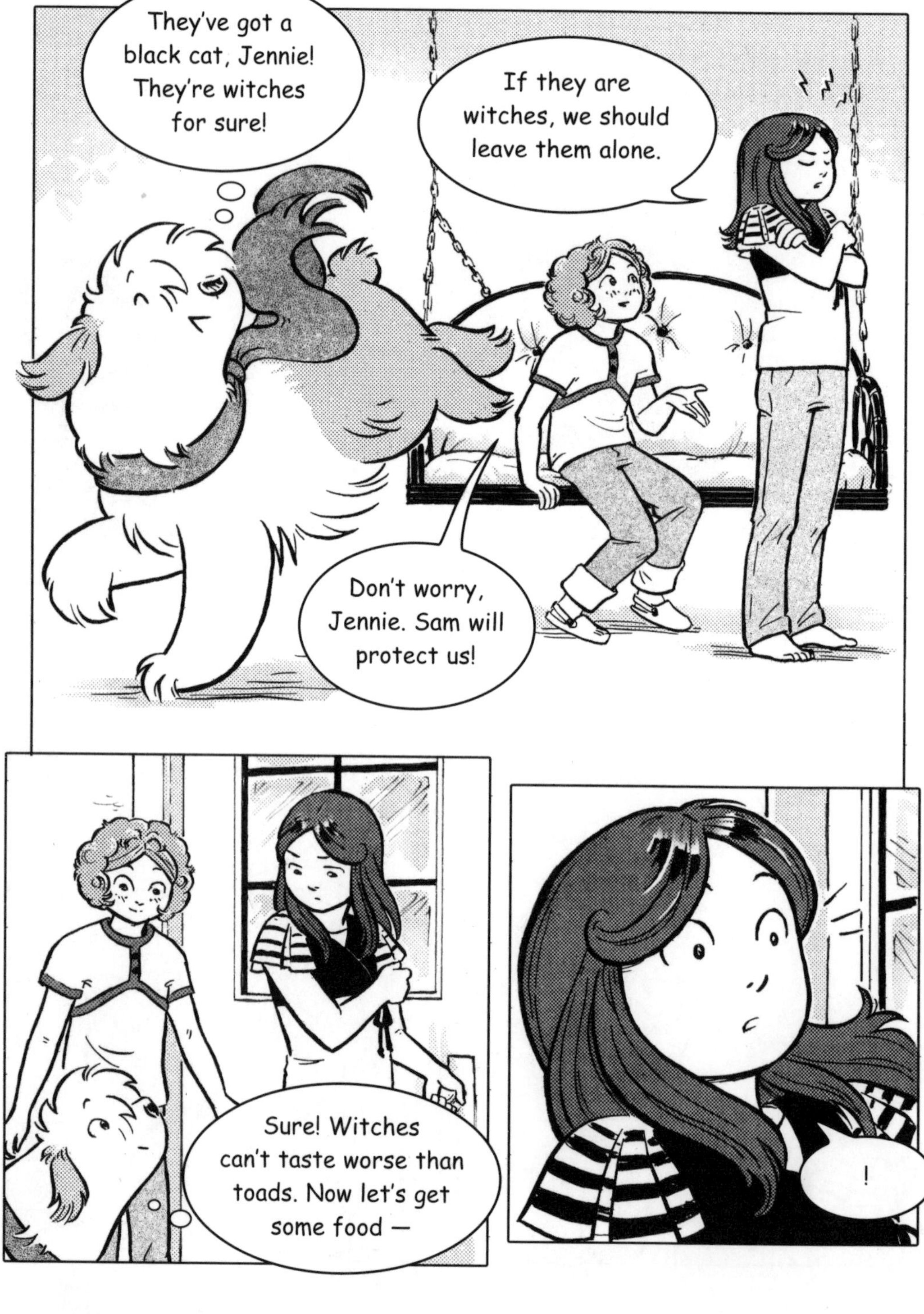
They've got a black cat, Jennie! They're witches for sure!
If they are witches, we should leave them alone.
Don't worry, Jennie. Sam will protect us!
Sure! Witches can't taste worse than toads. Now let's get some food –
!

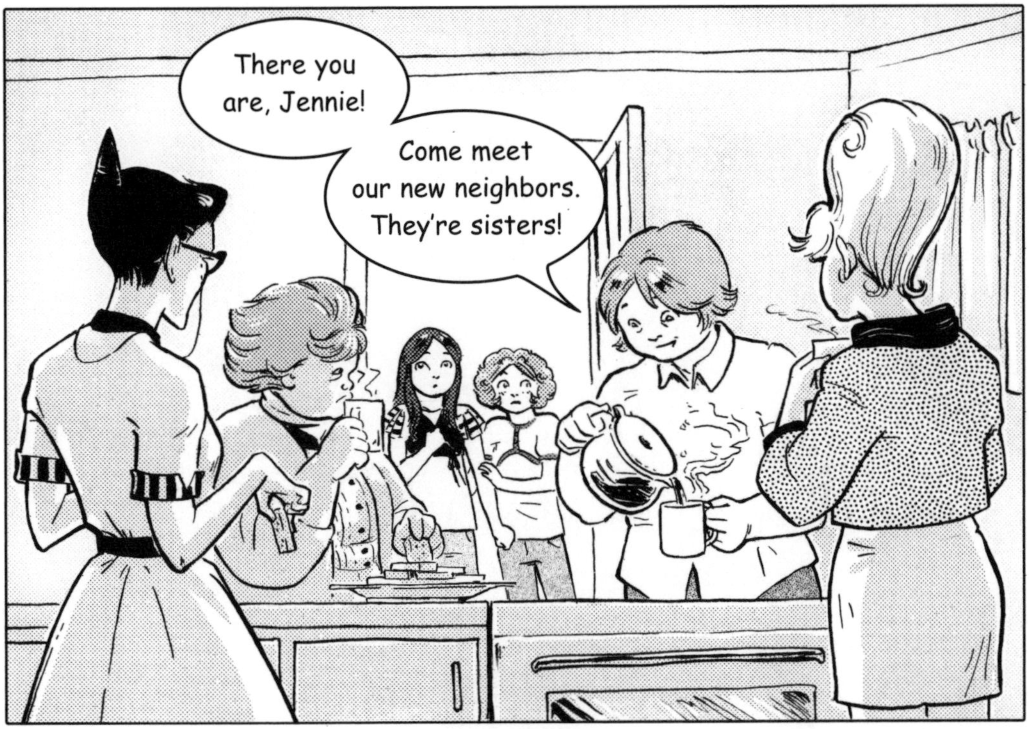
There you are, Jennie!
Come meet our new neighbors. They're sisters!

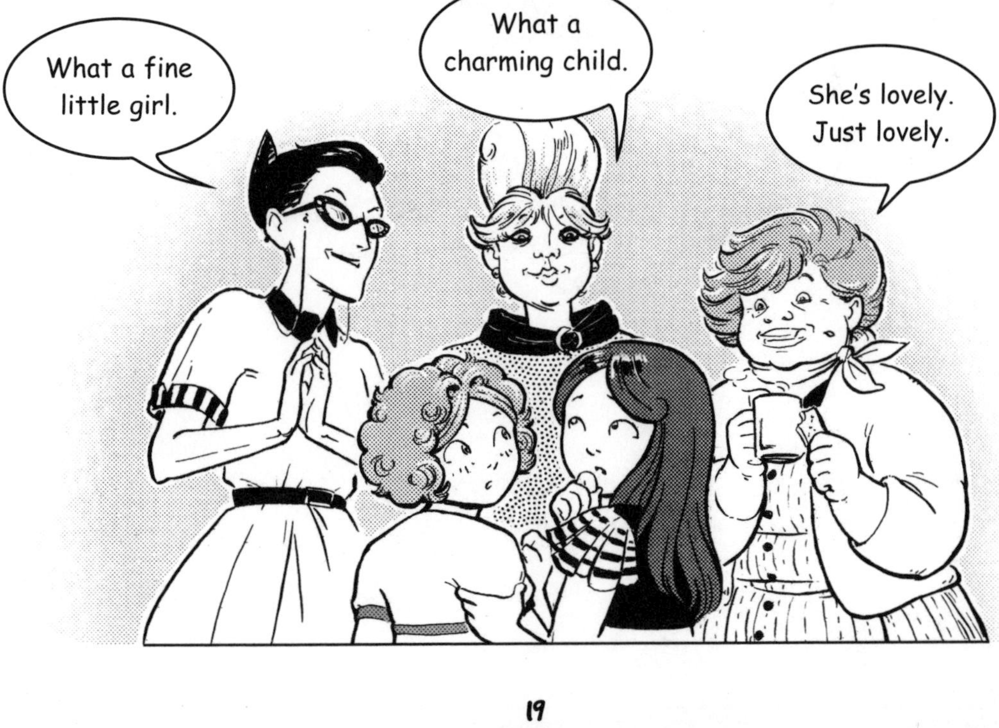
What a fine little girl.
What a charming child.
She's lovely. Just lovely.

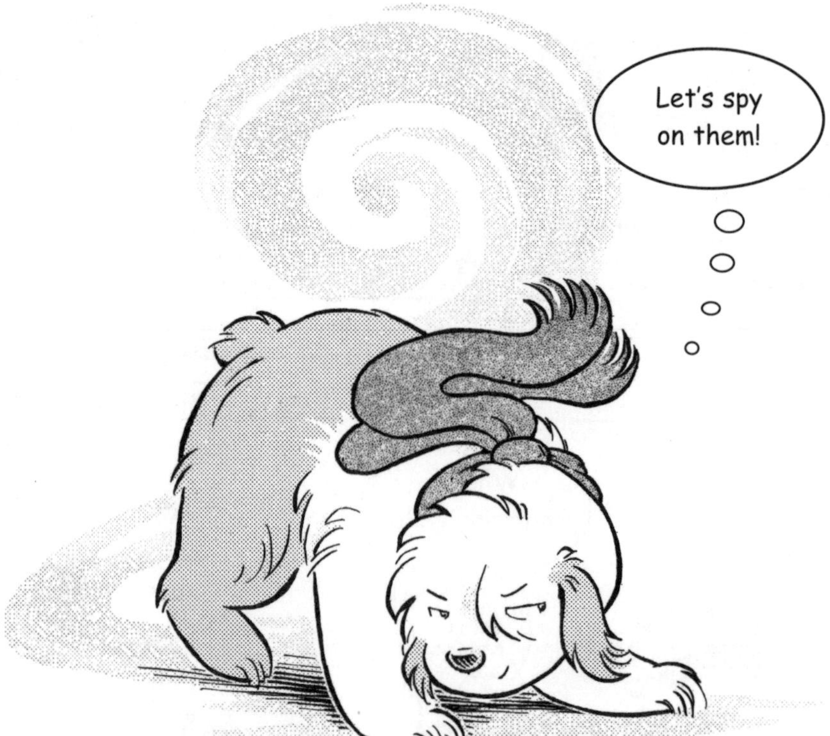
Let's spy on them!

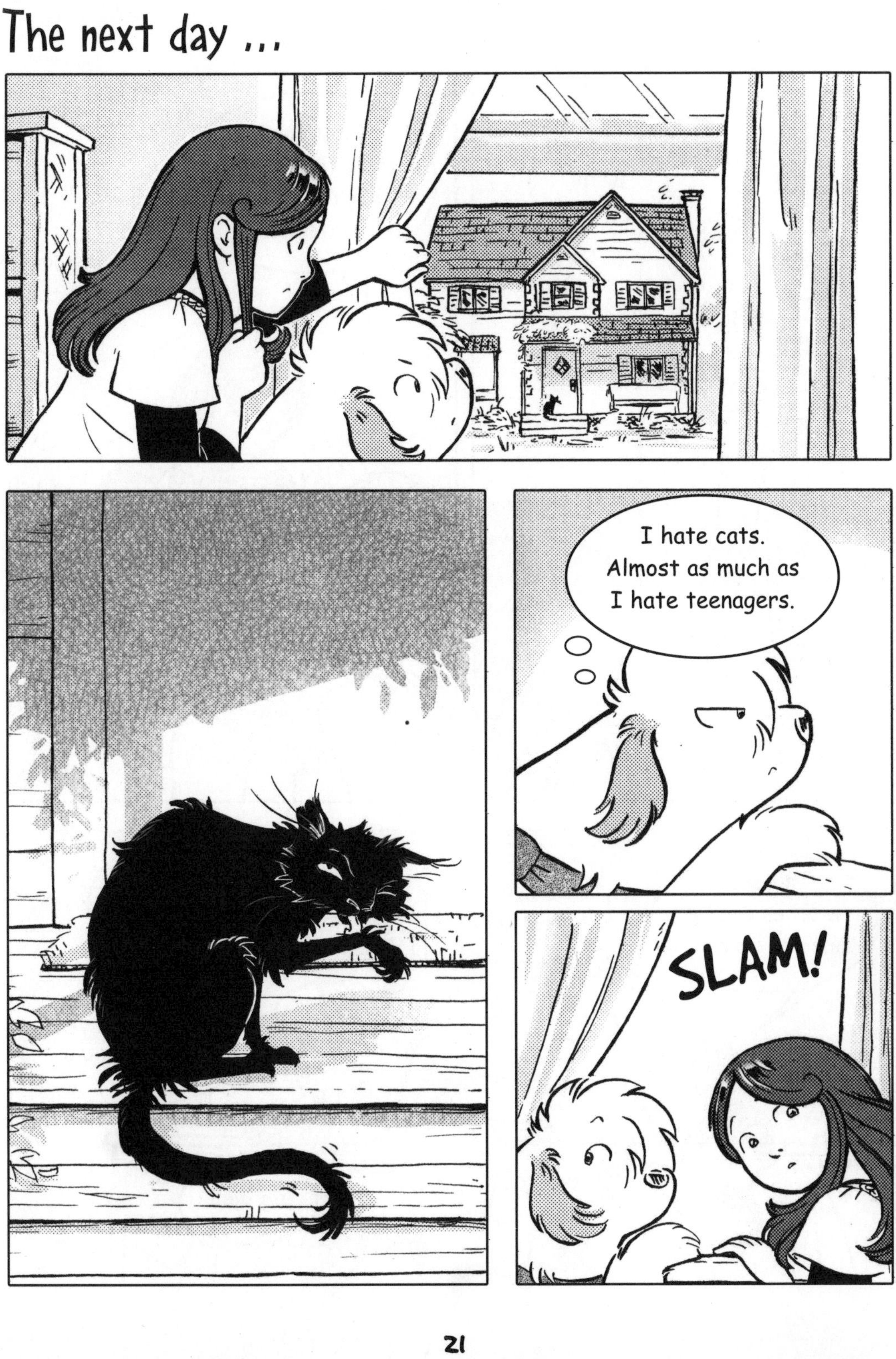
The next day ...
I hate cats.
Almost as much as
I hate teenagers.
SLAM!

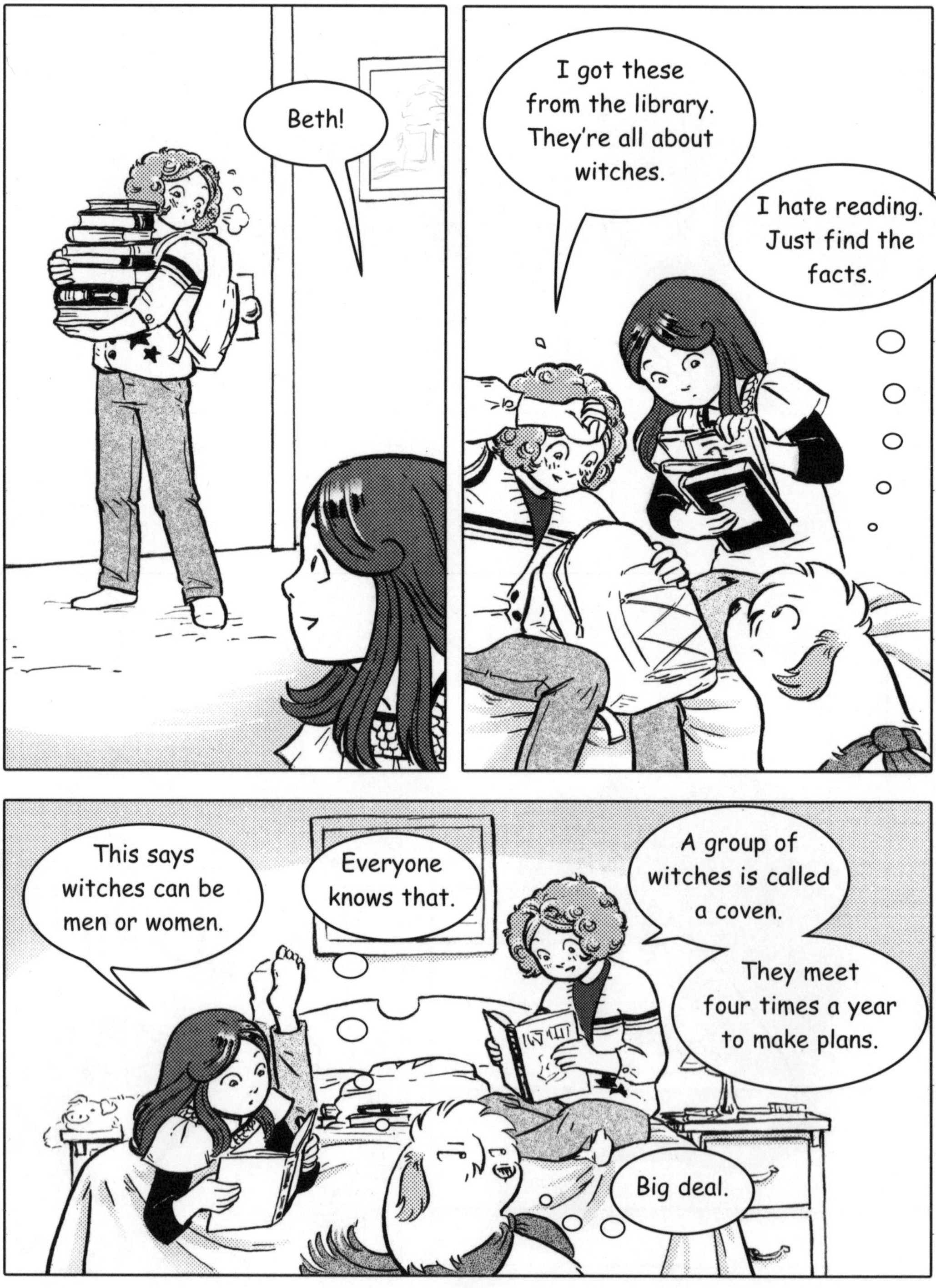
Beth!
I got these from the library. They're all about witches.
I hate reading. Just find the facts.
This says witches can be men or women.
Everyone knows that.
A group of witches is called a coven.
They meet four times a year to make plans.
Big deal.

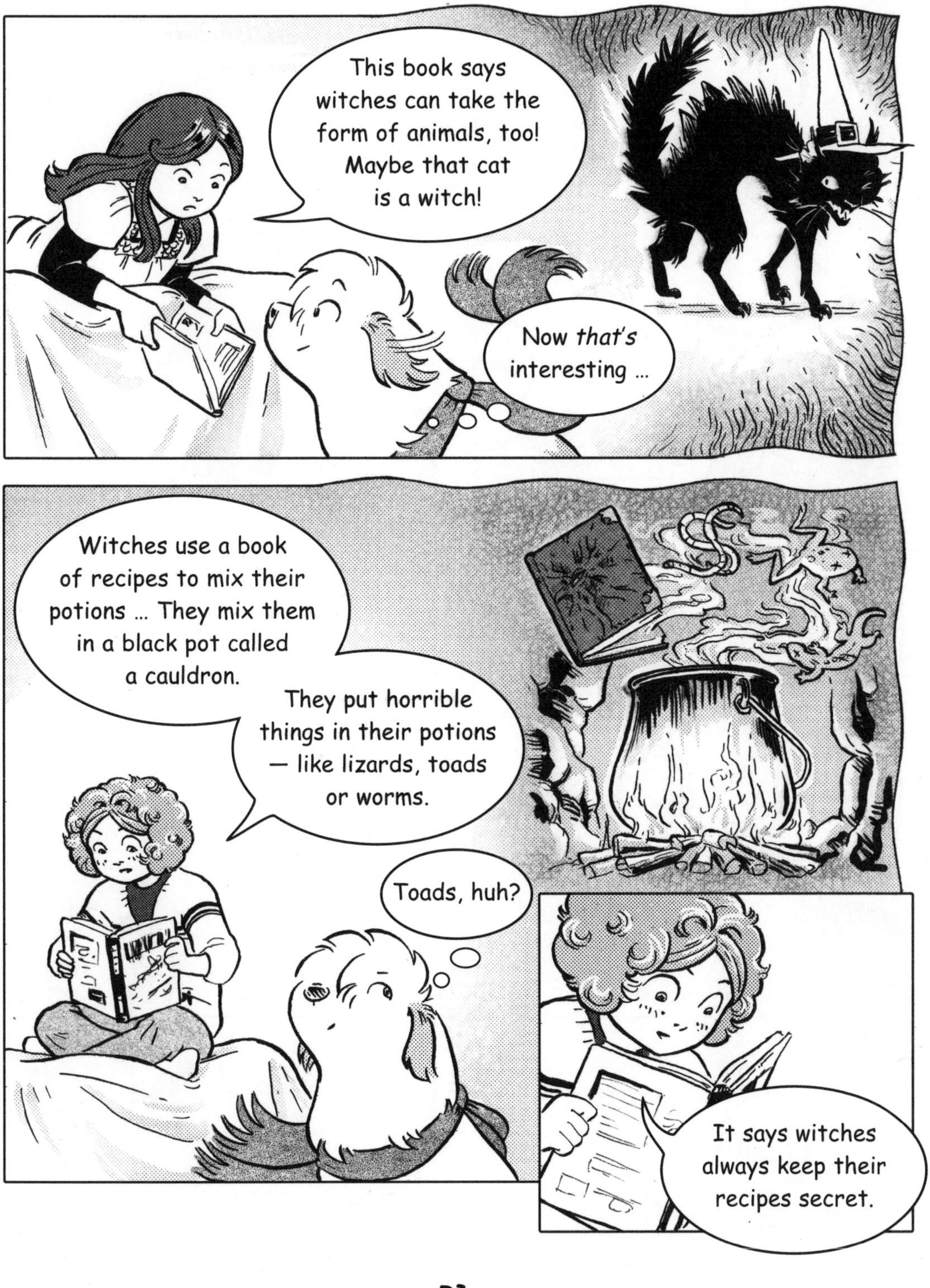
This book says witches can take the form of animals, too! Maybe that cat is a witch!
Now *that's* interesting ...
Witches use a book of recipes to mix their potions ... They mix them in a black pot called a cauldron.
They put horrible things in their potions — like lizards, toads or worms.
Toads, huh?
It says witches always keep their recipes secret.

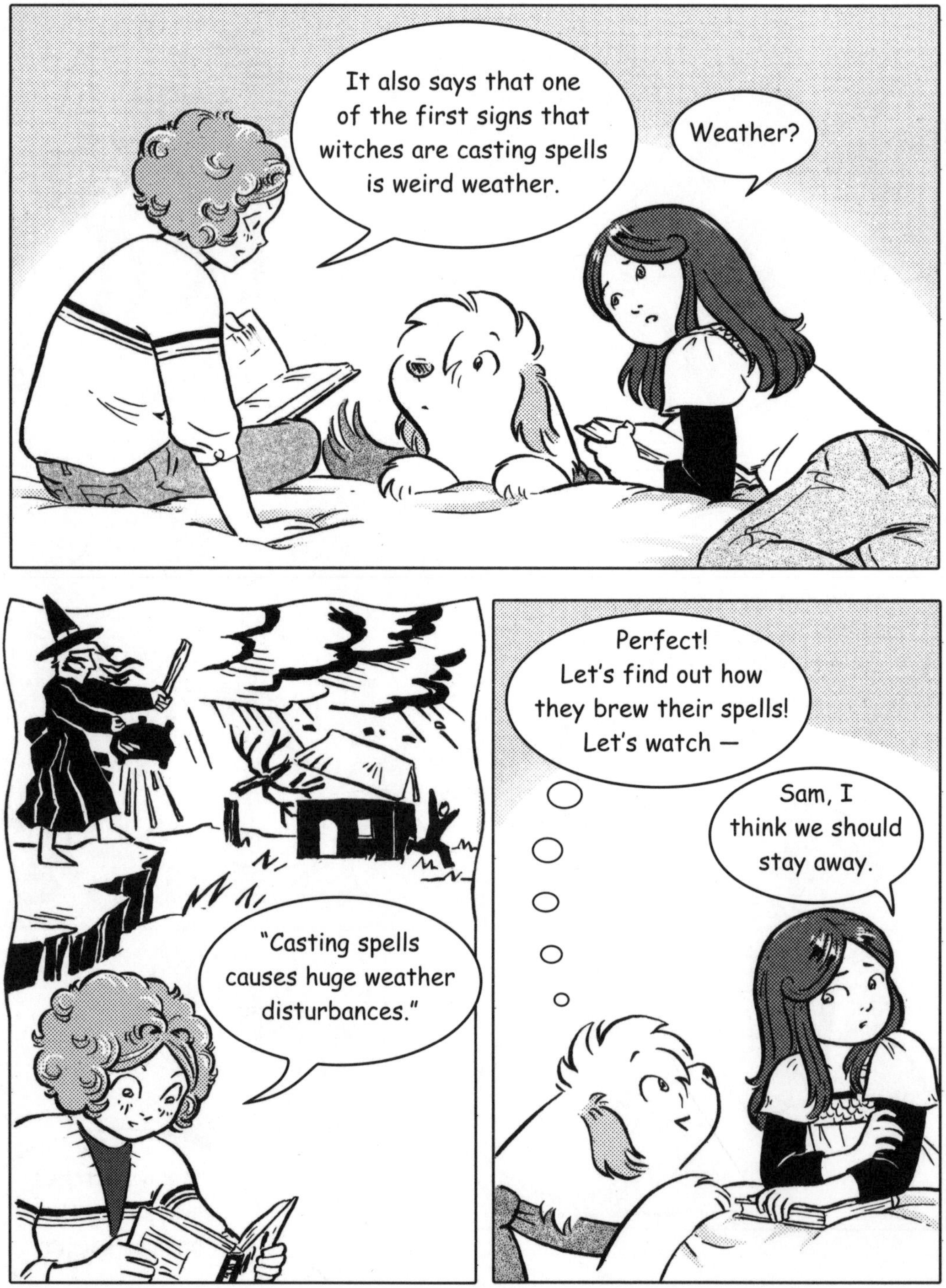
It also says that one of the first signs that witches are casting spells is weird weather.
Weather?
"Casting spells causes huge weather disturbances."
Perfect! Let's find out how they brew their spells! Let's watch —
Sam, I think we should stay away.

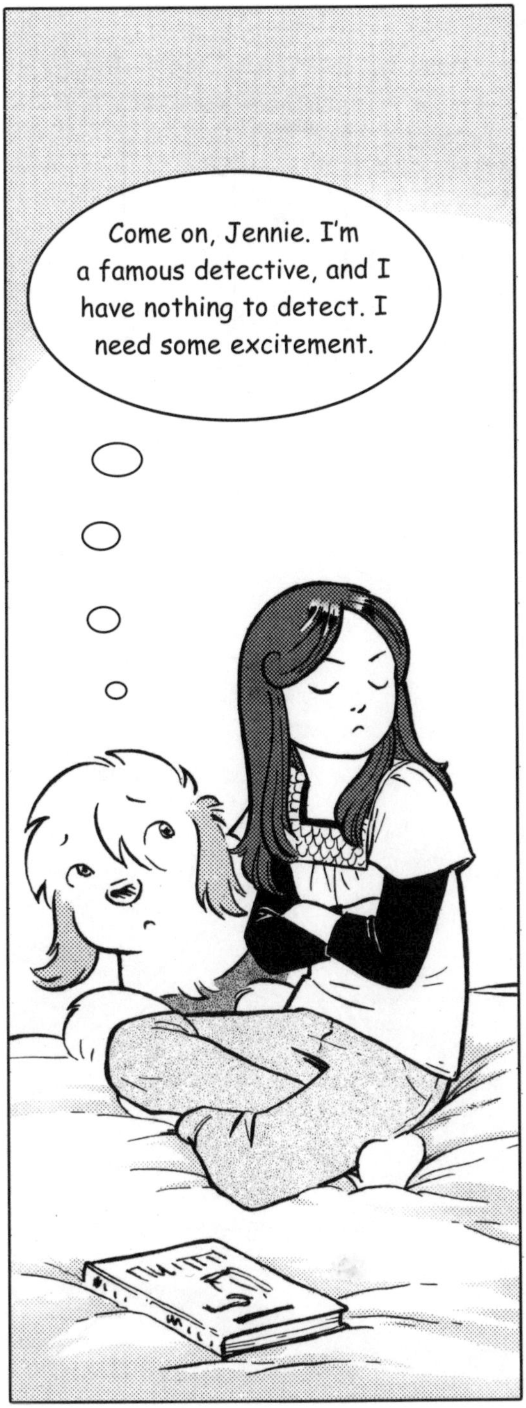
Come on, Jennie. I'm a famous detective, and I have nothing to detect. I need some excitement.

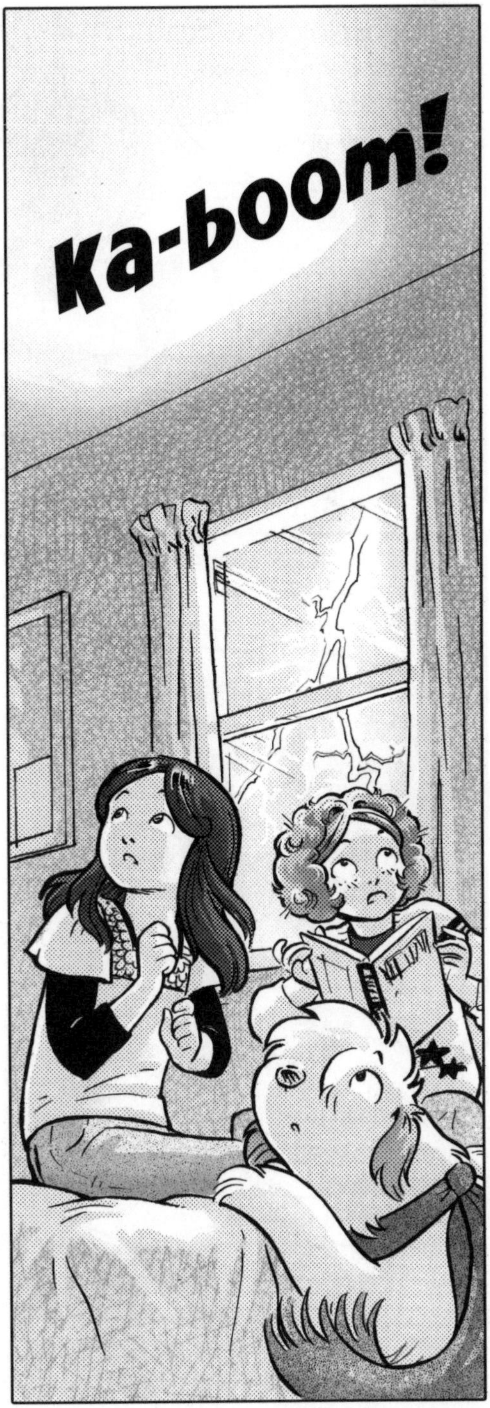
Ka-boom!

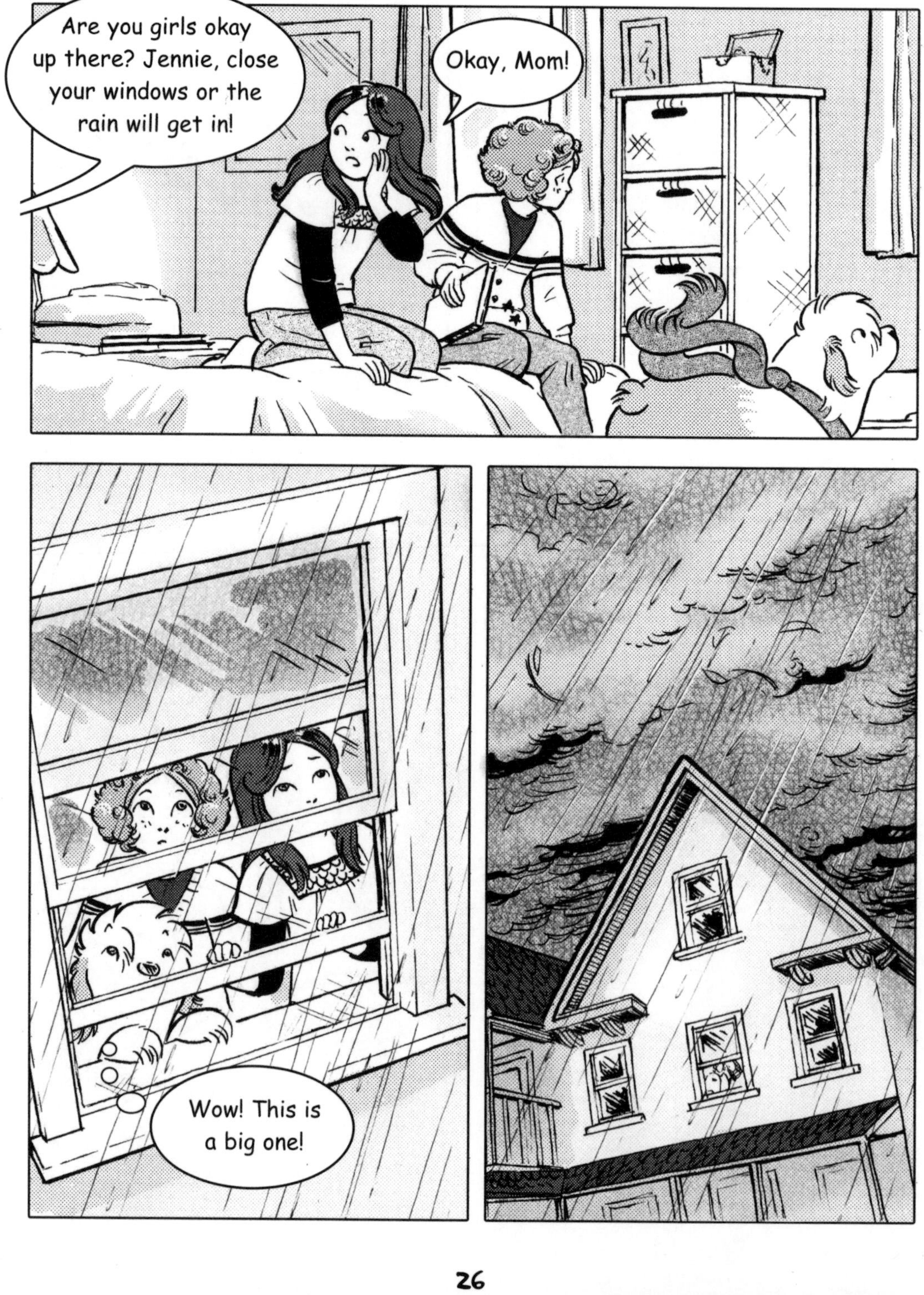
Are you girls okay up there? Jennie, close your windows or the rain will get in!
Okay, Mom!
Wow! This is a big one!

Those witches must be casting a spell.

Maybe they're putting a hex on the town.

Maybe they'll turn us all into toads!

I don't want to be a toad, Sam! I like being a person!

I hope that's not what they're doing. I would hate to be a toad.

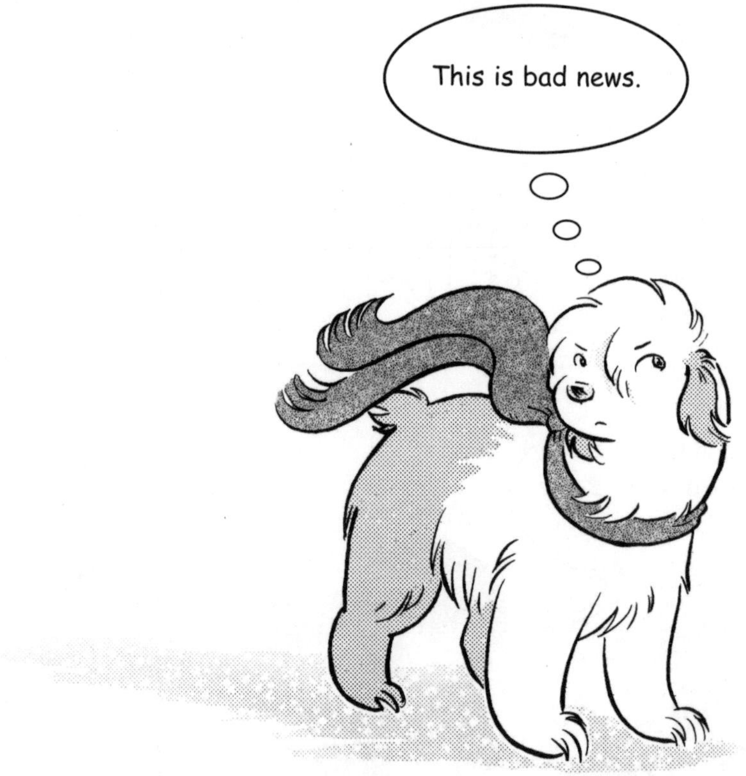
This is bad news.

The next night ...

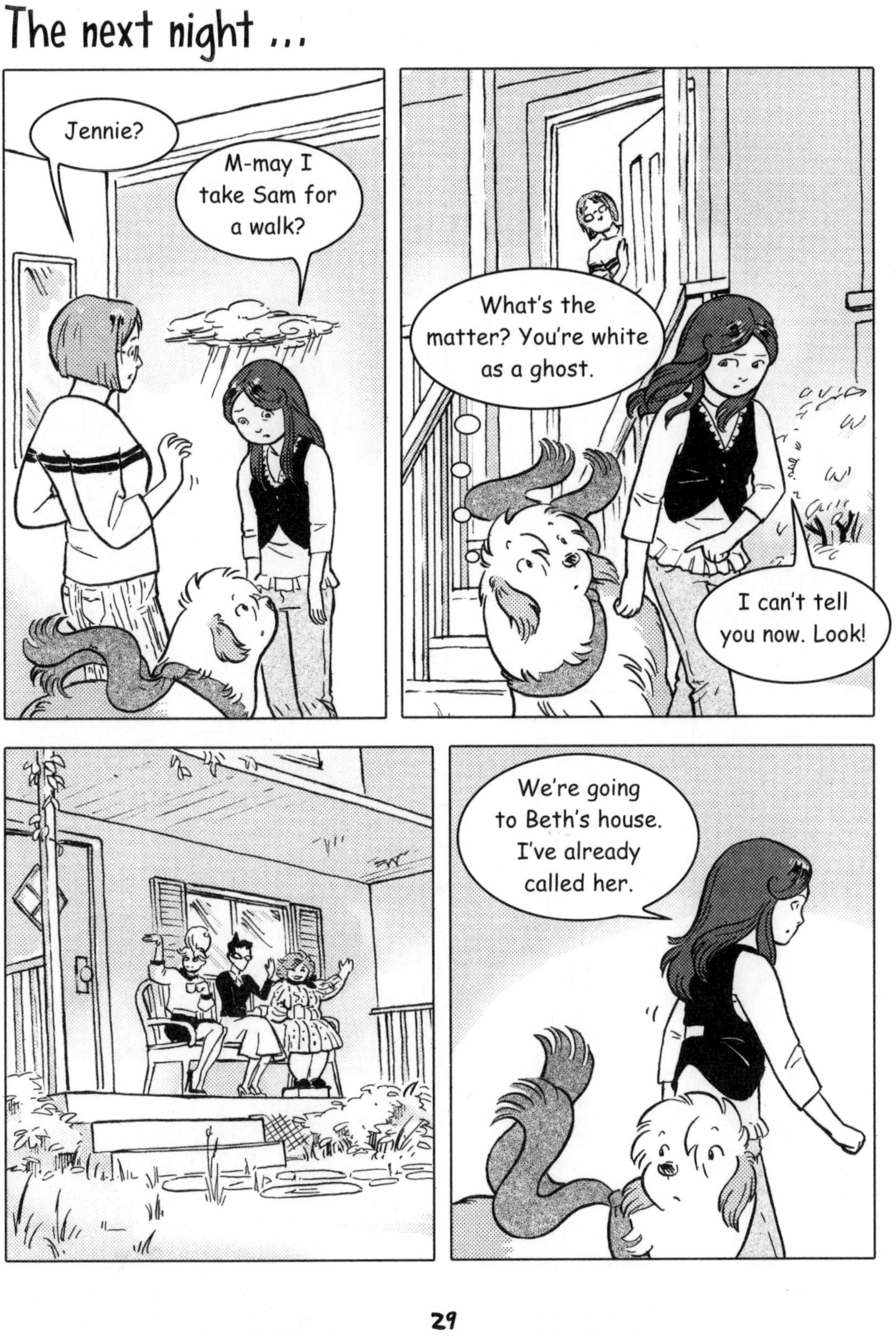
Jennie?
M-may I take Sam for a walk?
What's the matter? You're white as a ghost.
I can't tell you now. Look!
We're going to Beth's house. I've already called her.

We can go to my room.

Something terrible has happened!

So tell me!

Noel has football practice every day this month ...

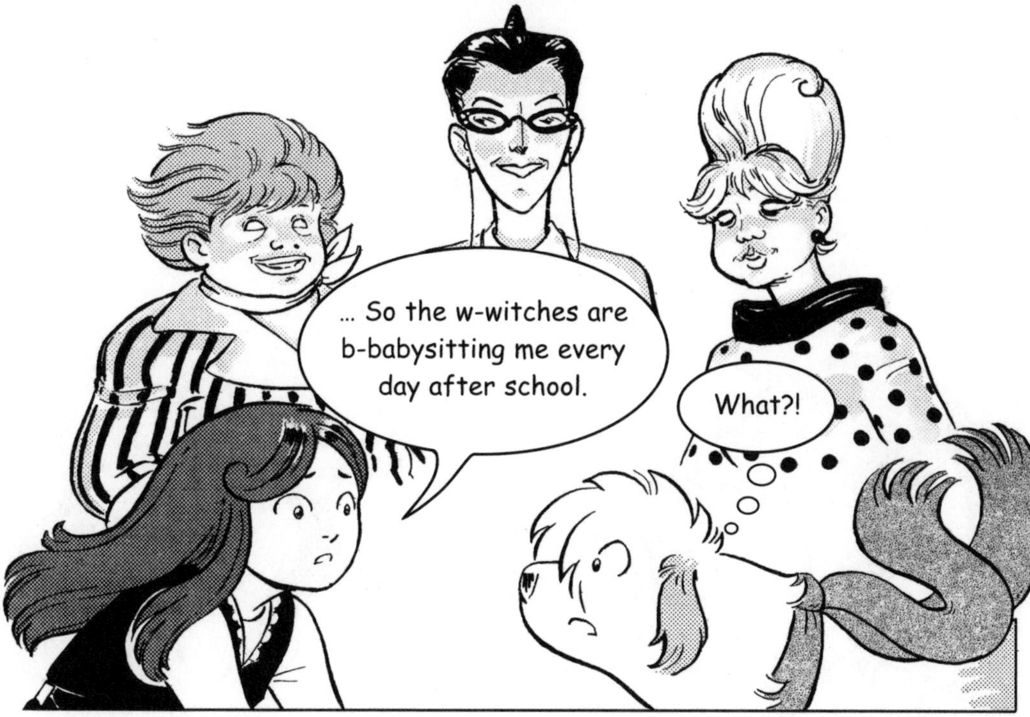
… So the w-witches are b-babysitting me every day after school.
What?!

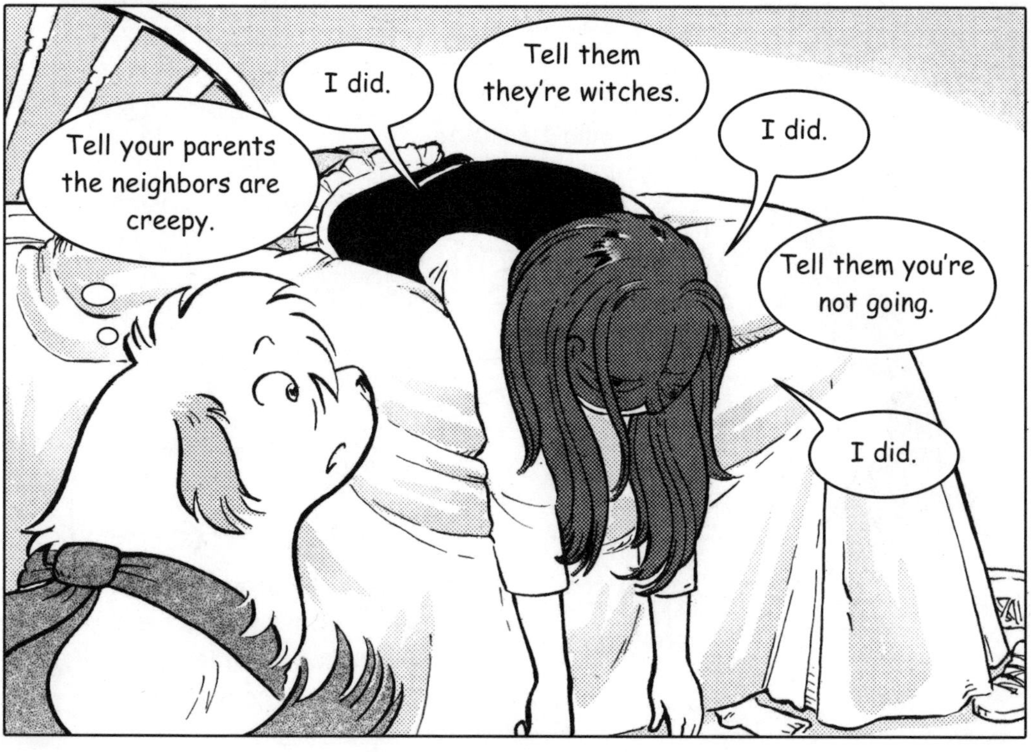
Tell your parents the neighbors are creepy.
I did.
Tell them they're witches.
I did.
Tell them you're not going.
I did.

Nothing worked. I have to go on Monday.

I know! Ask Beth's mom to babysit!

Could I come to your house instead, Beth?

I already asked. Mom's taking the twins to swimming lessons. I have to go with them.

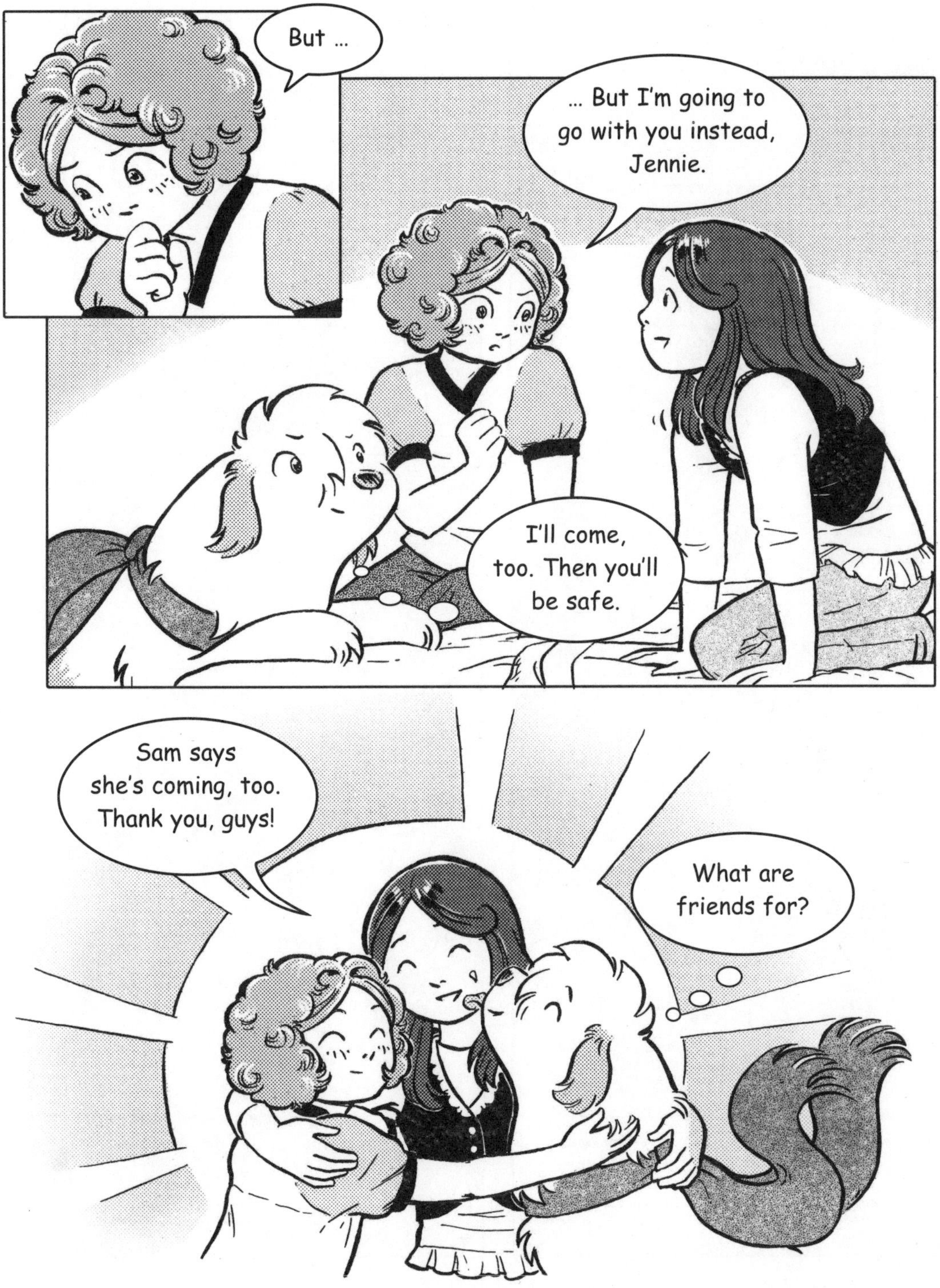
But ...
... But I'm going to go with you instead, Jennie.
I'll come, too. Then you'll be safe.
Sam says she's coming, too. Thank you, guys!
What are friends for?

The next day ...

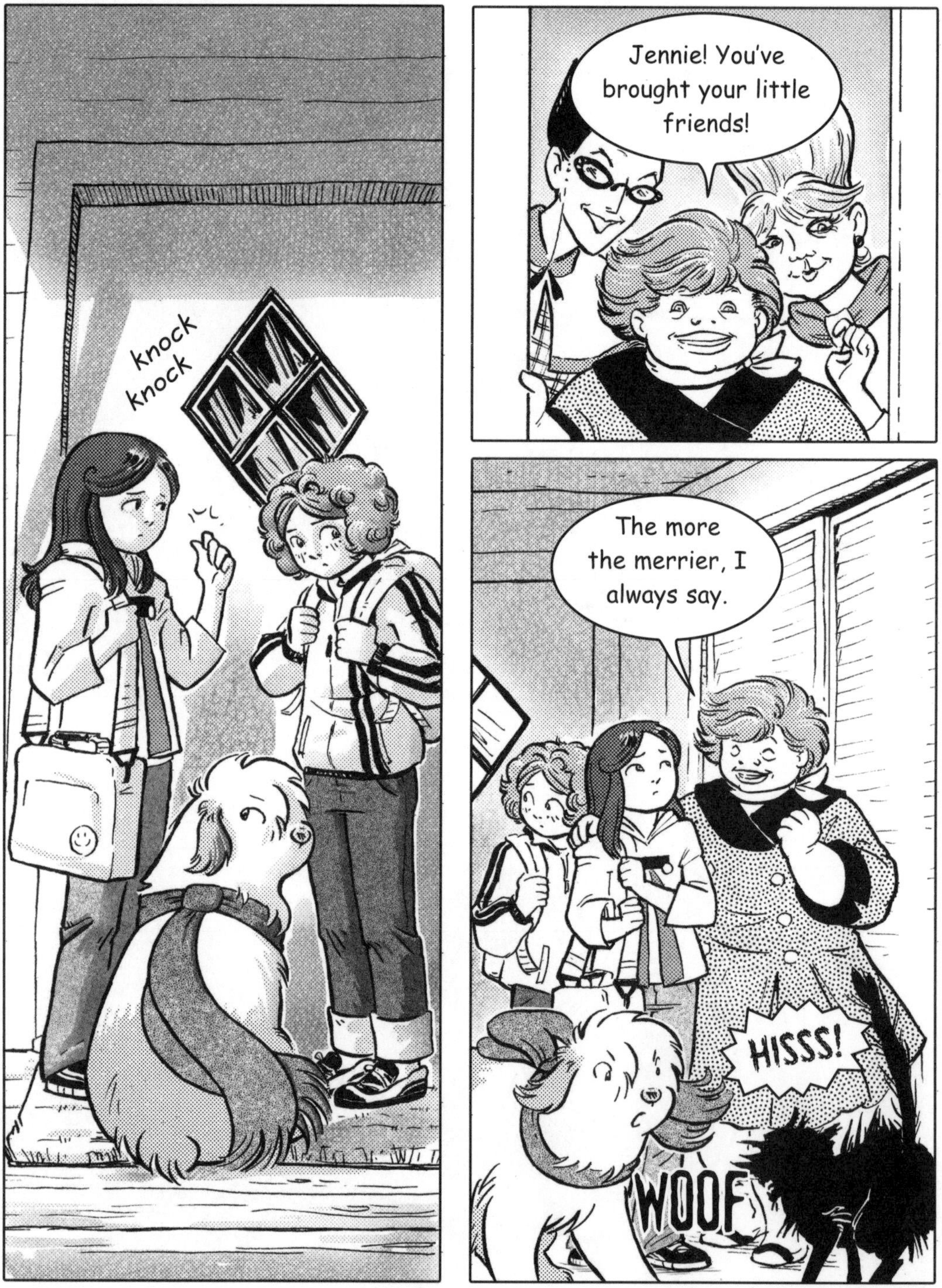
knock
knock
Jennie! You've brought your little friends!
The more the merrier, I always say.
HISSS!
WOOF

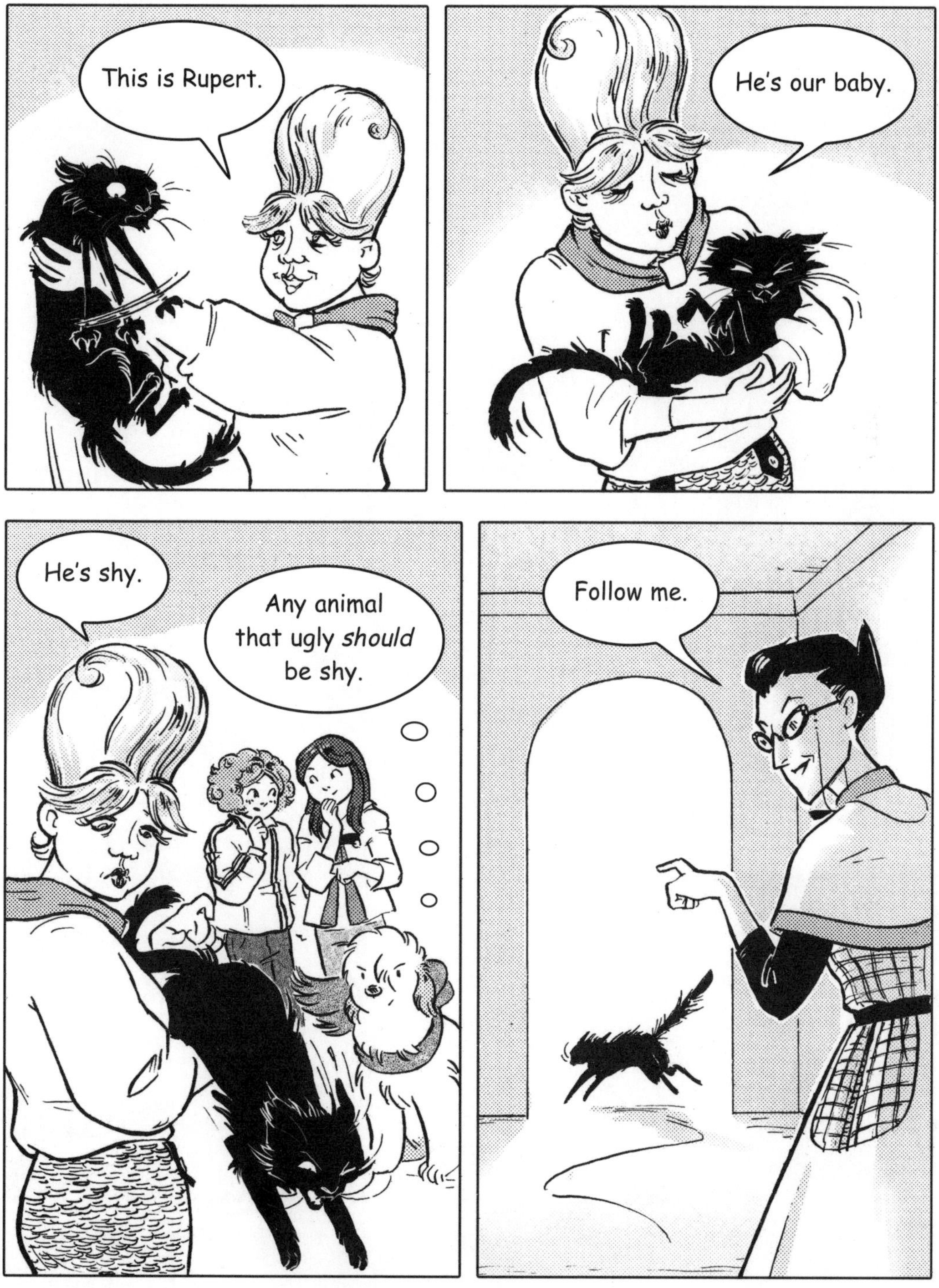
This is Rupert.
He's our baby.
He's shy.
Any animal that ugly *should* be shy.
Follow me.

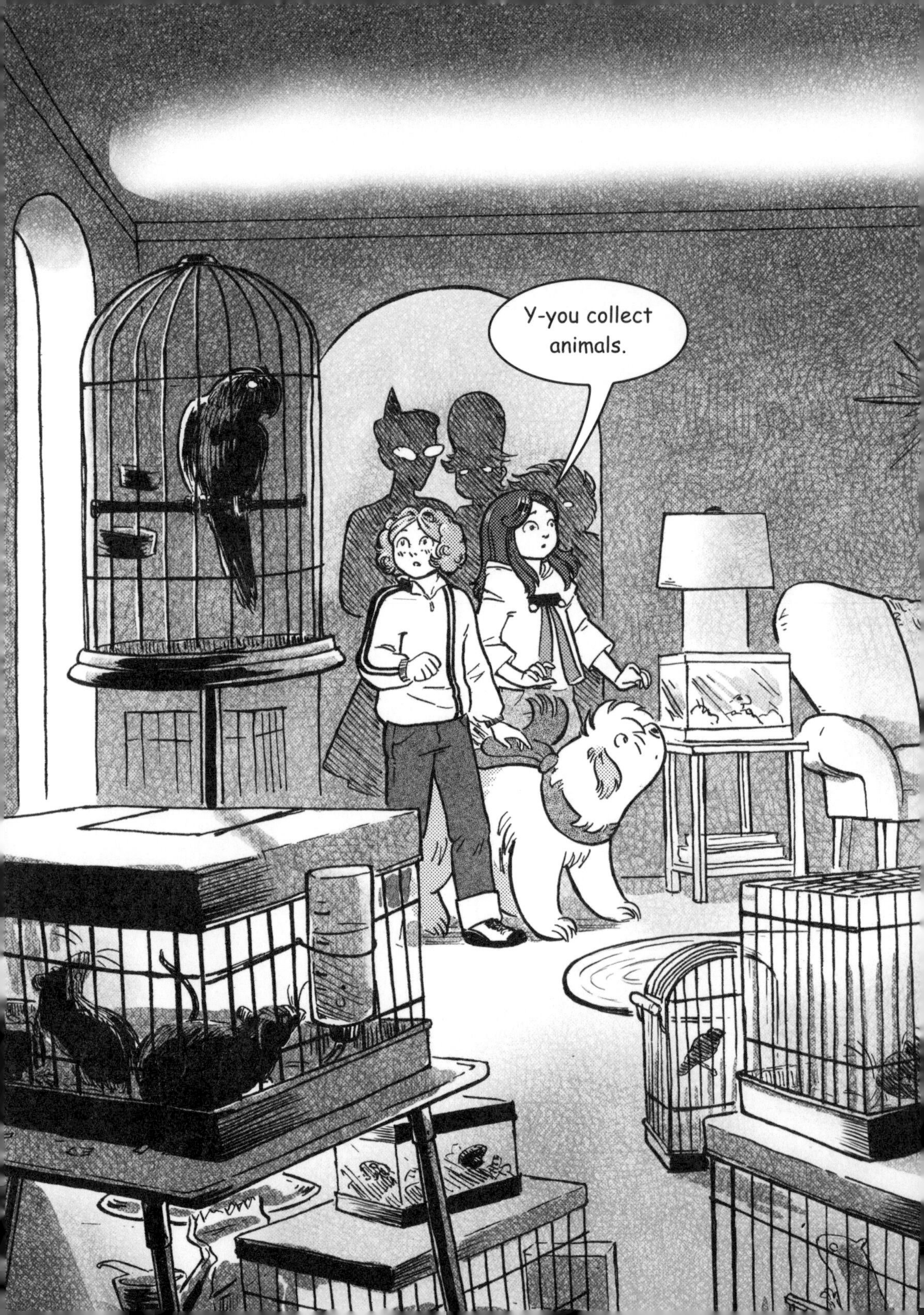
Y-you collect animals.

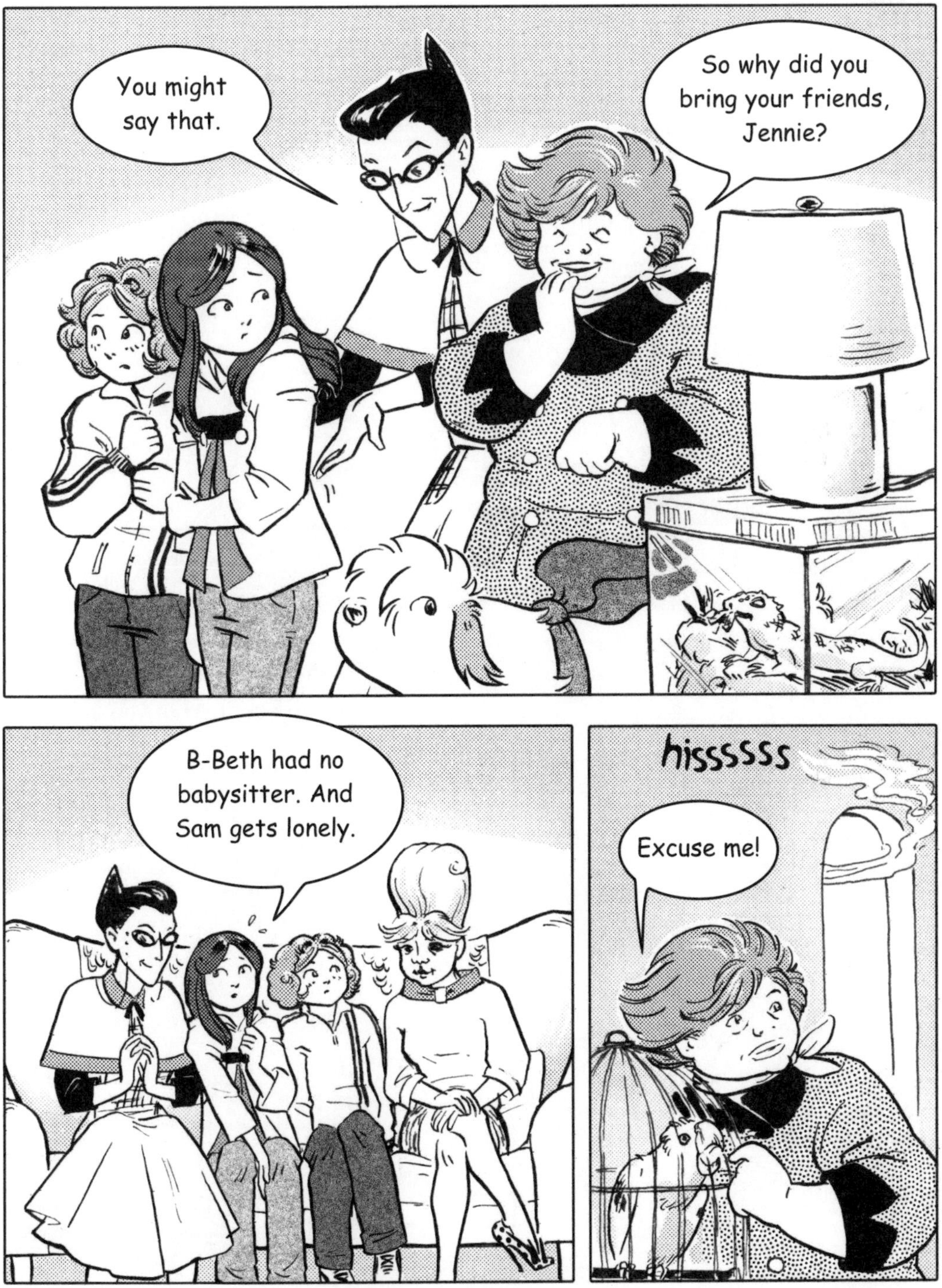
You might say that.
So why did you bring your friends, Jennie?
B-Beth had no babysitter. And Sam gets lonely.
hissssss
Excuse me!

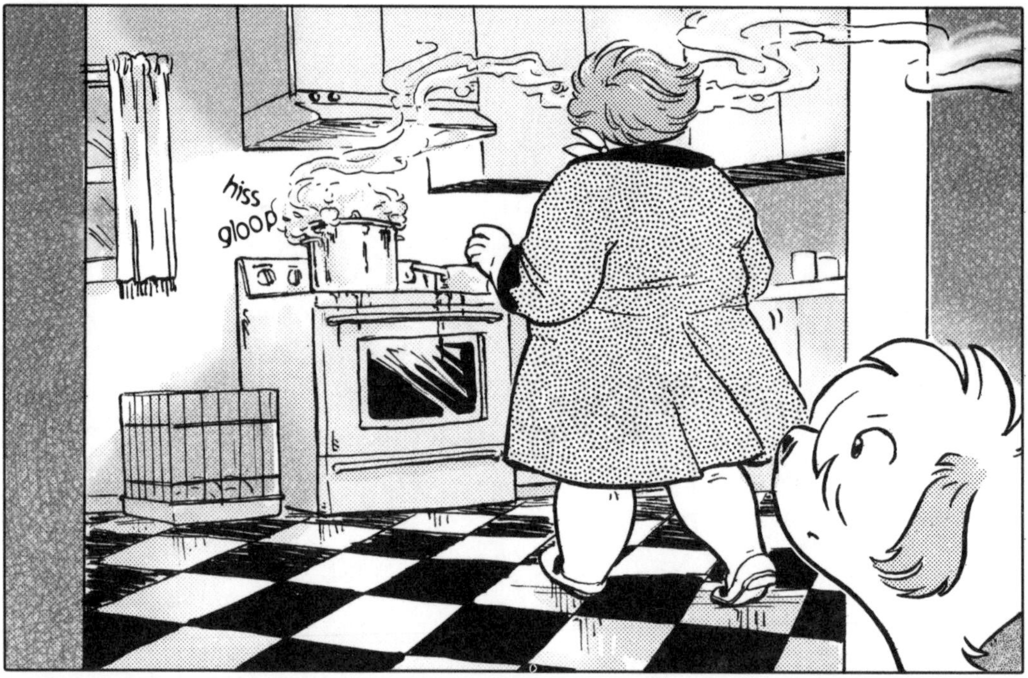
hiss
gloop

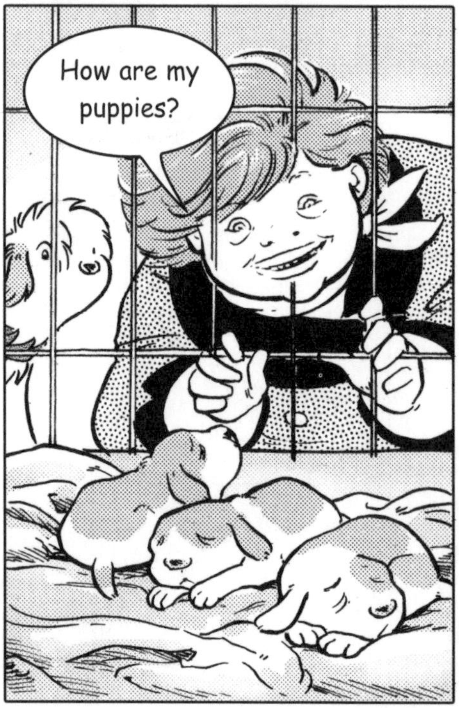
How are my puppies?

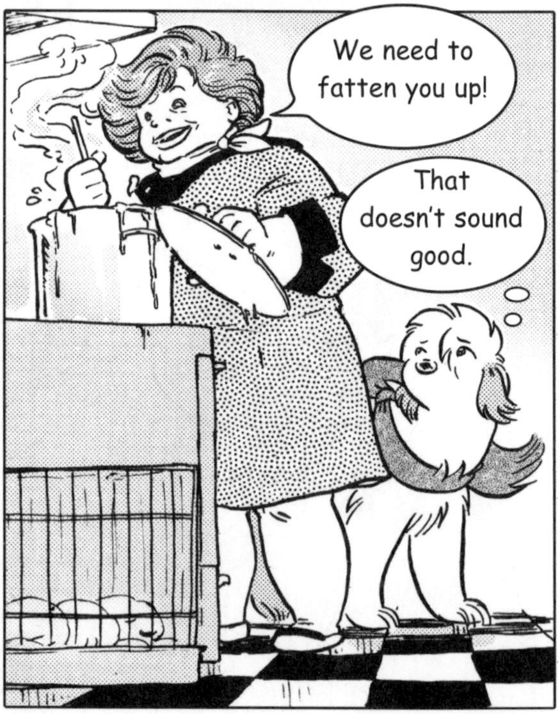
We need to fatten you up!
That doesn't sound good.

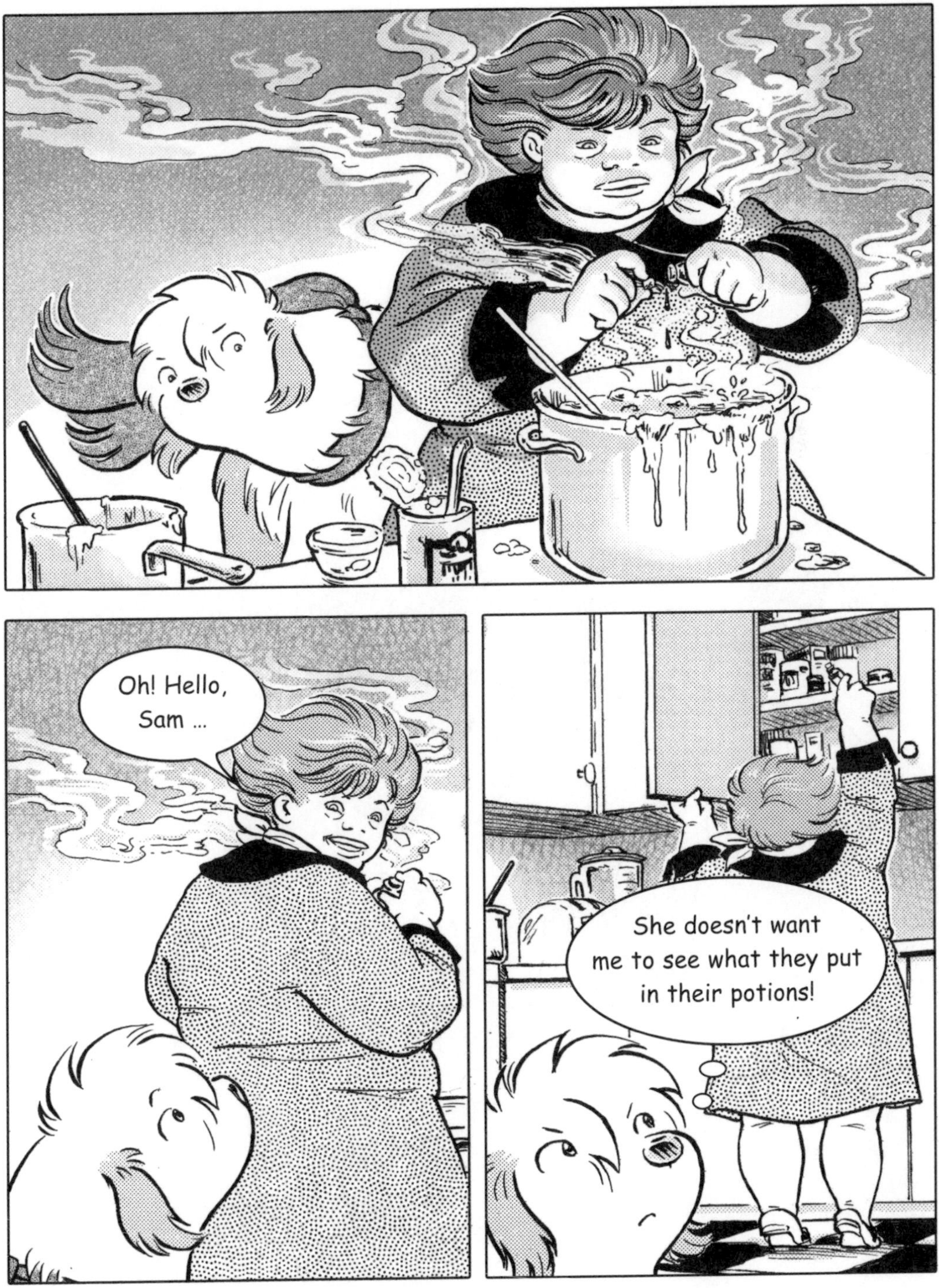
Oh! Hello, Sam ...
She doesn't want me to see what they put in their potions!

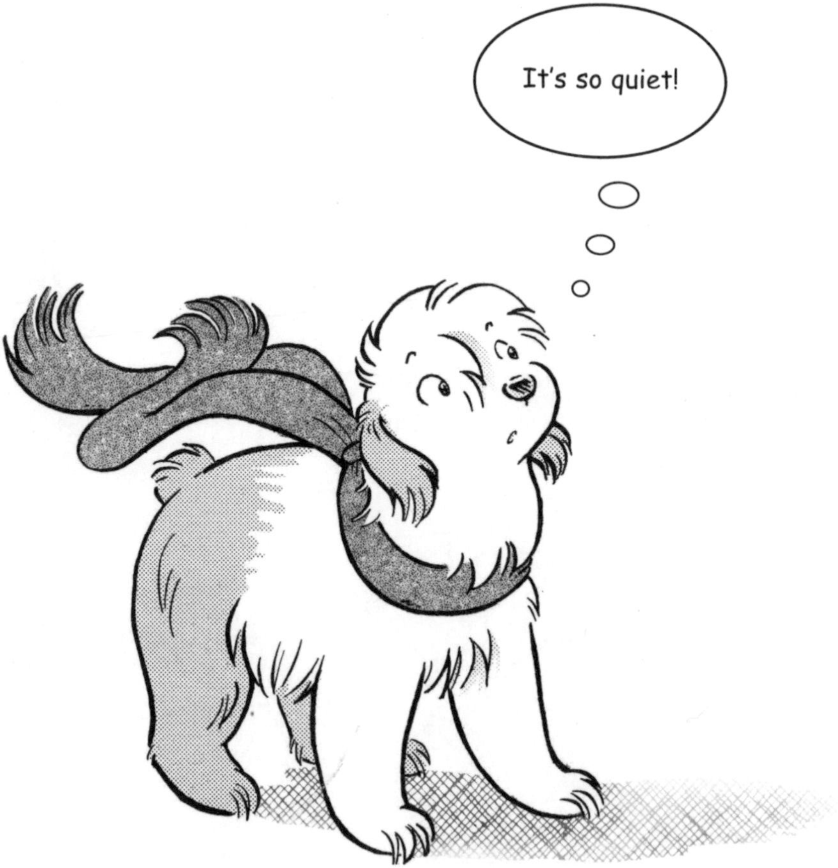
It's so quiet!

Later that week ...

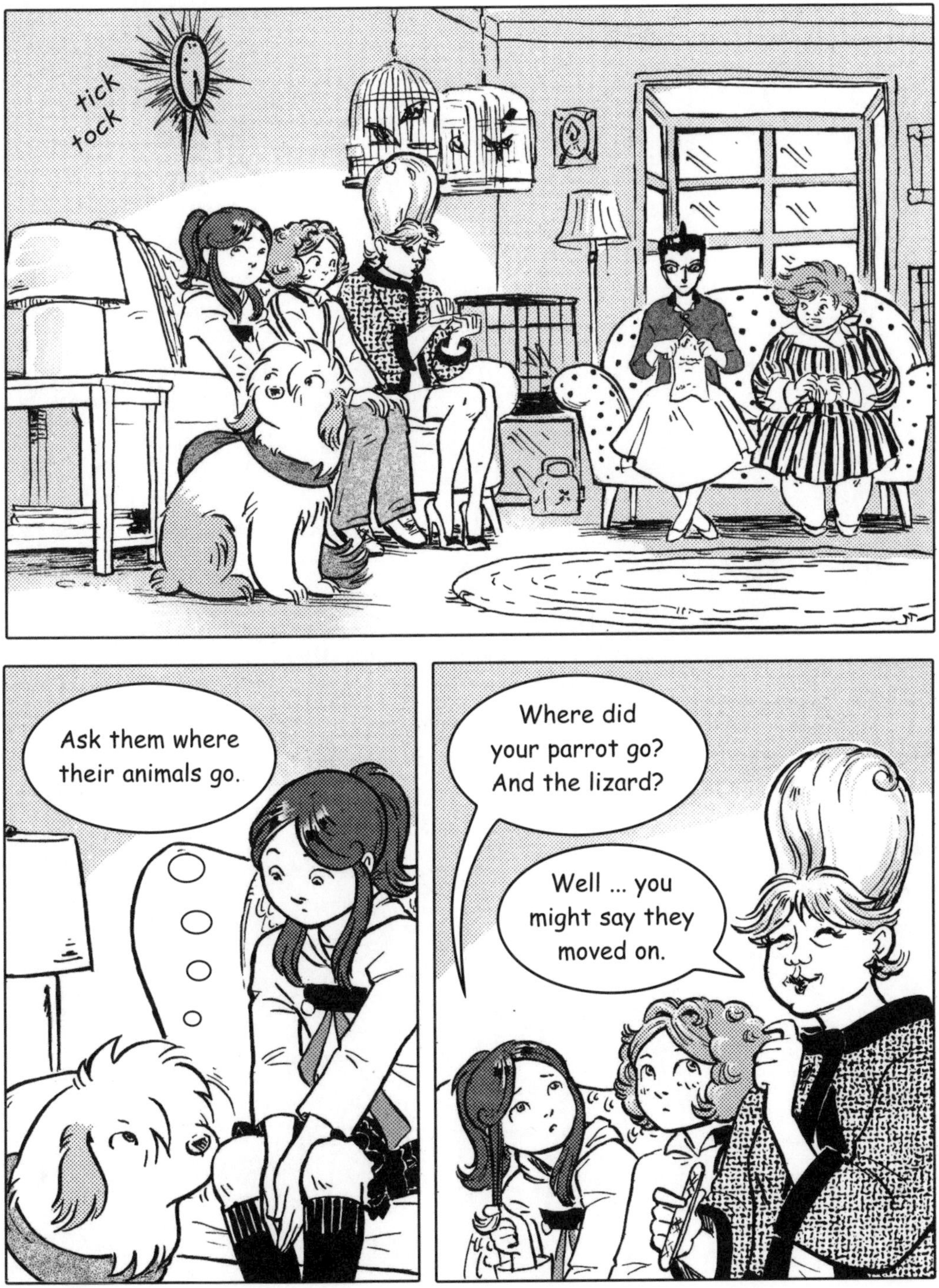
tick
tock
Ask them where their animals go.
Where did your parrot go? And the lizard?
Well ... you might say they moved on.

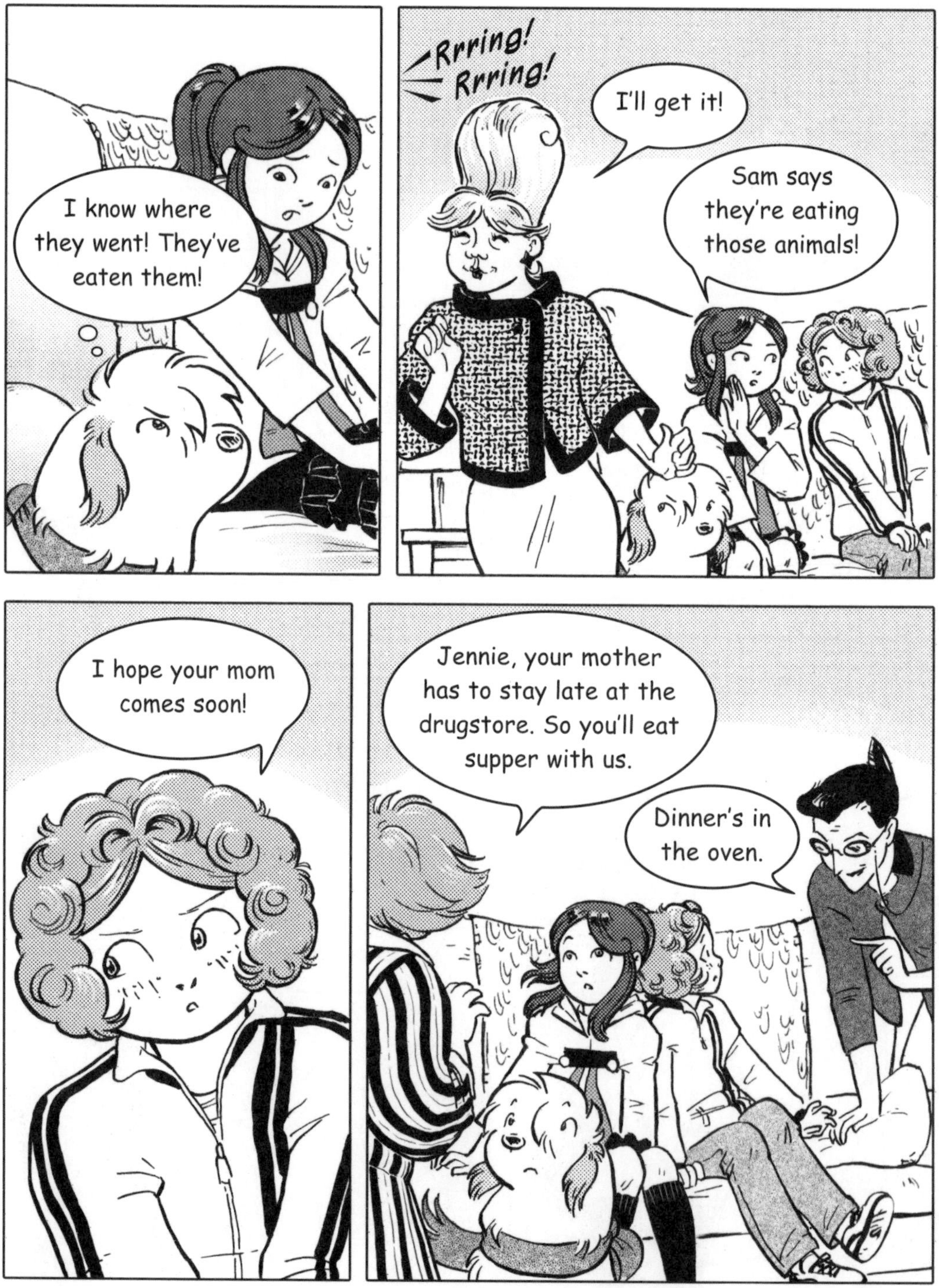
I know where they went! They've eaten them!
Rrring! Rrring!
I'll get it!
Sam says they're eating those animals!
I hope your mom comes soon!
Jennie, your mother has to stay late at the drugstore. So you'll eat supper with us.
Dinner's in the oven.

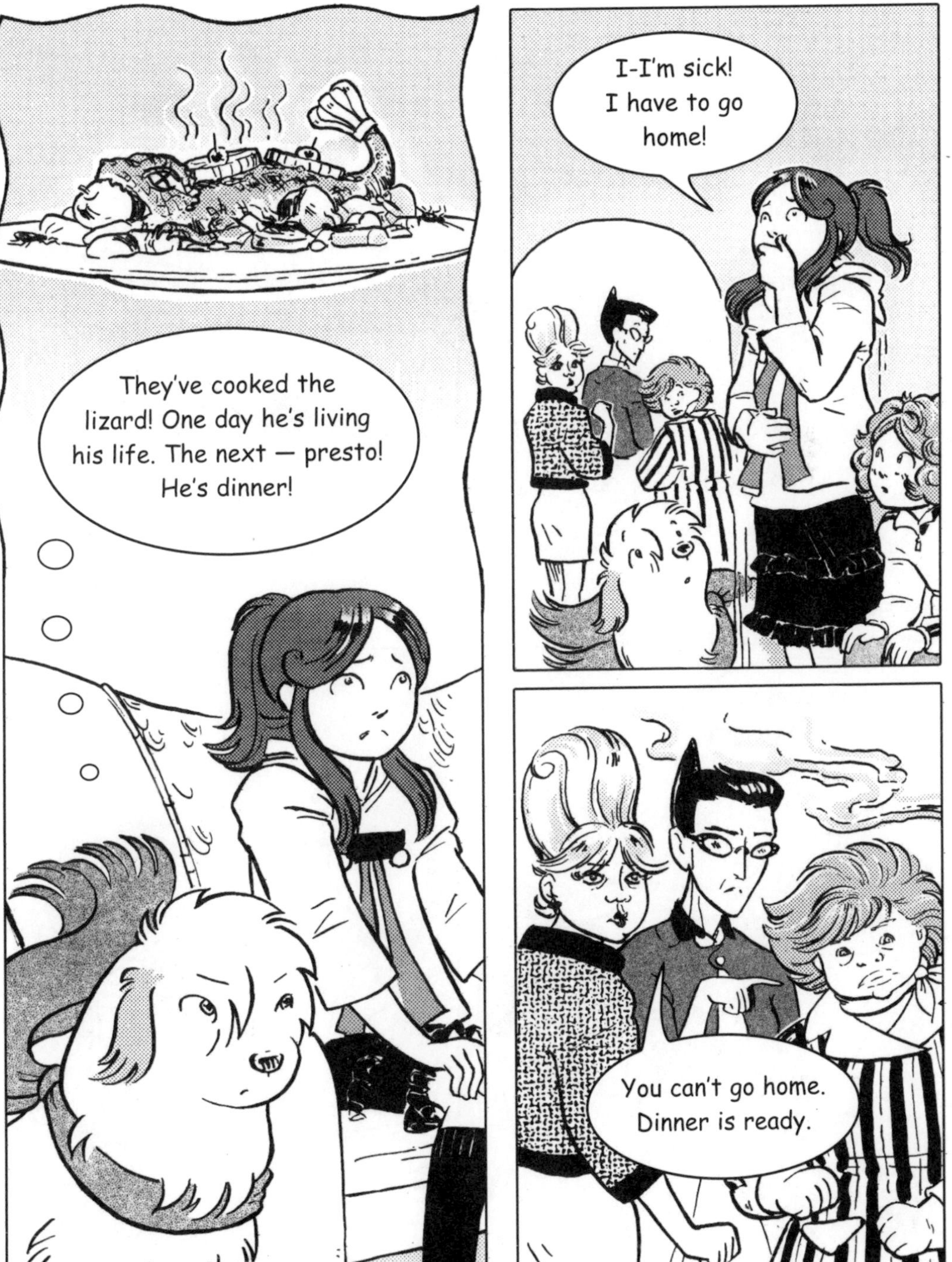
They've cooked the lizard! One day he's living his life. The next — presto! He's dinner!
I-I'm sick! I have to go home!
You can't go home. Dinner is ready.

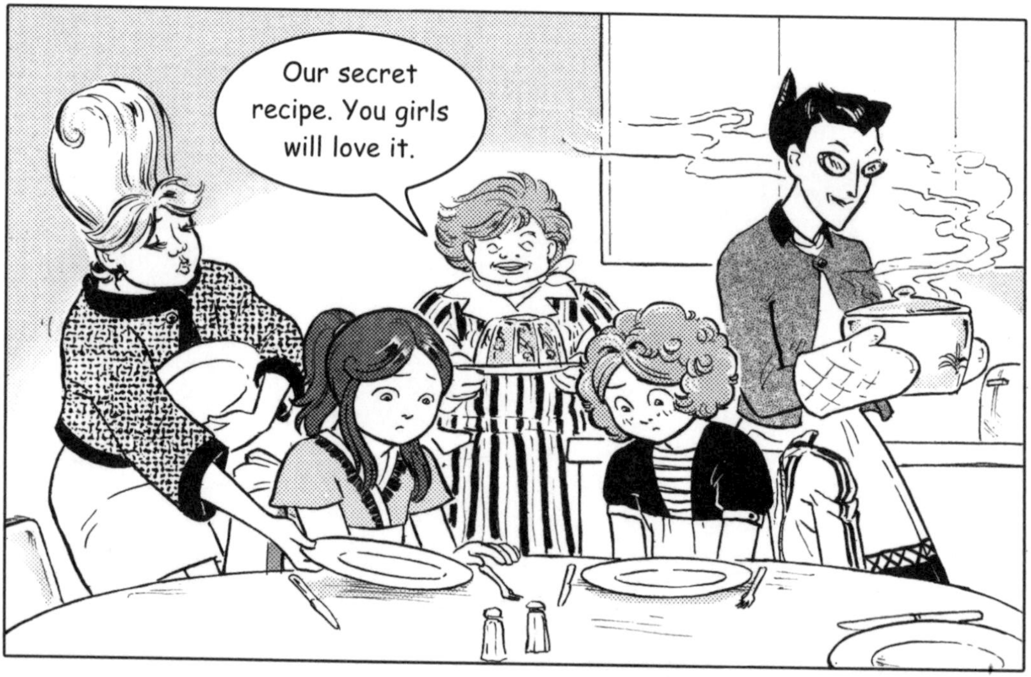
Our secret recipe. You girls will love it.

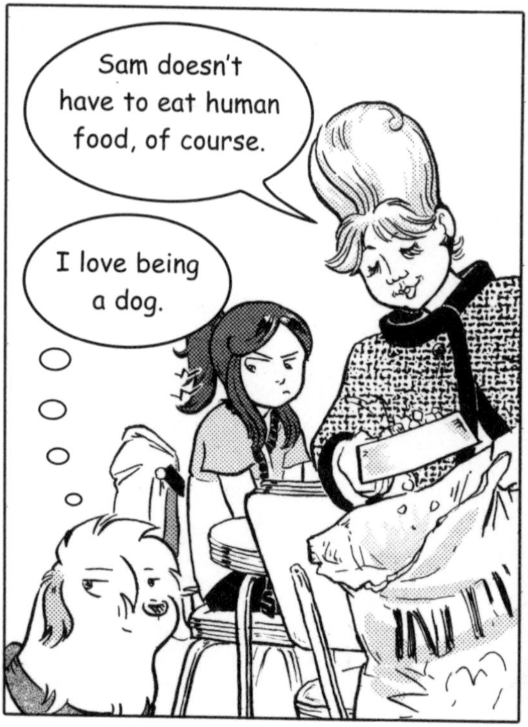
Sam doesn't have to eat human food, of course.
I love being a dog.

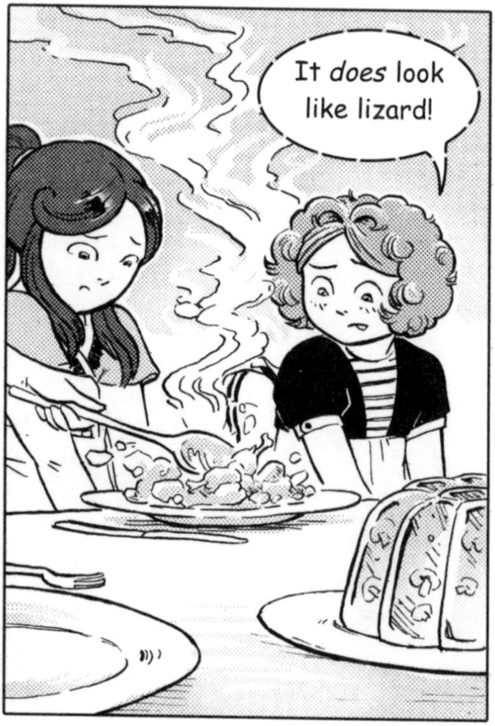
It *does* look like lizard!

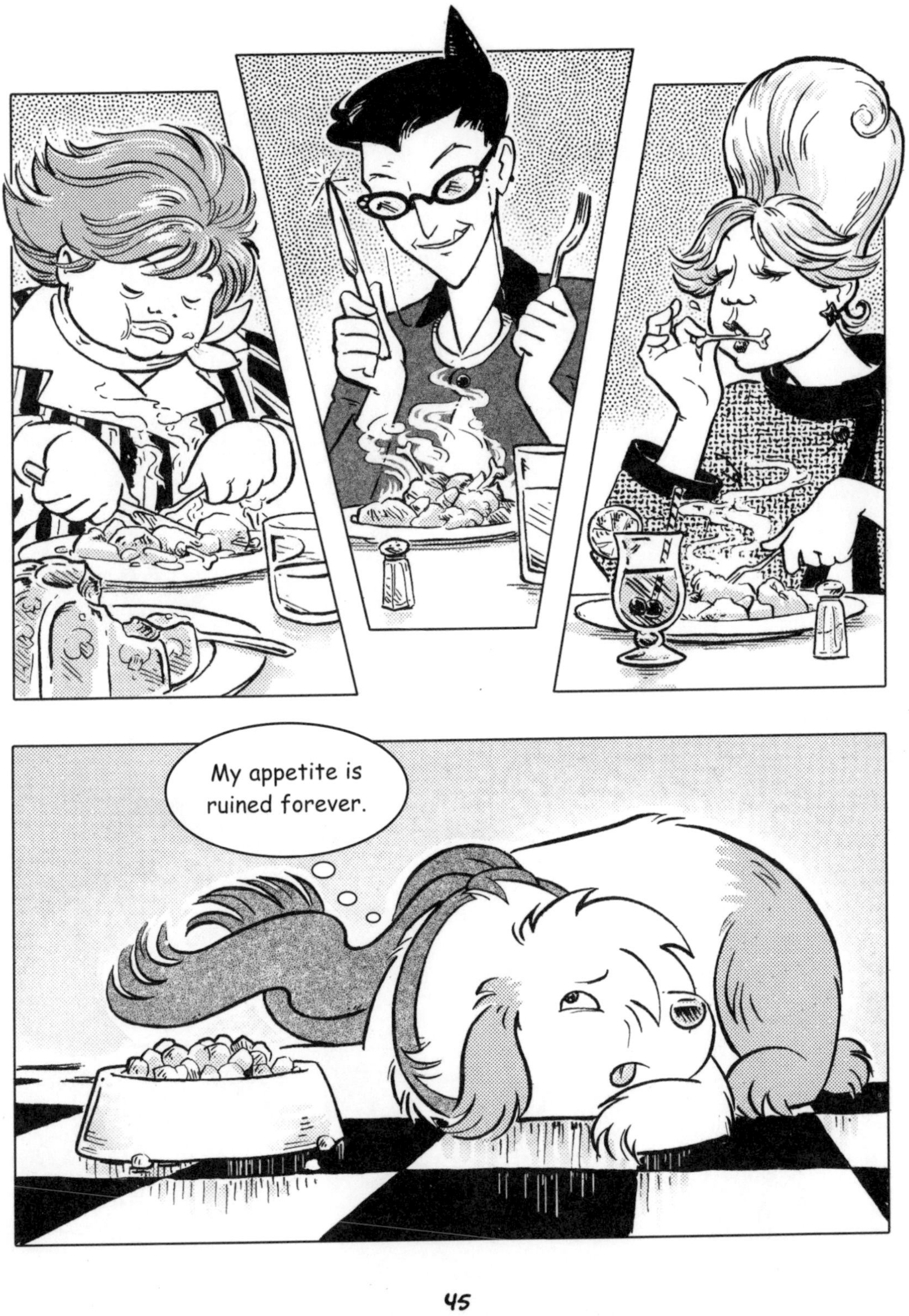
My appetite is
ruined forever.

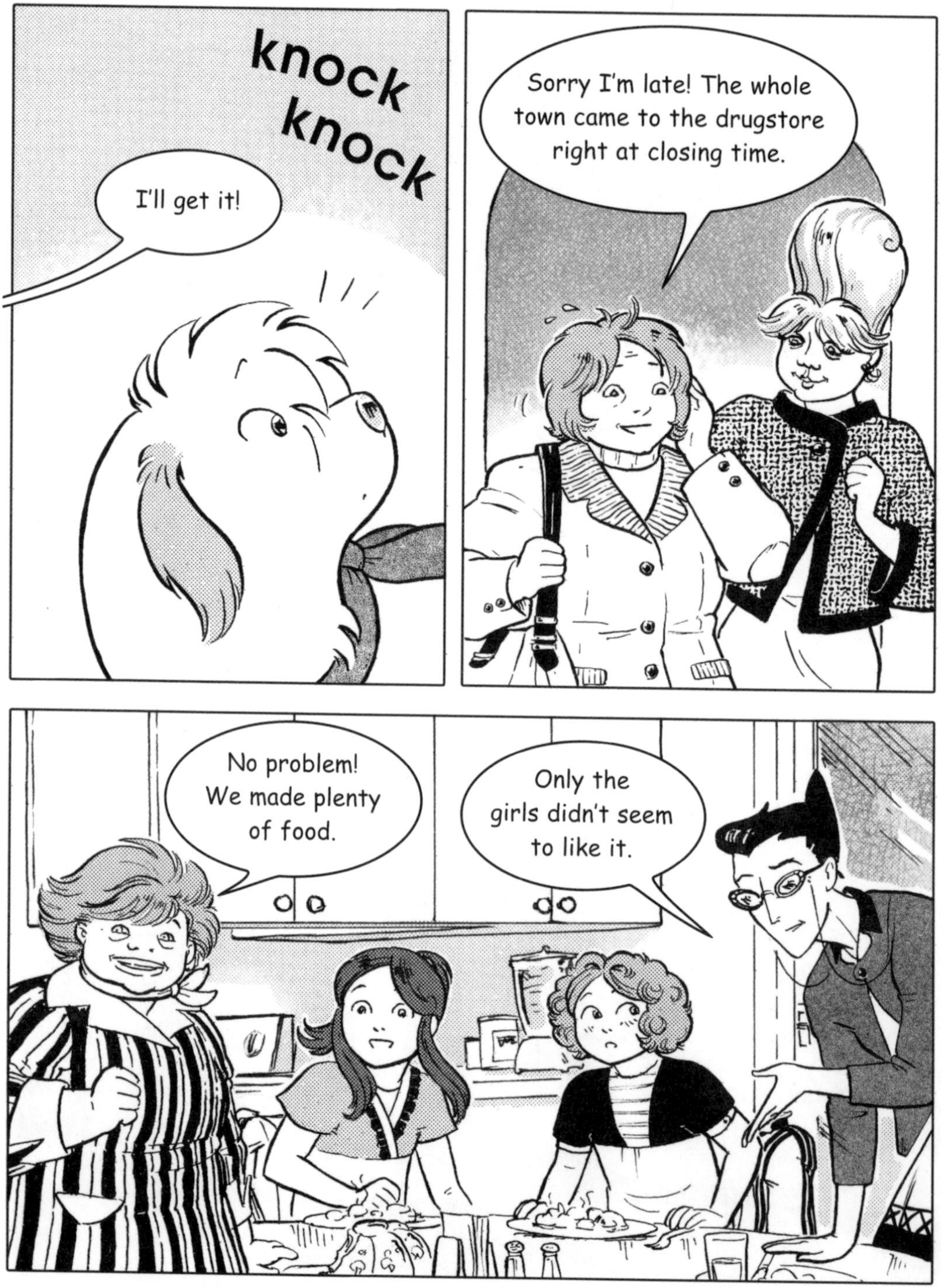
knock knock
I'll get it!
Sorry I'm late! The whole town came to the drugstore right at closing time.
No problem! We made plenty of food.
Only the girls didn't seem to like it.

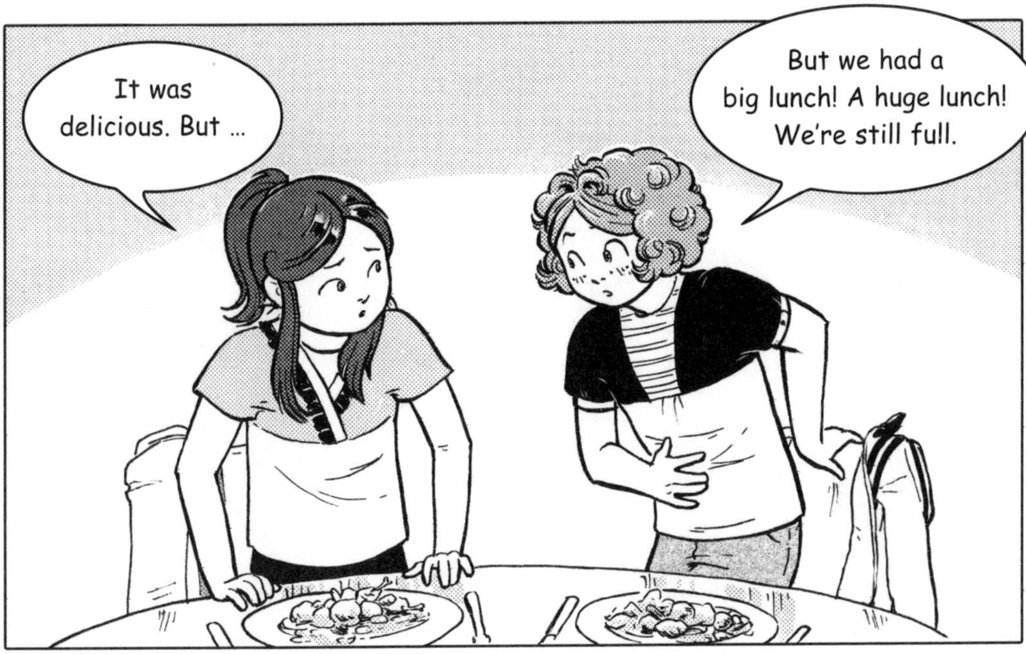
It was delicious. But ...
But we had a big lunch! A huge lunch! We're still full.

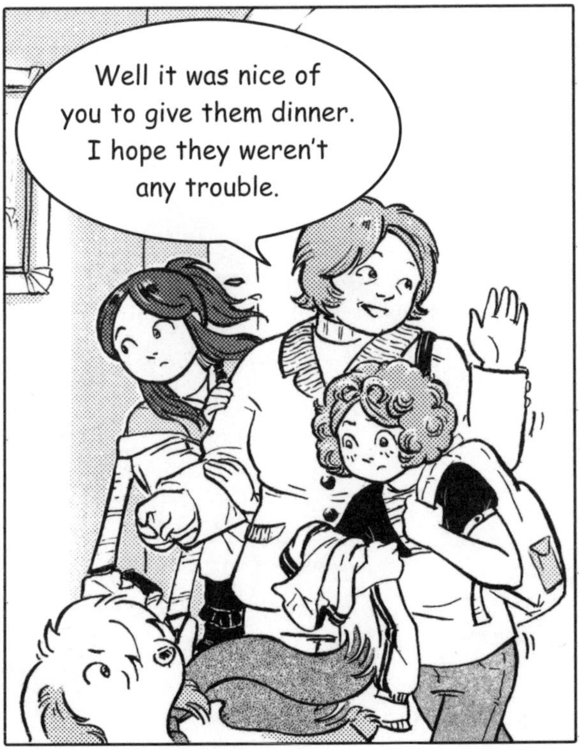
Well it was nice of you to give them dinner. I hope they weren't any trouble.

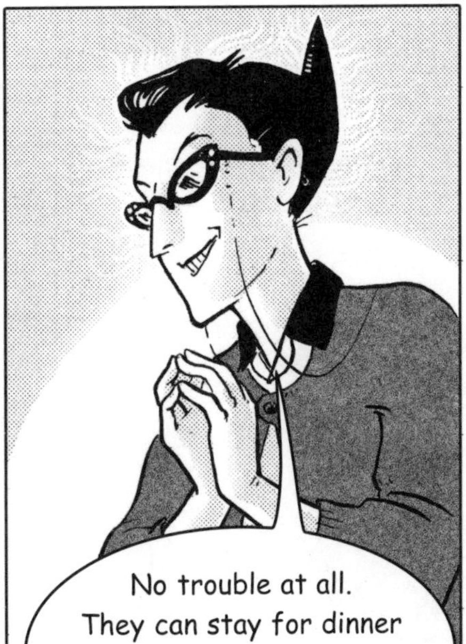
No trouble at all. They can stay for dinner any time. We have many more secret recipes.

That weekend ...

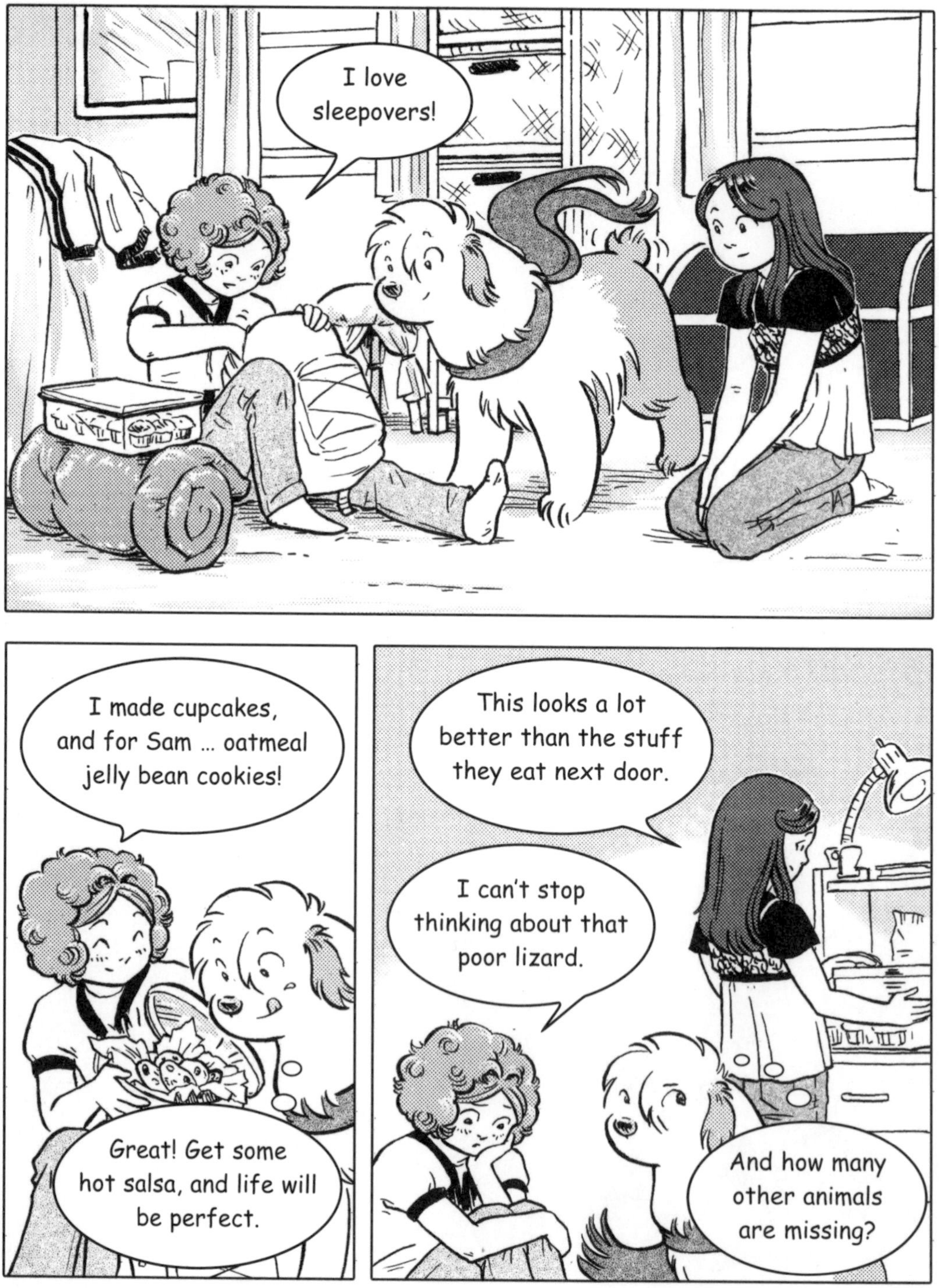
I love sleepovers!
I made cupcakes, and for Sam ... oatmeal jelly bean cookies!
Great! Get some hot salsa, and life will be perfect.
This looks a lot better than the stuff they eat next door.
I can't stop thinking about that poor lizard.
And how many other animals are missing?

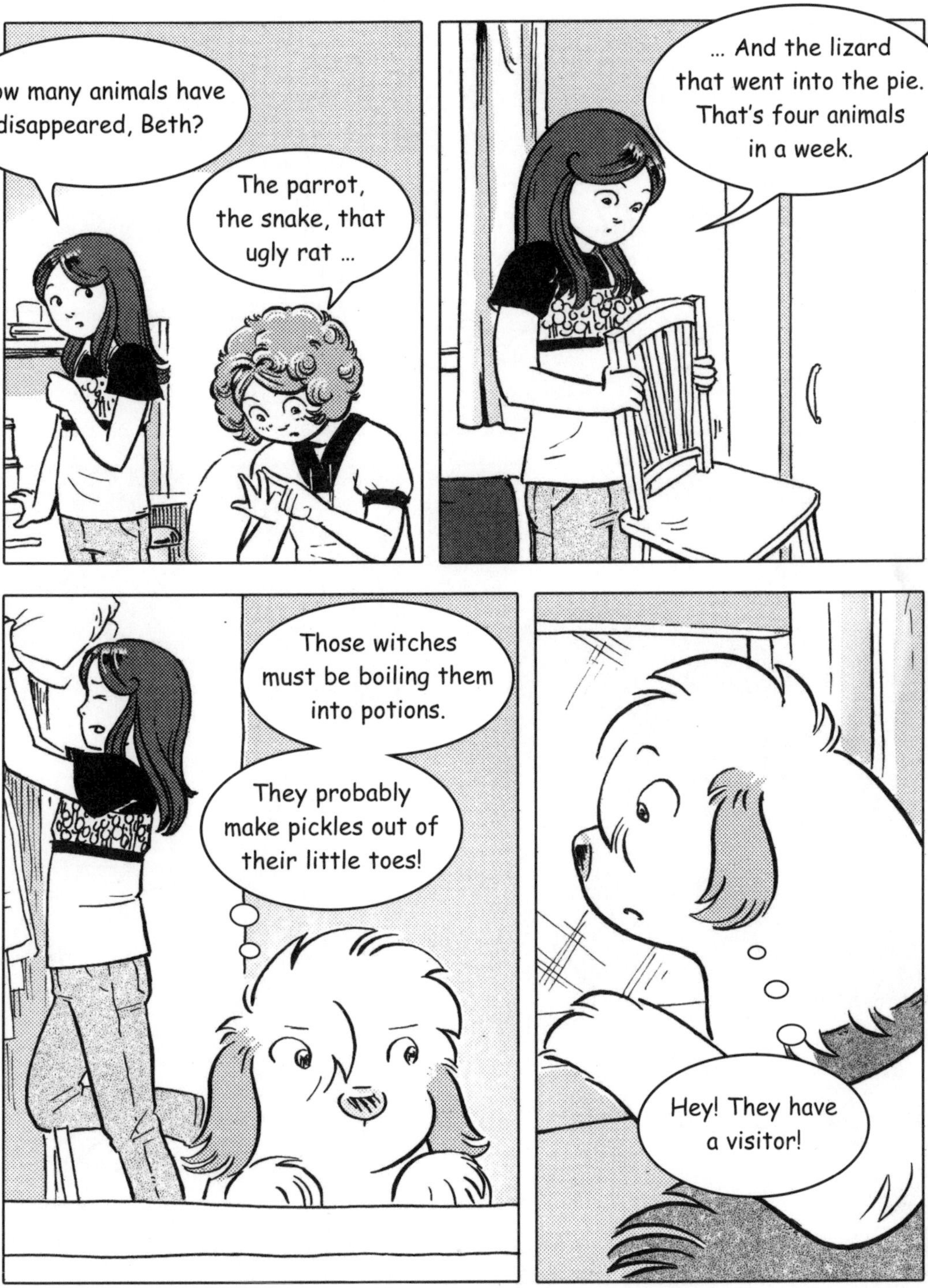
How many animals have disappeared, Beth?
The parrot, the snake, that ugly rat ...
... And the lizard that went into the pie. That's four animals in a week.
Those witches must be boiling them into potions.
They probably make pickles out of their little toes!
Hey! They have a visitor!

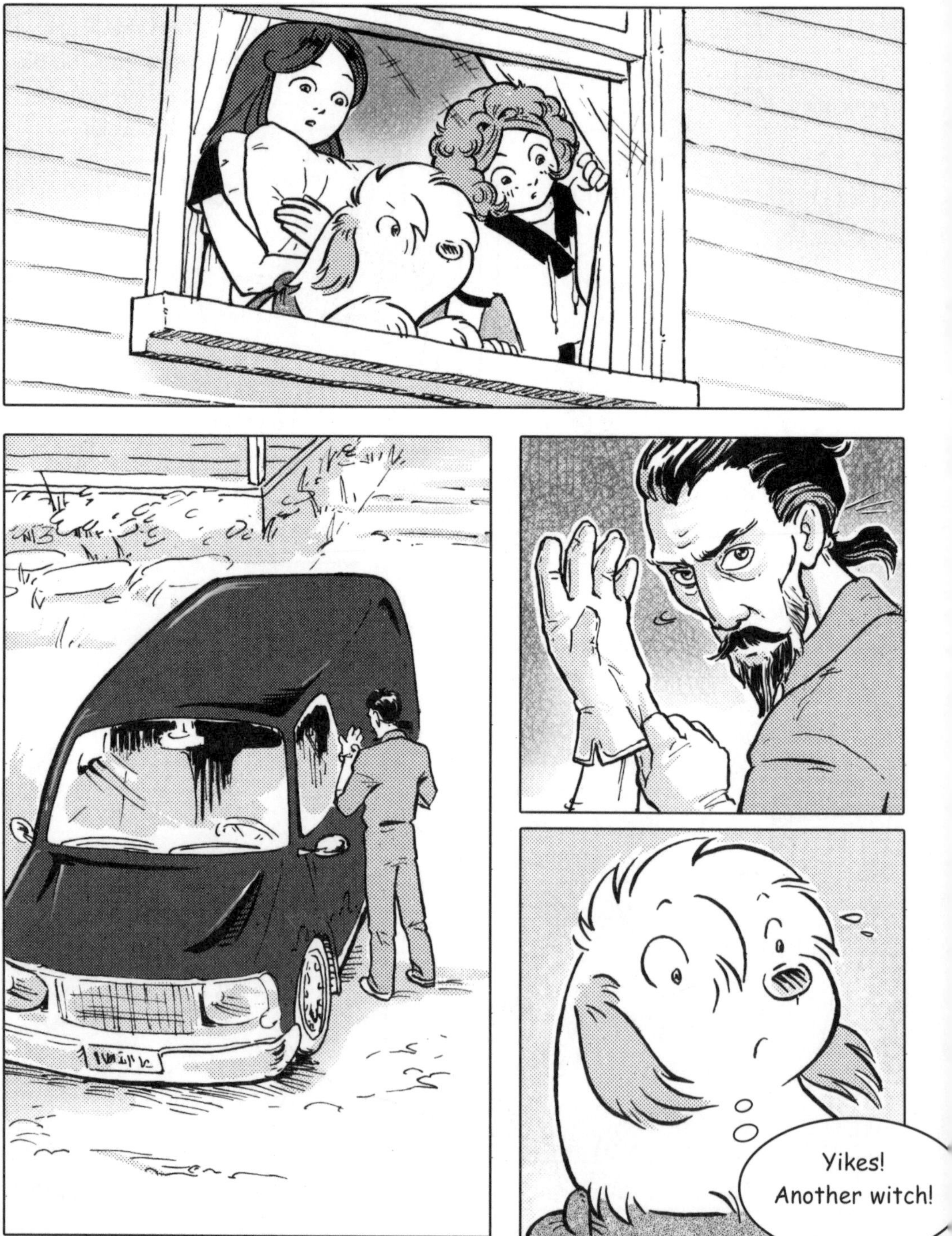
Yikes!
Another witch!

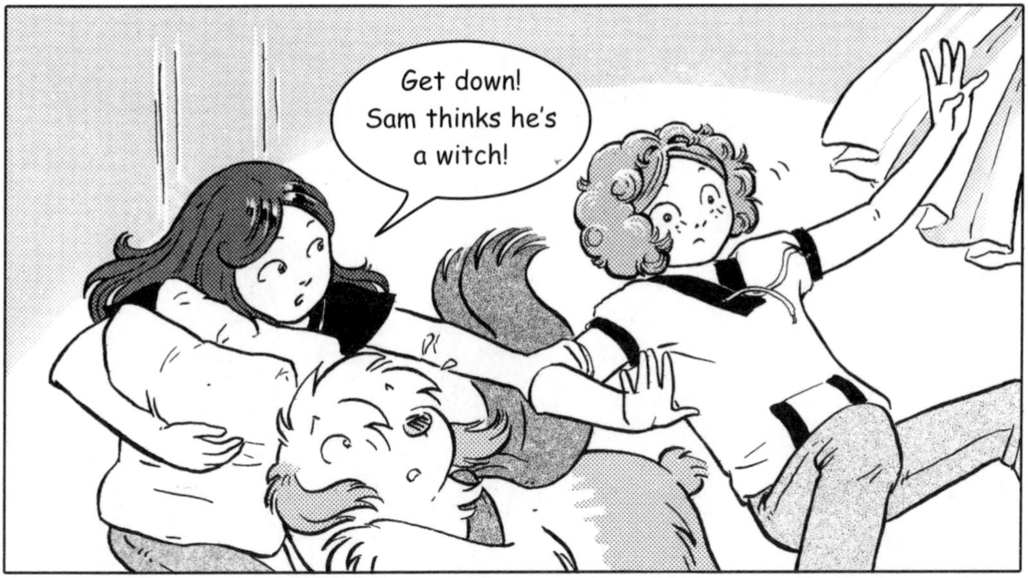
Get down! Sam thinks he's a witch!

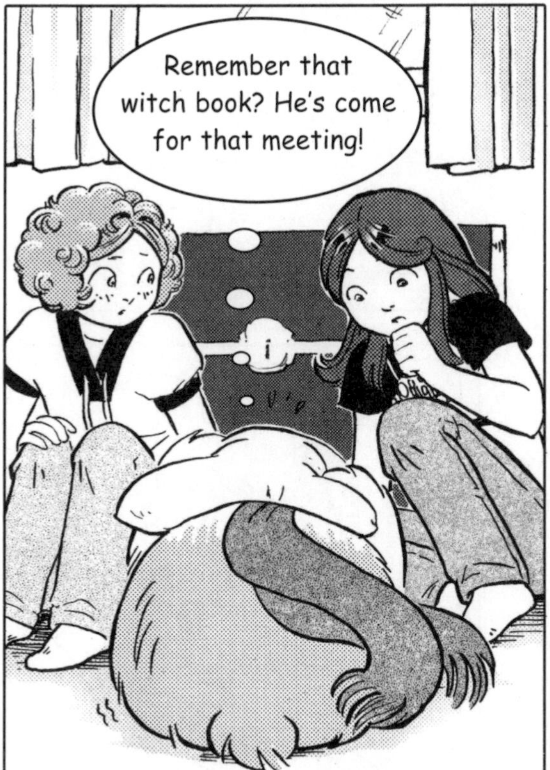
Remember that witch book? He's come for that meeting!

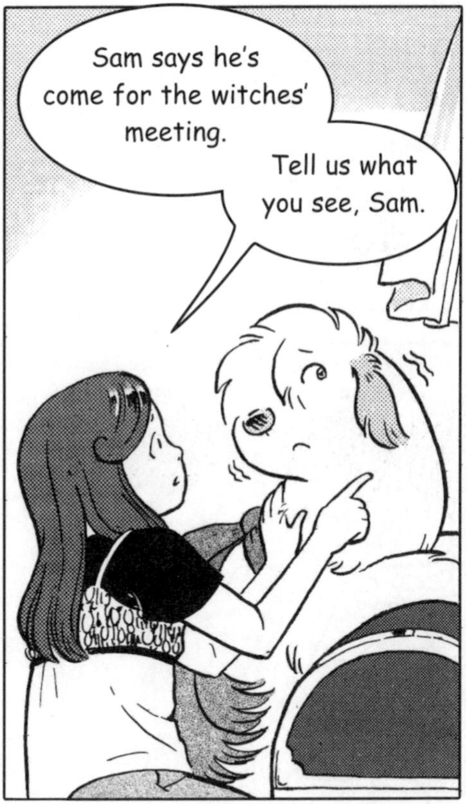
Sam says he's come for the witches' meeting.
Tell us what you see, Sam.

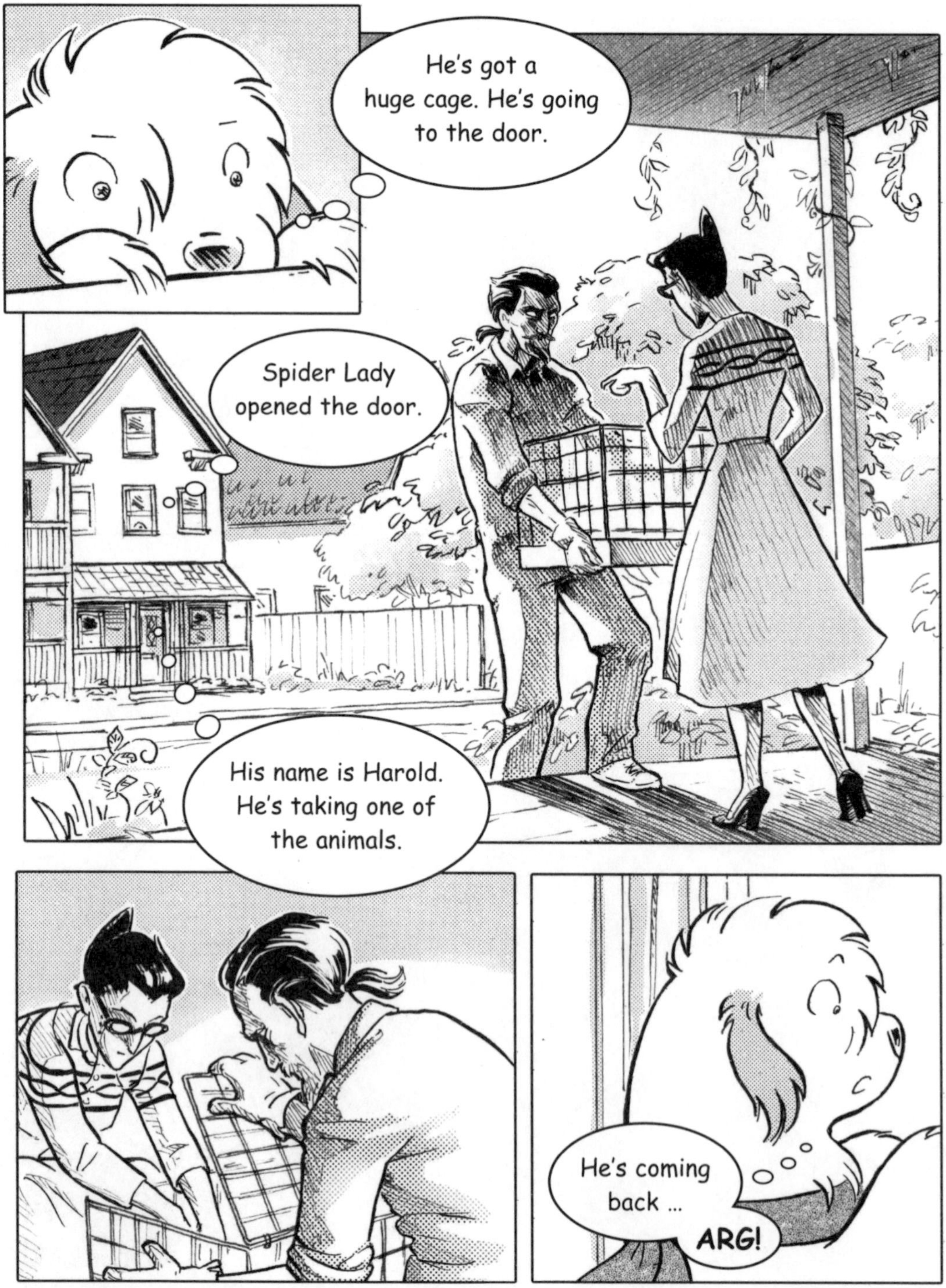
He's got a huge cage. He's going to the door.
Spider Lady opened the door.
His name is Harold. He's taking one of the animals.
He's coming back ...
ARG!

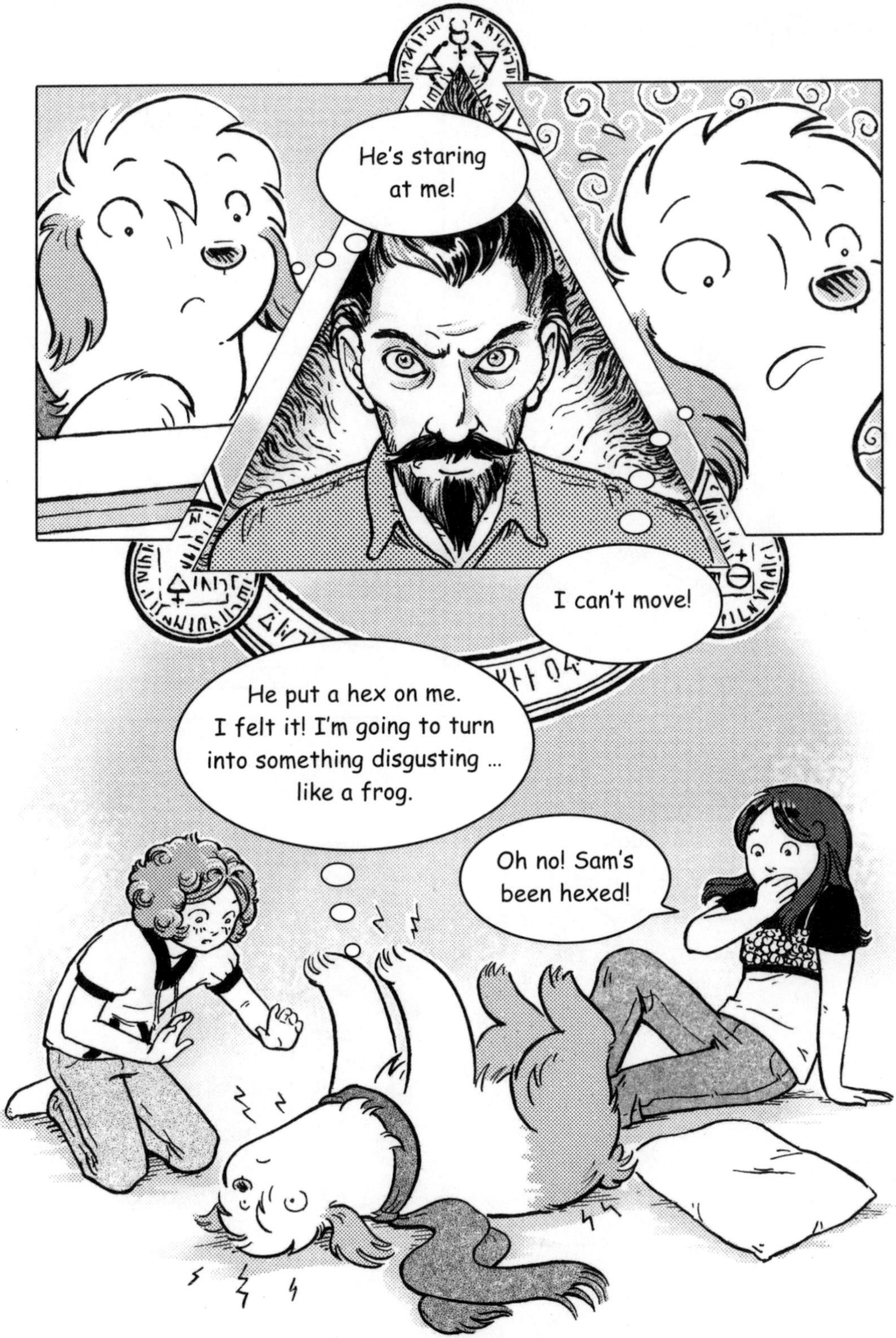
He's staring at me!
I can't move!
He put a hex on me. I felt it! I'm going to turn into something disgusting ... like a frog.
Oh no! Sam's been hexed!

Later that afternoon ...

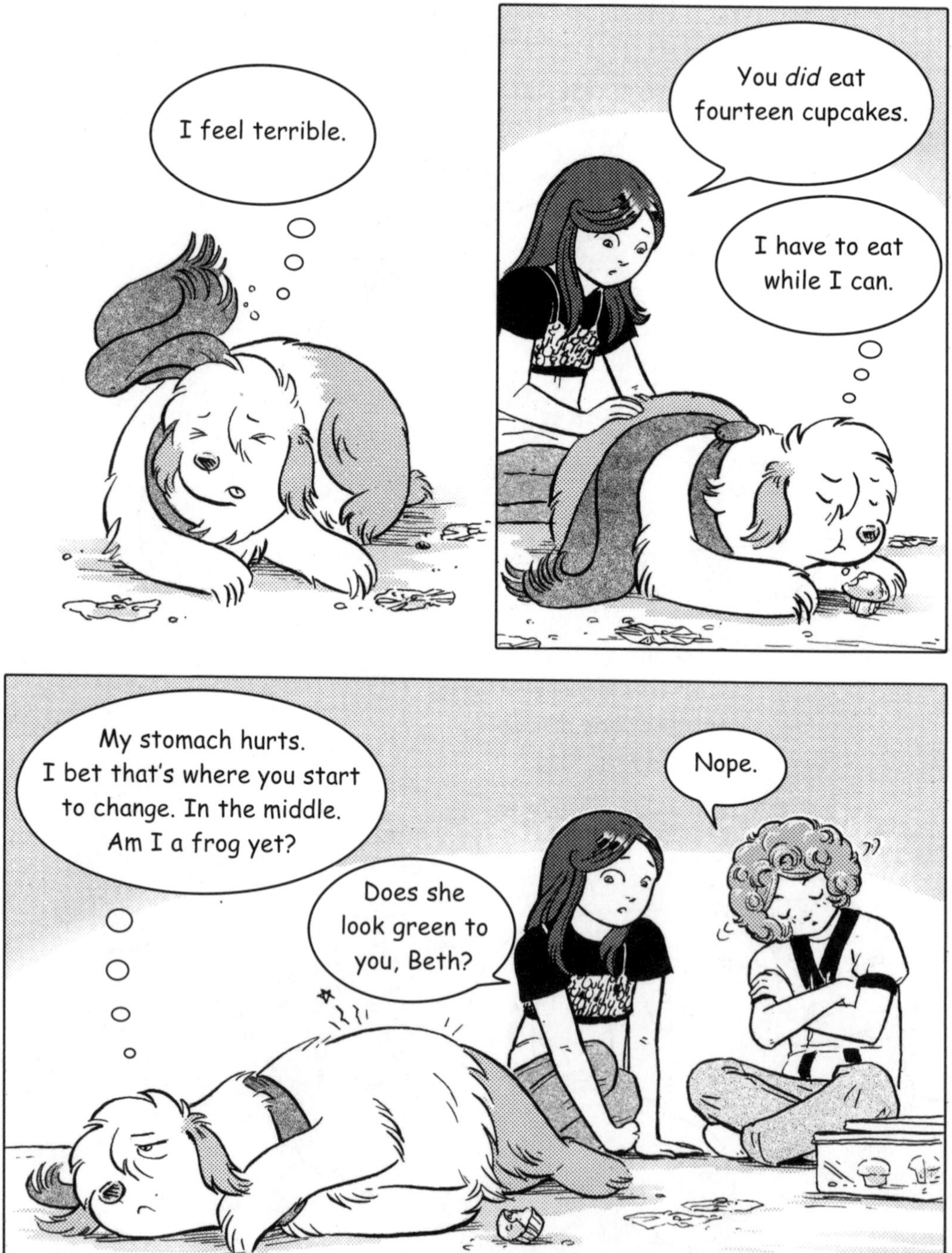

I feel terrible.
You *did* eat fourteen cupcakes.
I have to eat while I can.
My stomach hurts. I bet that's where you start to change. In the middle. Am I a frog yet?
Does she look green to you, Beth?
Nope.

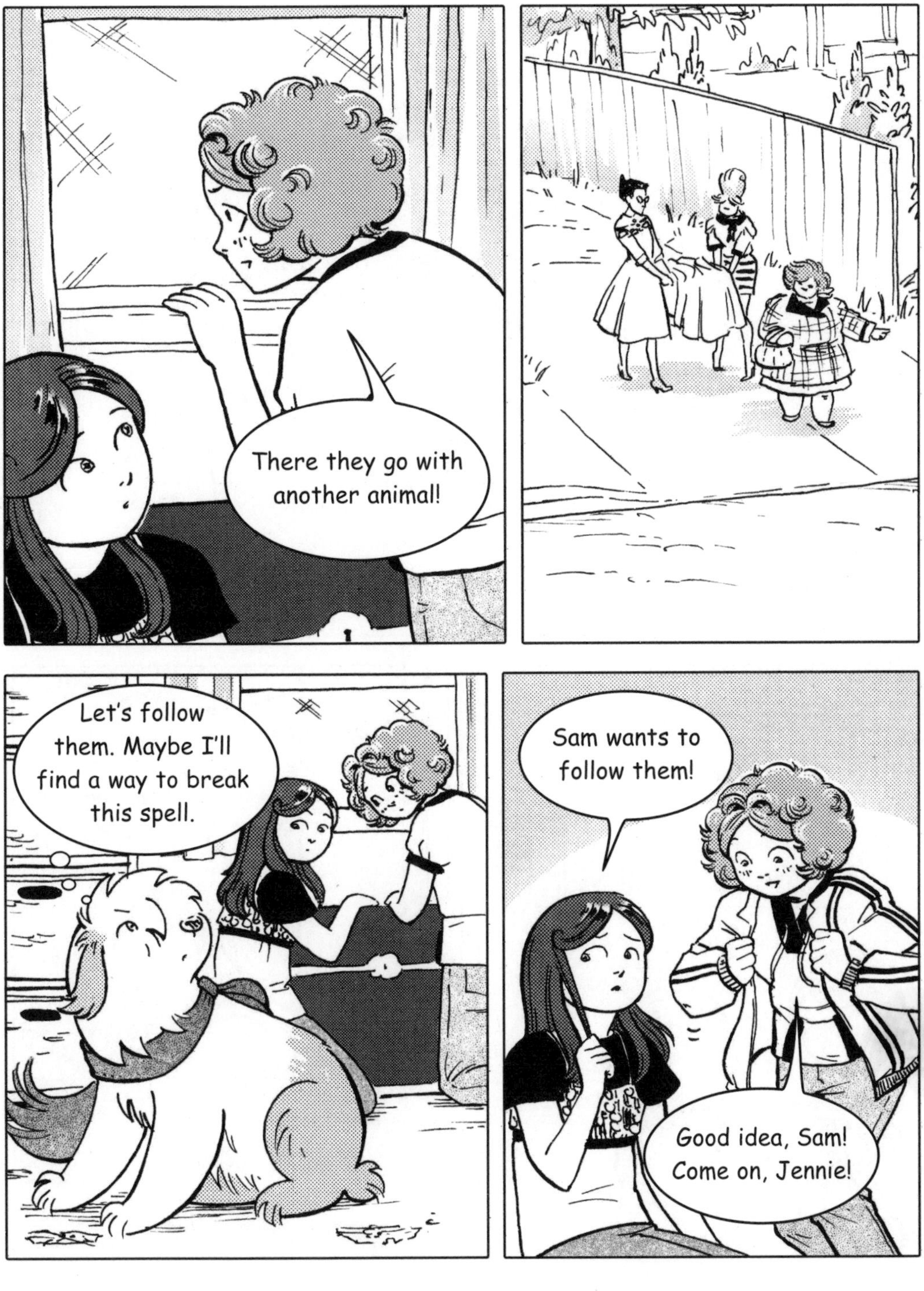
There they go with another animal!
Let's follow them. Maybe I'll find a way to break this spell.
Sam wants to follow them!
Good idea, Sam! Come on, Jennie!

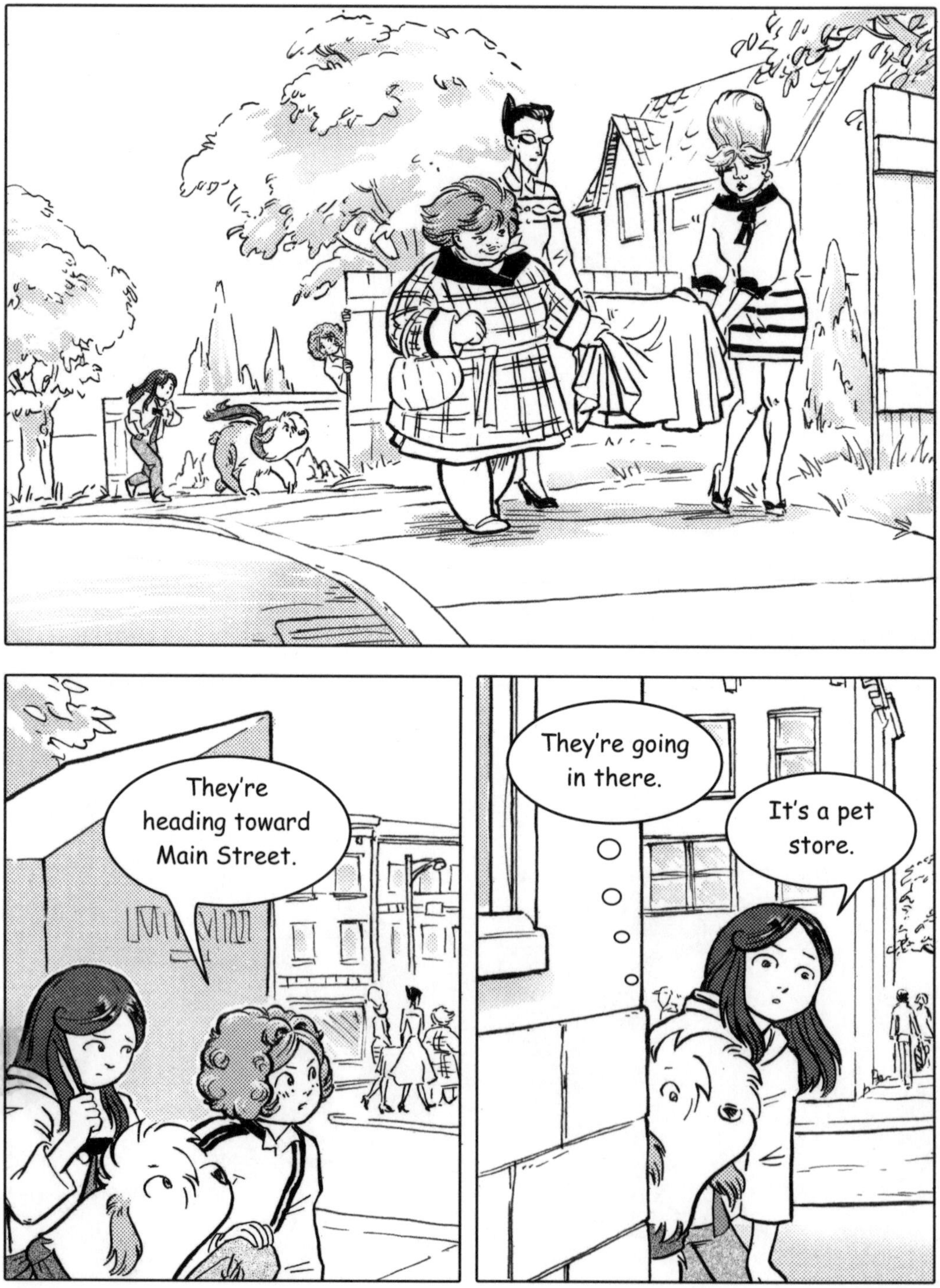
They're heading toward Main Street.
They're going in there.
It's a pet store.

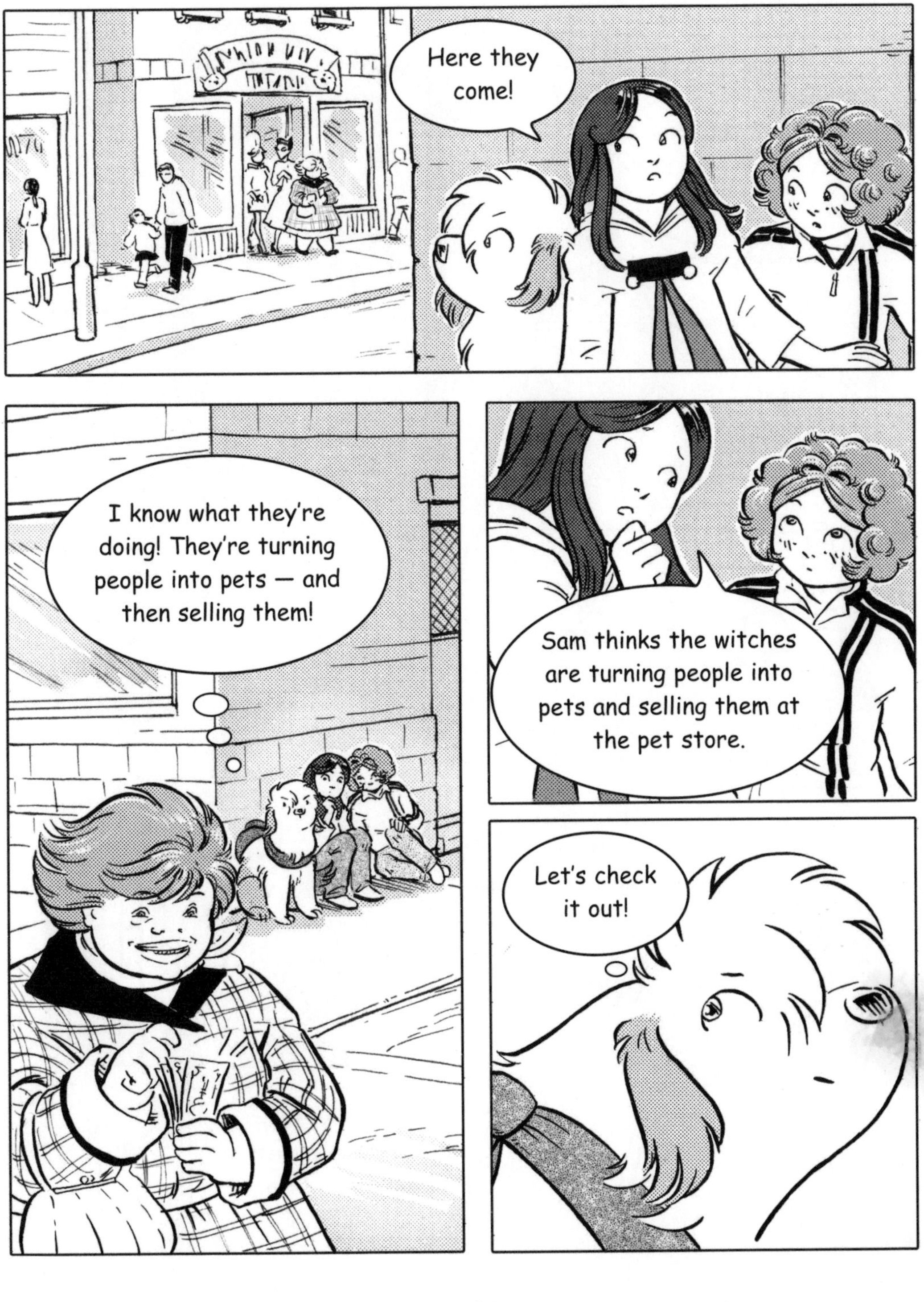
Here they come!
I know what they're doing! They're turning people into pets — and then selling them!
Sam thinks the witches are turning people into pets and selling them at the pet store.
Let's check it out!

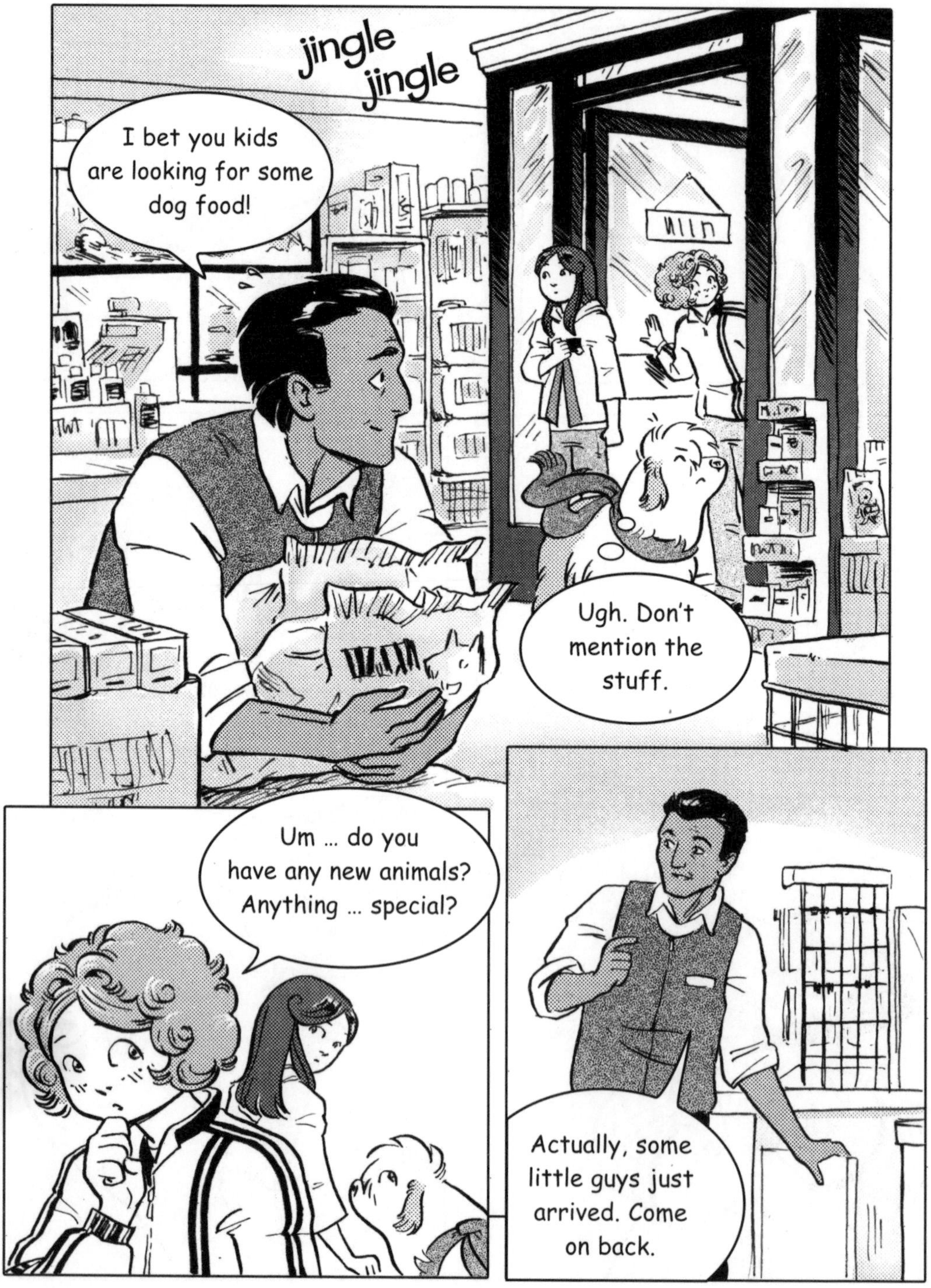
jingle jingle
I bet you kids are looking for some dog food!
Ugh. Don't mention the stuff.
Um ... do you have any new animals? Anything ... special?
Actually, some little guys just arrived. Come on back.

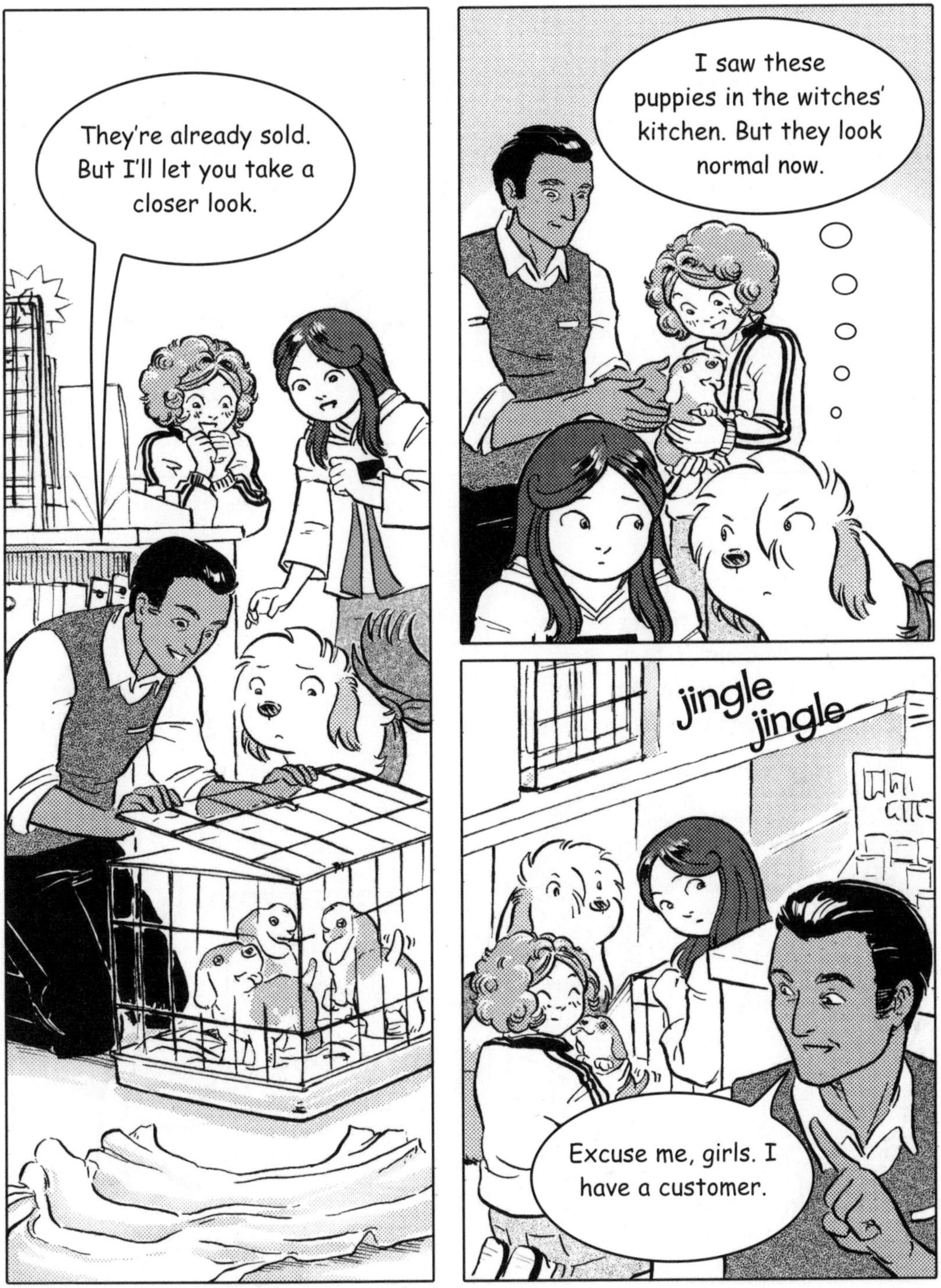
They're already sold. But I'll let you take a closer look.
I saw these puppies in the witches' kitchen. But they look normal now.
jingle jingle
Excuse me, girls. I have a customer.

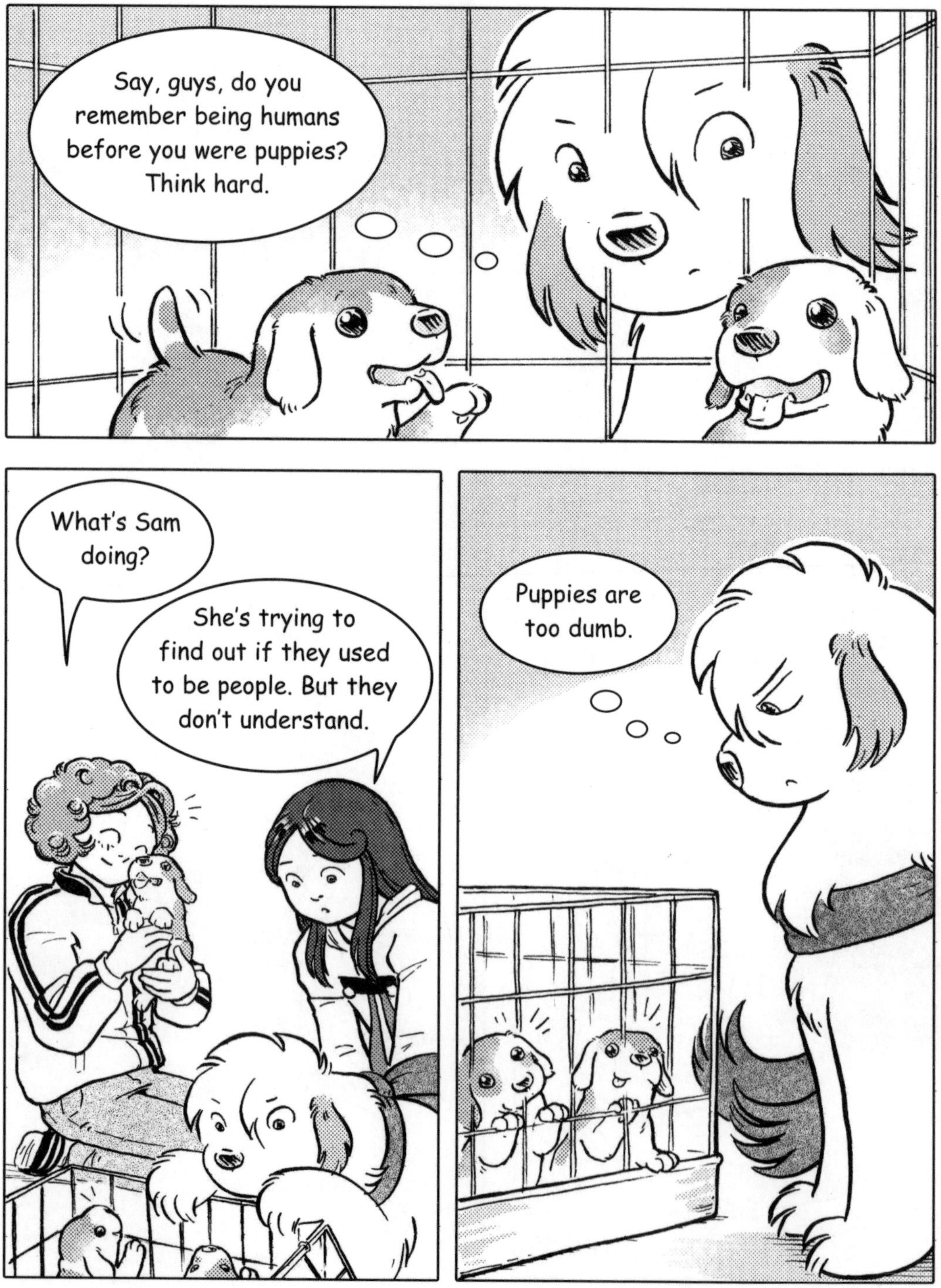
Say, guys, do you remember being humans before you were puppies? Think hard.
What's Sam doing?
She's trying to find out if they used to be people. But they don't understand.
Puppies are too dumb.

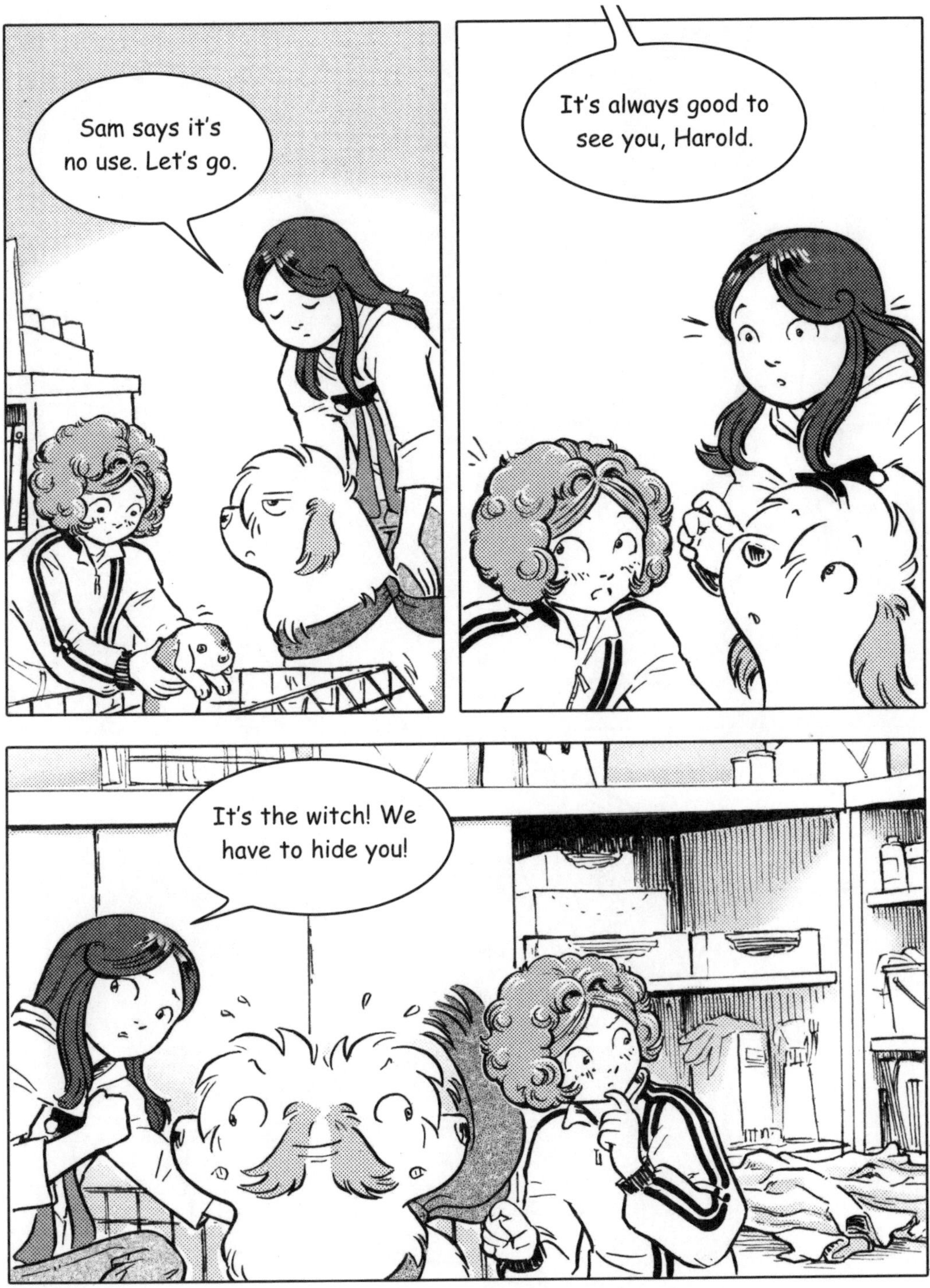
Sam says it's no use. Let's go.
It's always good to see you, Harold.
It's the witch! We have to hide you!

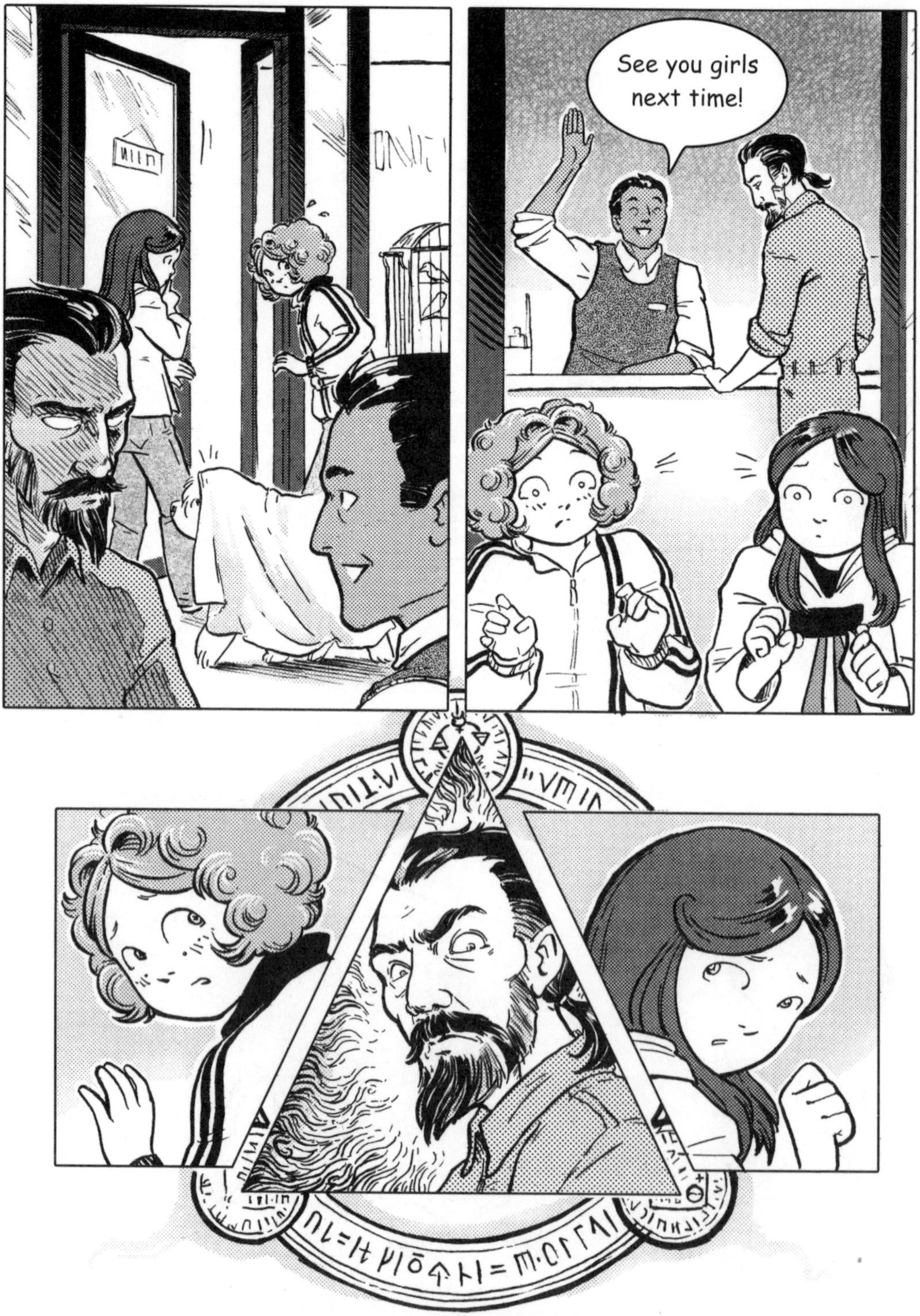
See you girls next time!

Later ...

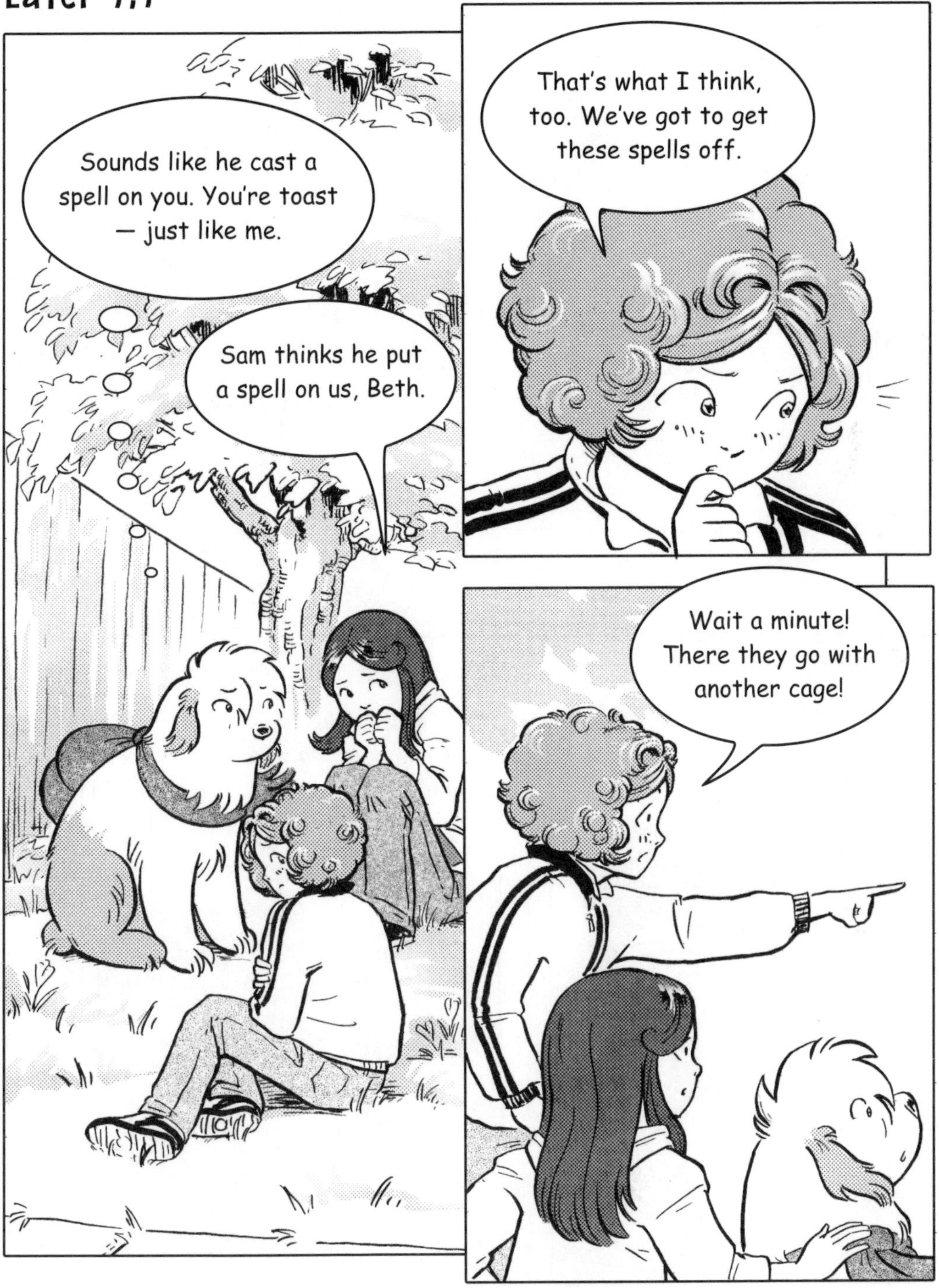
Sounds like he cast a spell on you. You're toast — just like me.
Sam thinks he put a spell on us, Beth.
That's what I think, too. We've got to get these spells off.
Wait a minute! There they go with another cage!

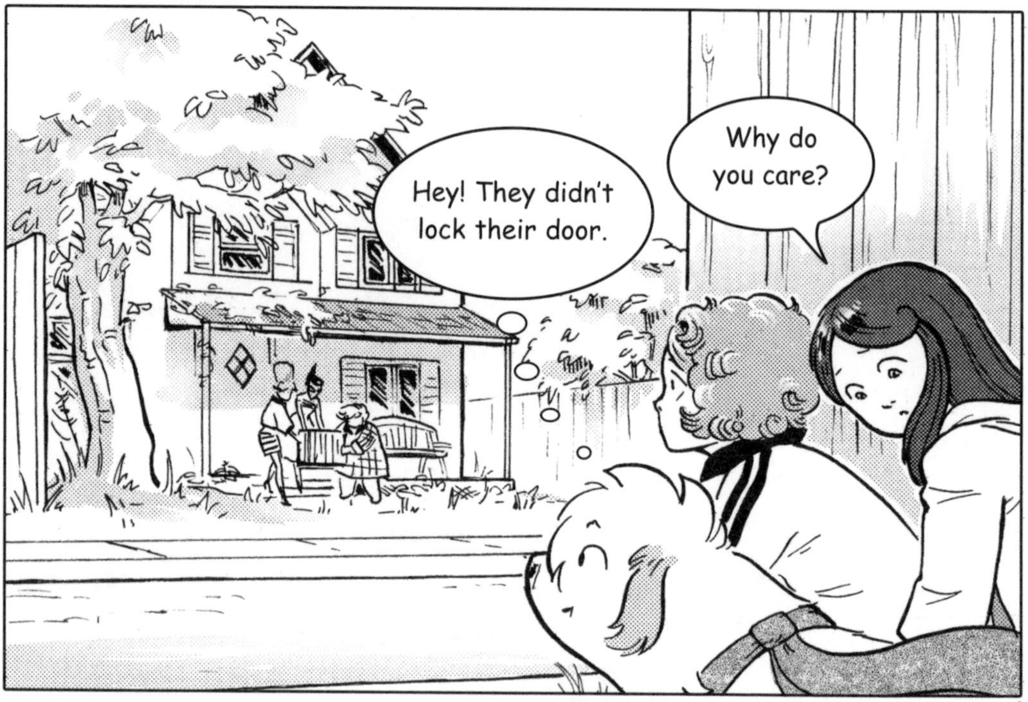
Hey! They didn't lock their door.
Why do you care?

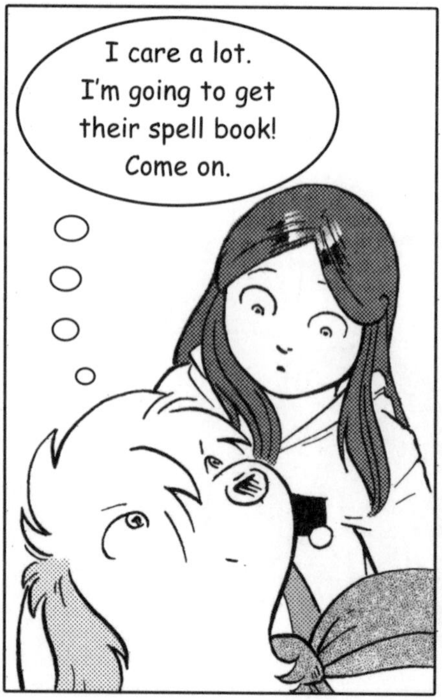
I care a lot. I'm going to get their spell book! Come on.

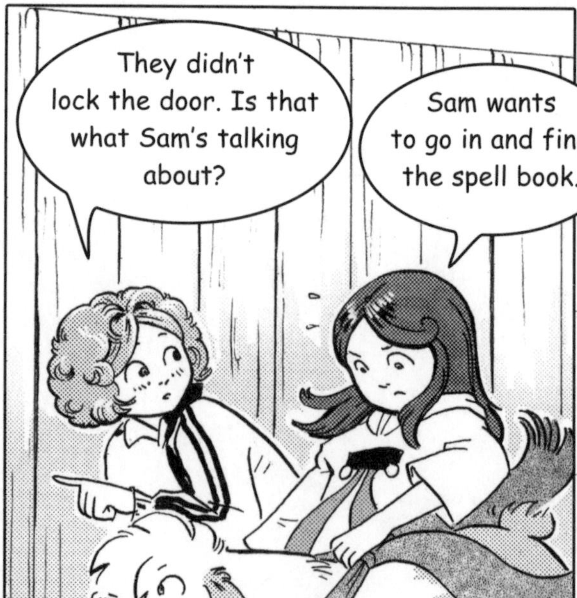
They didn't lock the door. Is that what Sam's talking about?
Sam wants to go in and find the spell book.

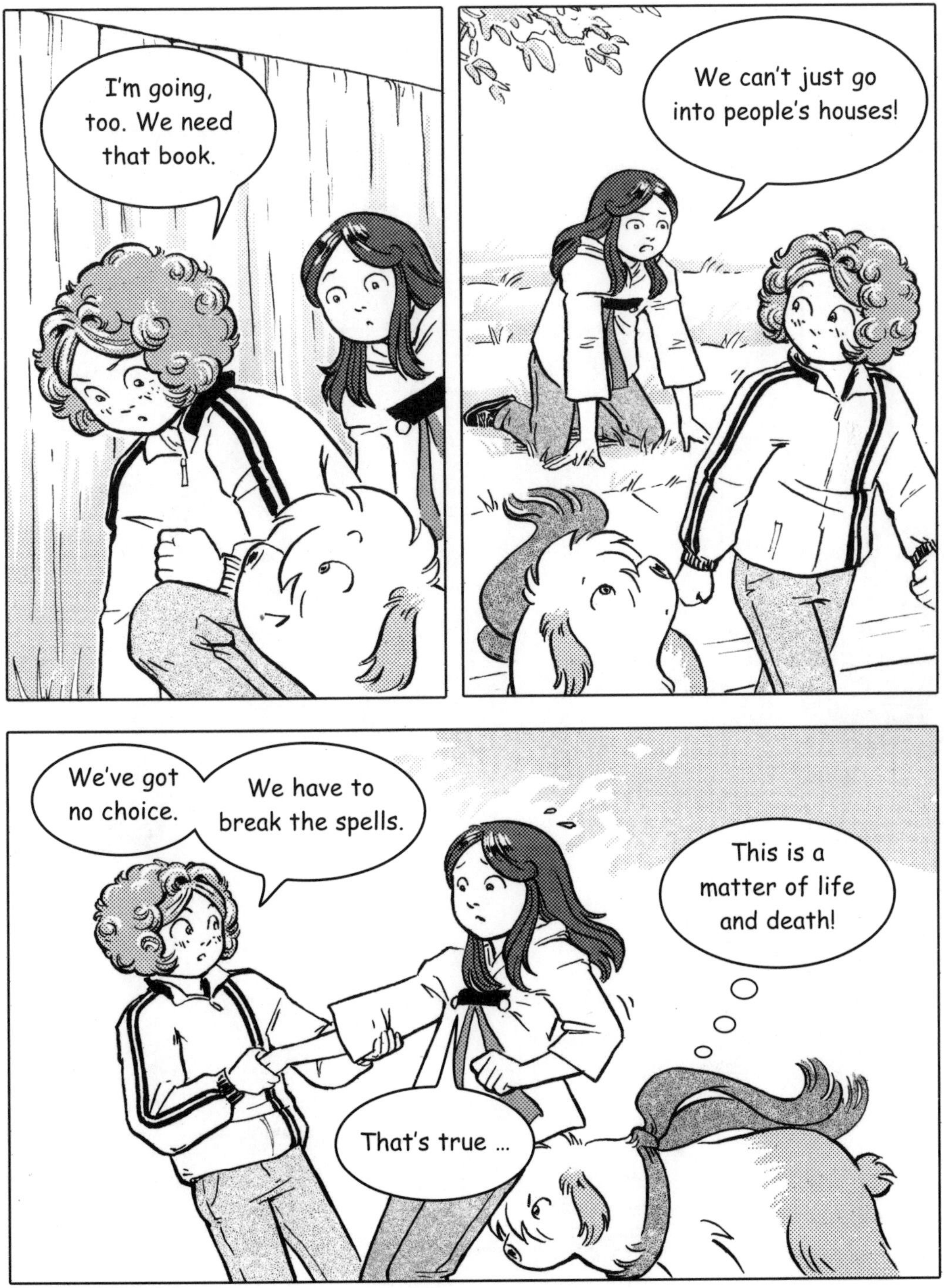
I'm going, too. We need that book.
We can't just go into people's houses!
We've got no choice.
We have to break the spells.
This is a matter of life and death!
That's true ...

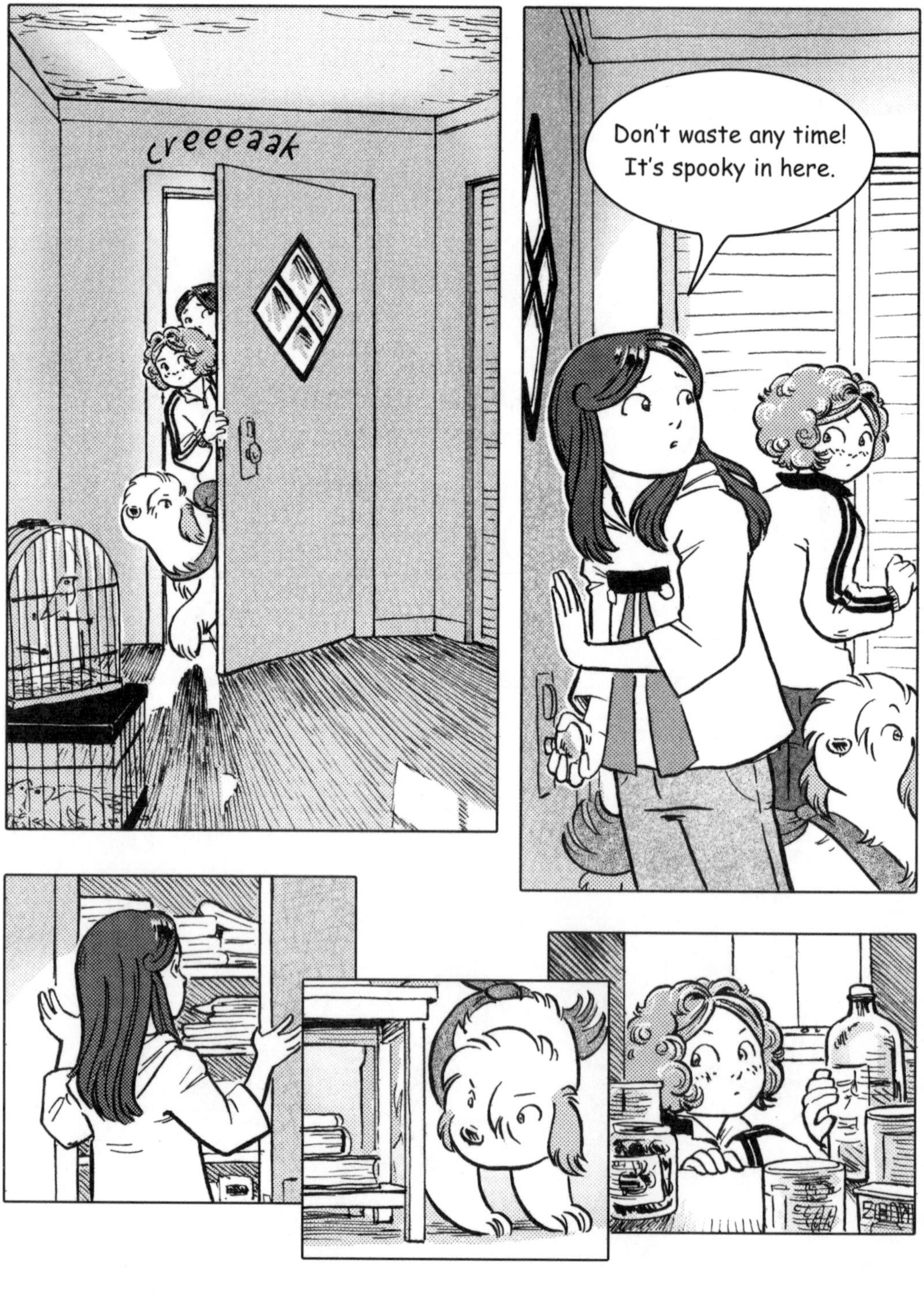
creeeaak
Don't waste any time! It's spooky in here.

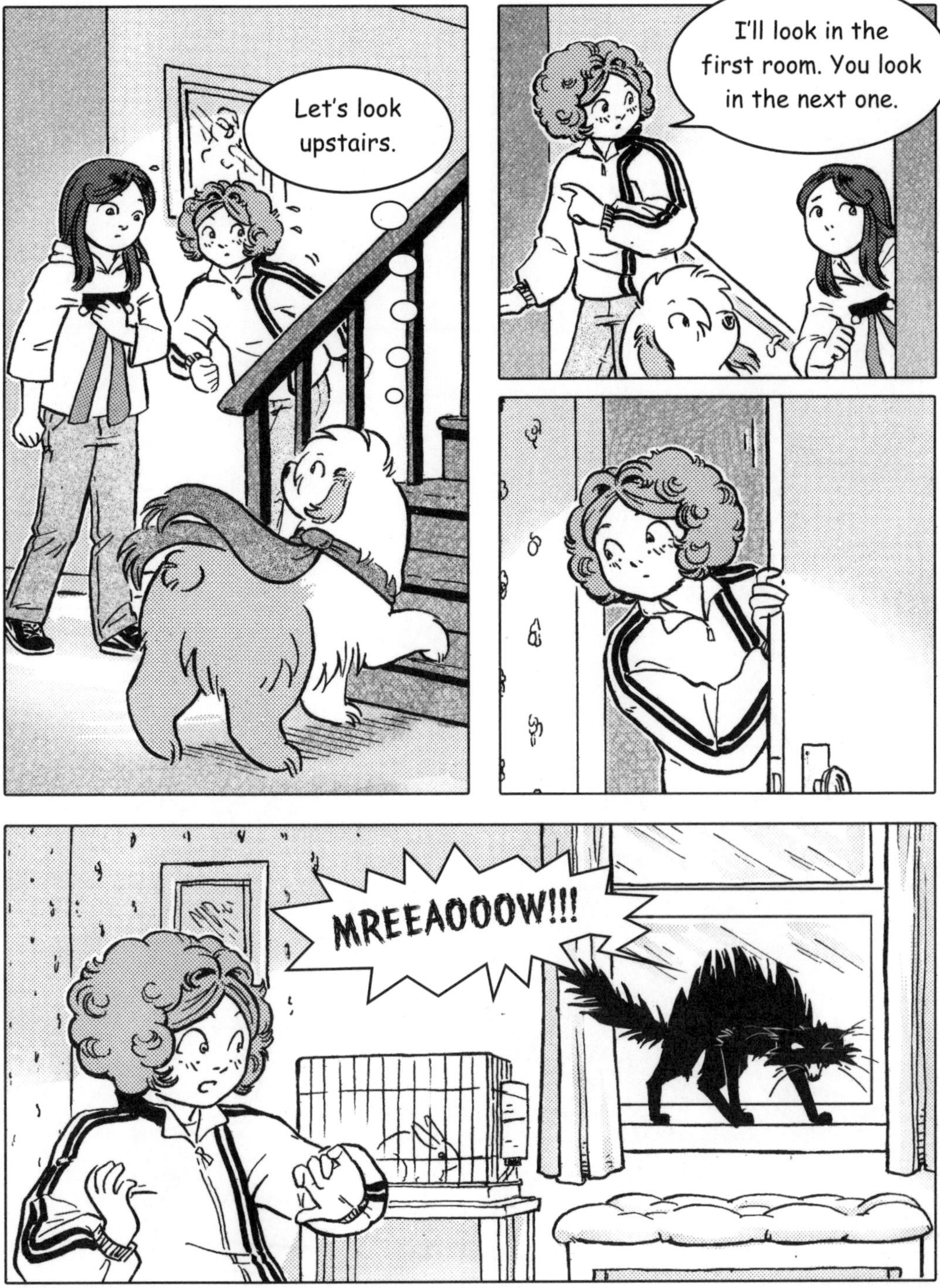
Let's look upstairs.
I'll look in the first room. You look in the next one.
MREEAOOOW!!!

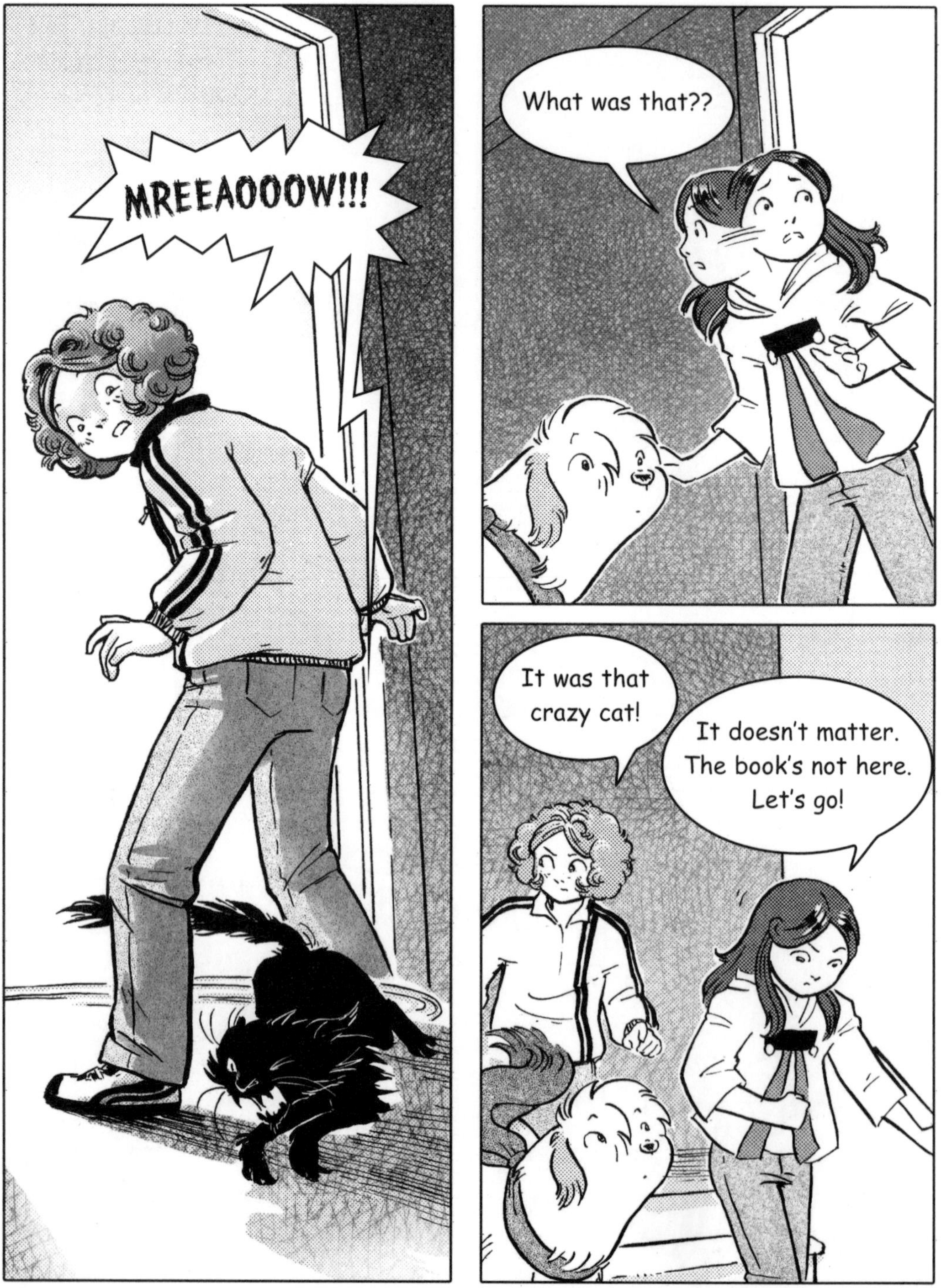
MREEAOOOW!!!
What was that??
It was that crazy cat!
It doesn't matter. The book's not here. Let's go!

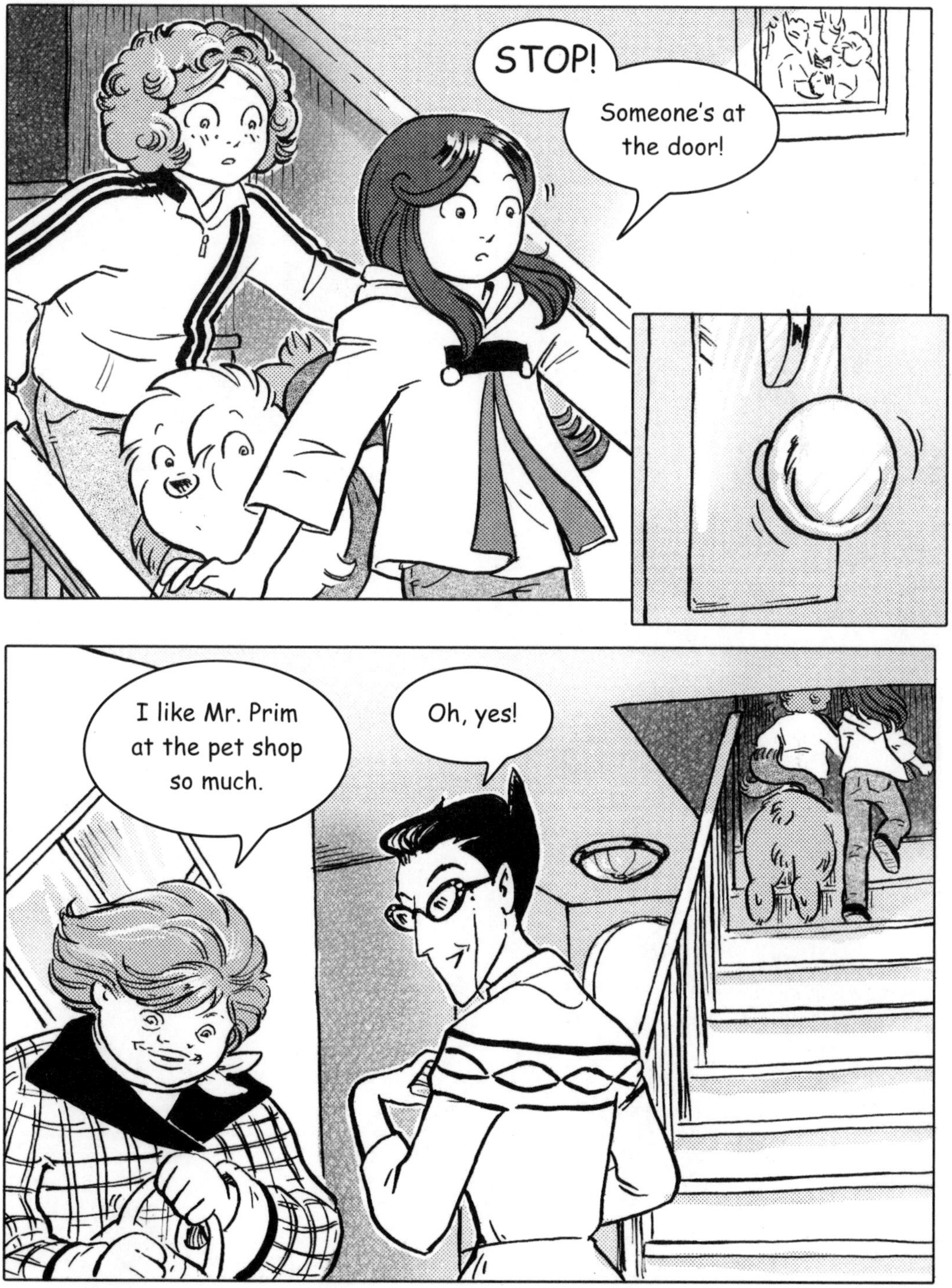
STOP!
Someone's at the door!
I like Mr. Prim at the pet shop so much.
Oh, yes!

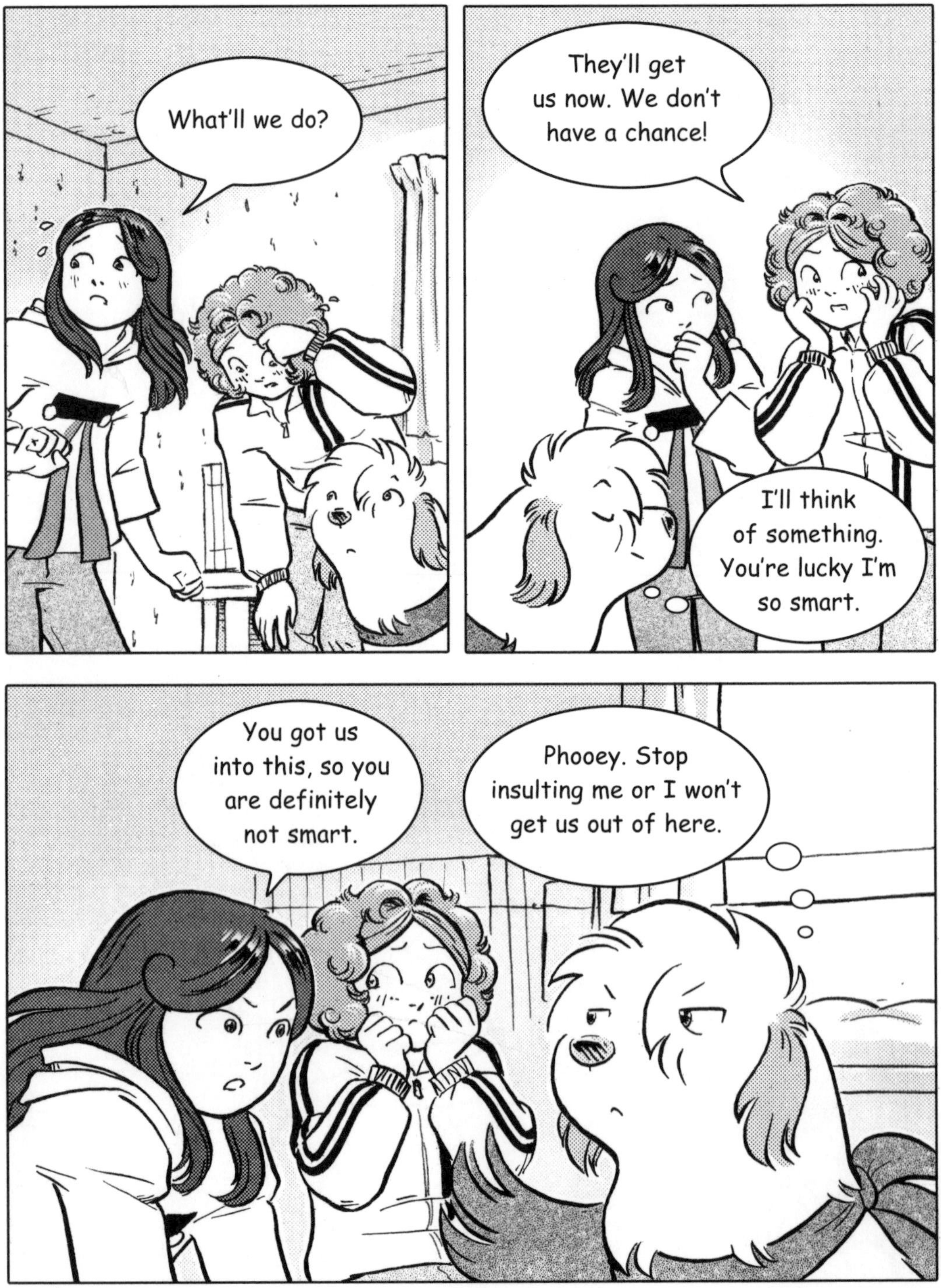
What'll we do?
They'll get us now. We don't have a chance!
I'll think of something. You're lucky I'm so smart.
You got us into this, so you are definitely not smart.
Phooey. Stop insulting me or I won't get us out of here.

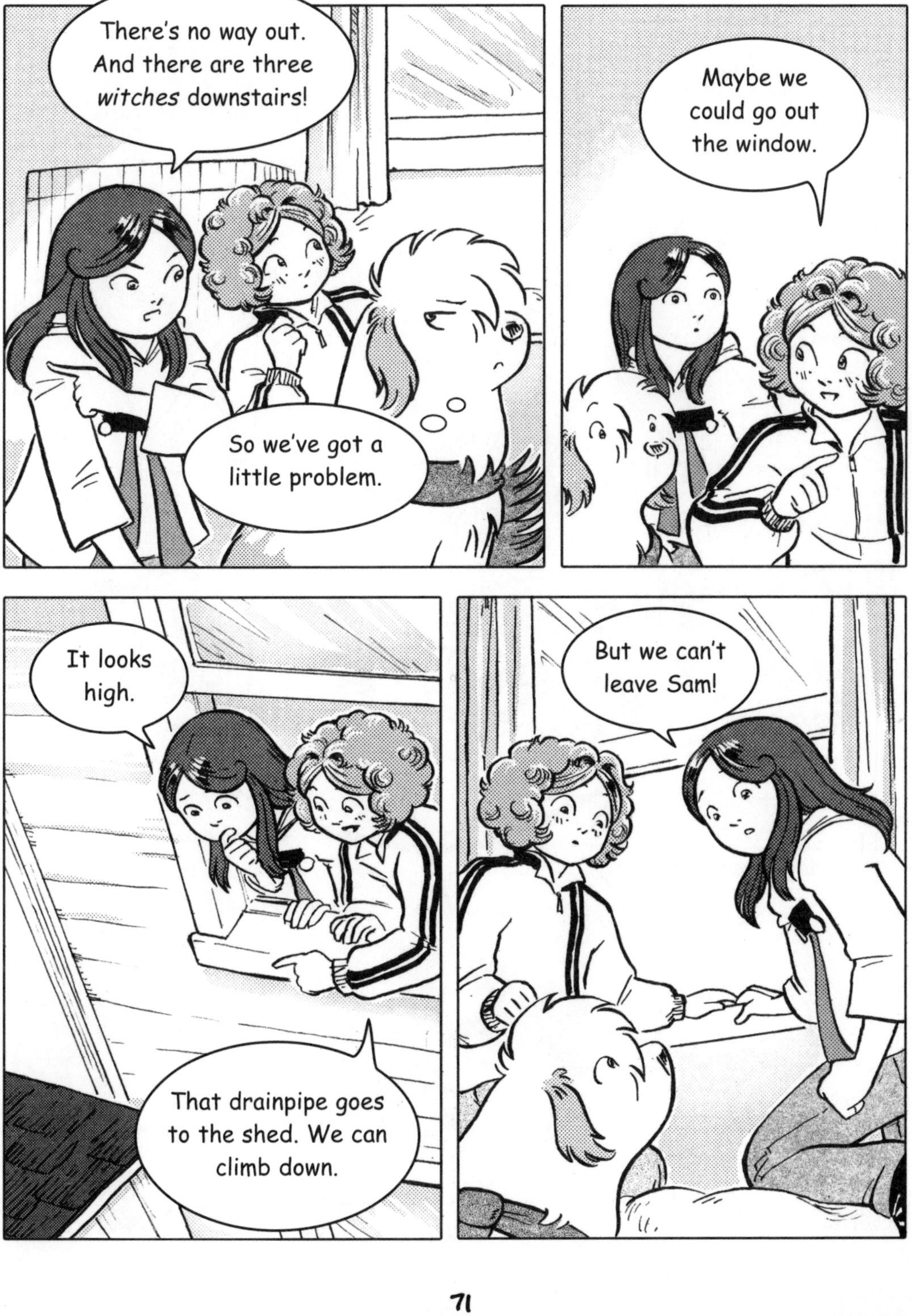
There's no way out. And there are three *witches* downstairs!
So we've got a little problem.
Maybe we could go out the window.
It looks high.
That drainpipe goes to the shed. We can climb down.
But we can't leave Sam!

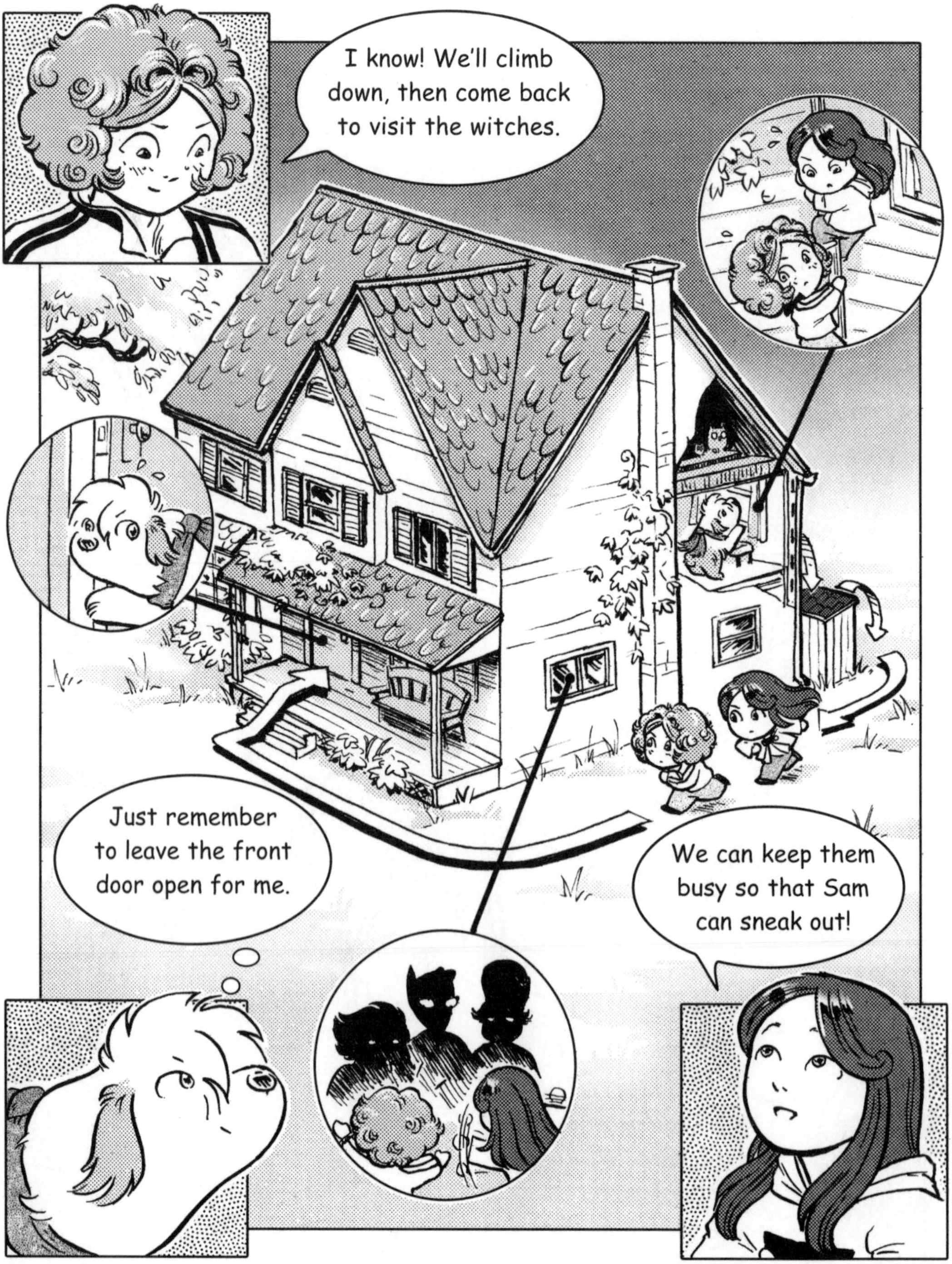
I know! We'll climb down, then come back to visit the witches.
Just remember to leave the front door open for me.
We can keep them busy so that Sam can sneak out!

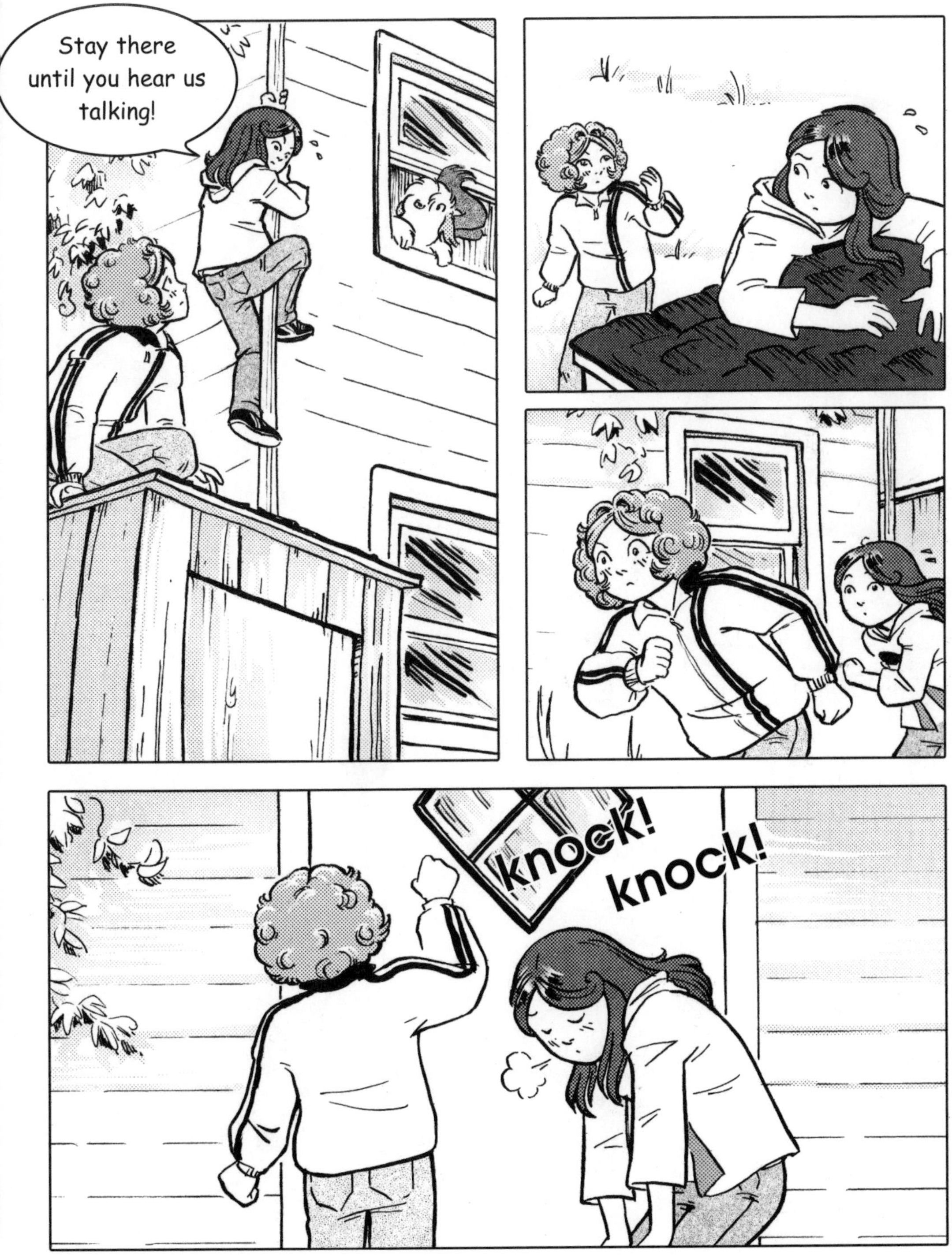
Stay there until you hear us talking!
knock!
knock!

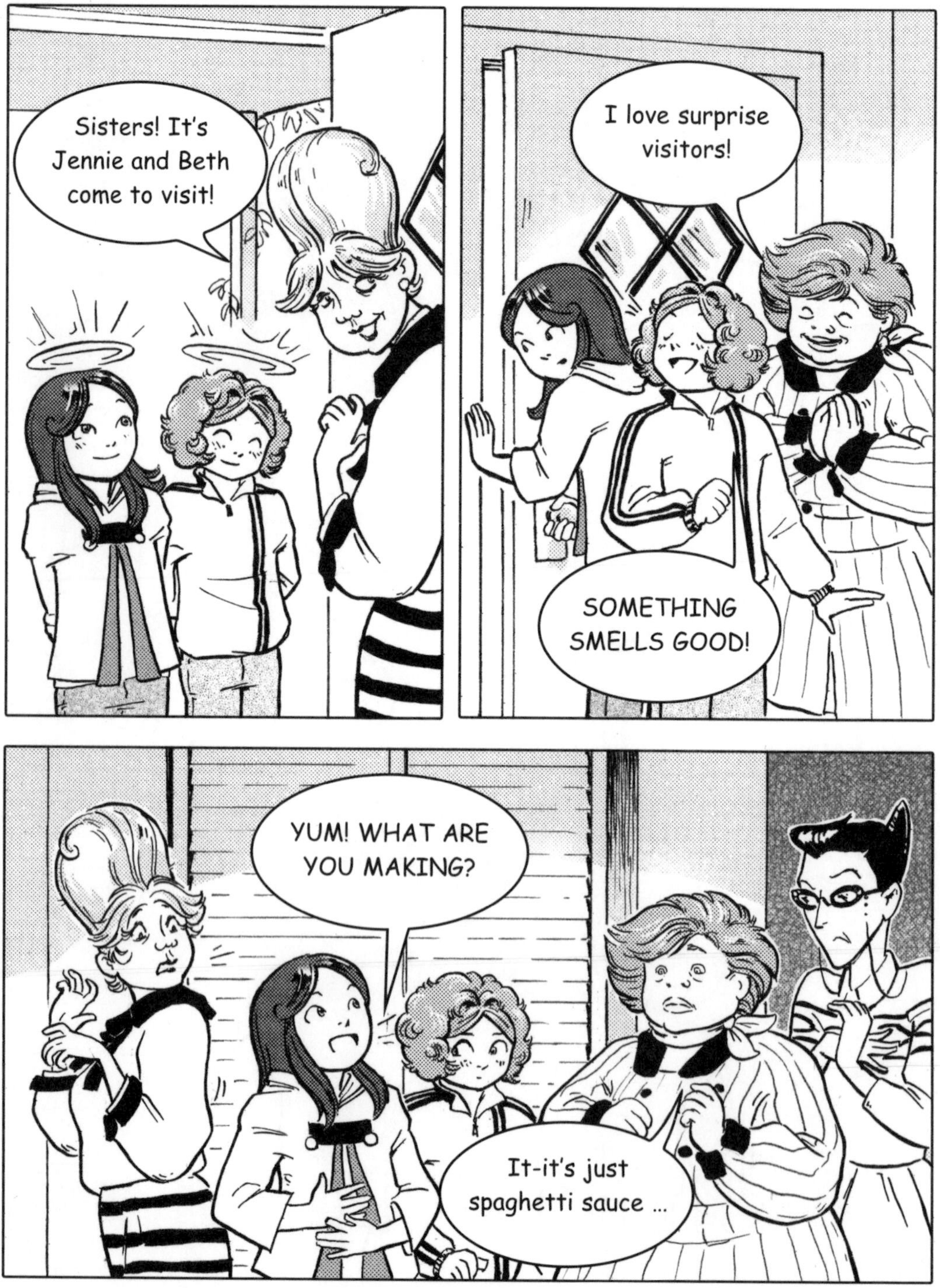

Sisters! It's Jennie and Beth come to visit!
I love surprise visitors!
SOMETHING SMELLS GOOD!
YUM! WHAT ARE YOU MAKING?
It-it's just spaghetti sauce ...

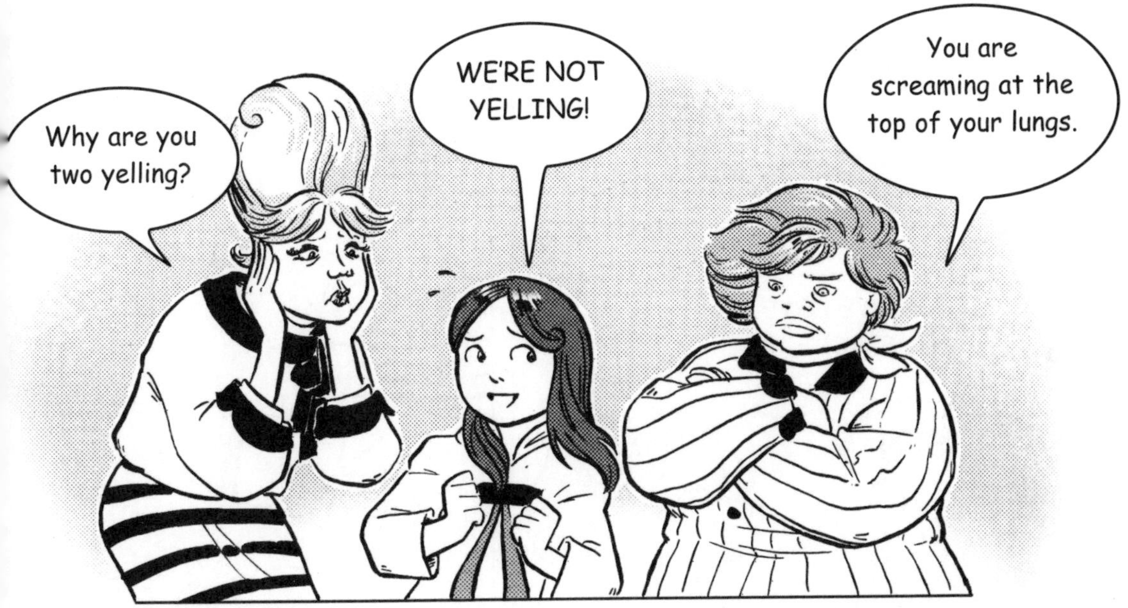
Why are you two yelling?
WE'RE NOT YELLING!
You are screaming at the top of your lungs.

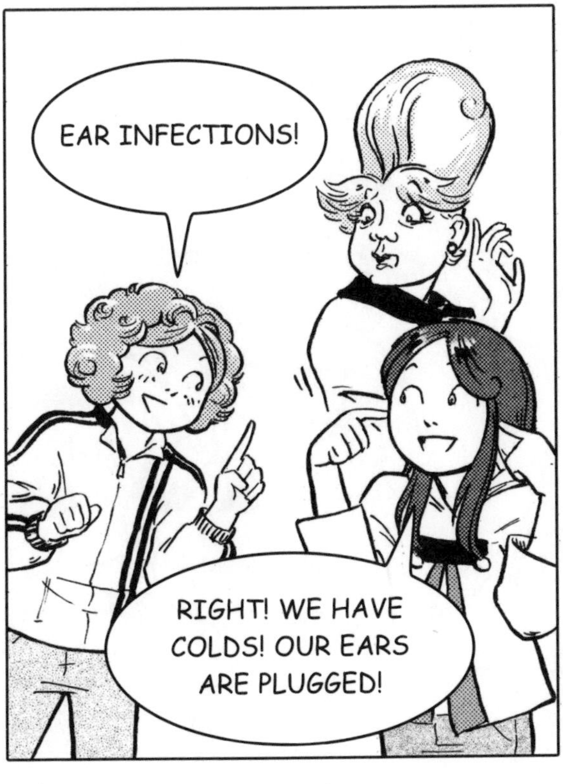
EAR INFECTIONS!
RIGHT! WE HAVE COLDS! OUR EARS ARE PLUGGED!

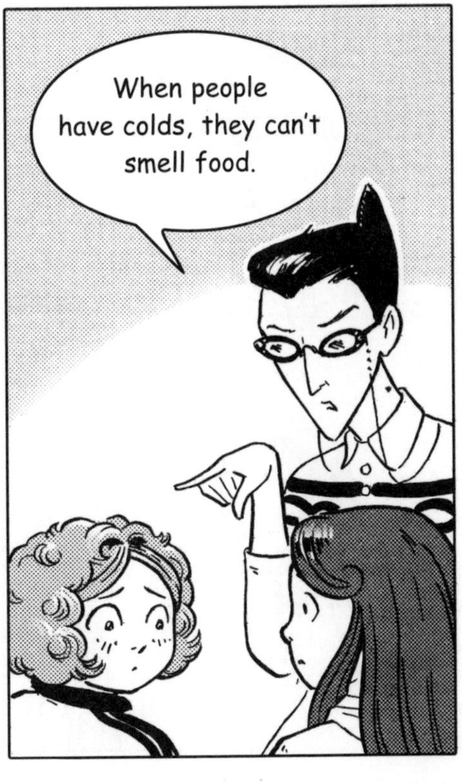
When people have colds, they can't smell food.

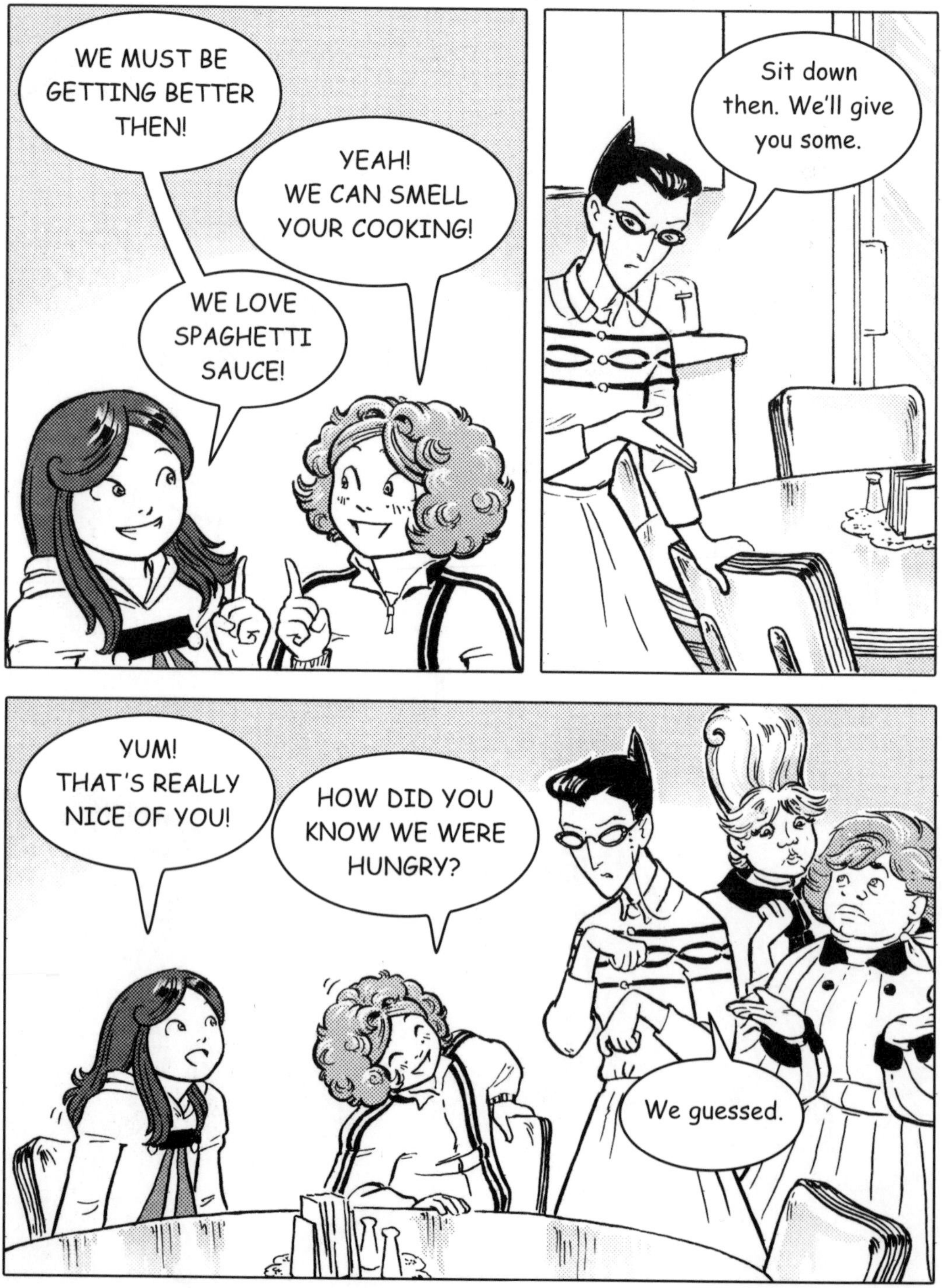
WE MUST BE GETTING BETTER THEN!
YEAH! WE CAN SMELL YOUR COOKING!
WE LOVE SPAGHETTI SAUCE!
Sit down then. We'll give you some.
YUM! THAT'S REALLY NICE OF YOU!
HOW DID YOU KNOW WE WERE HUNGRY?
We guessed.

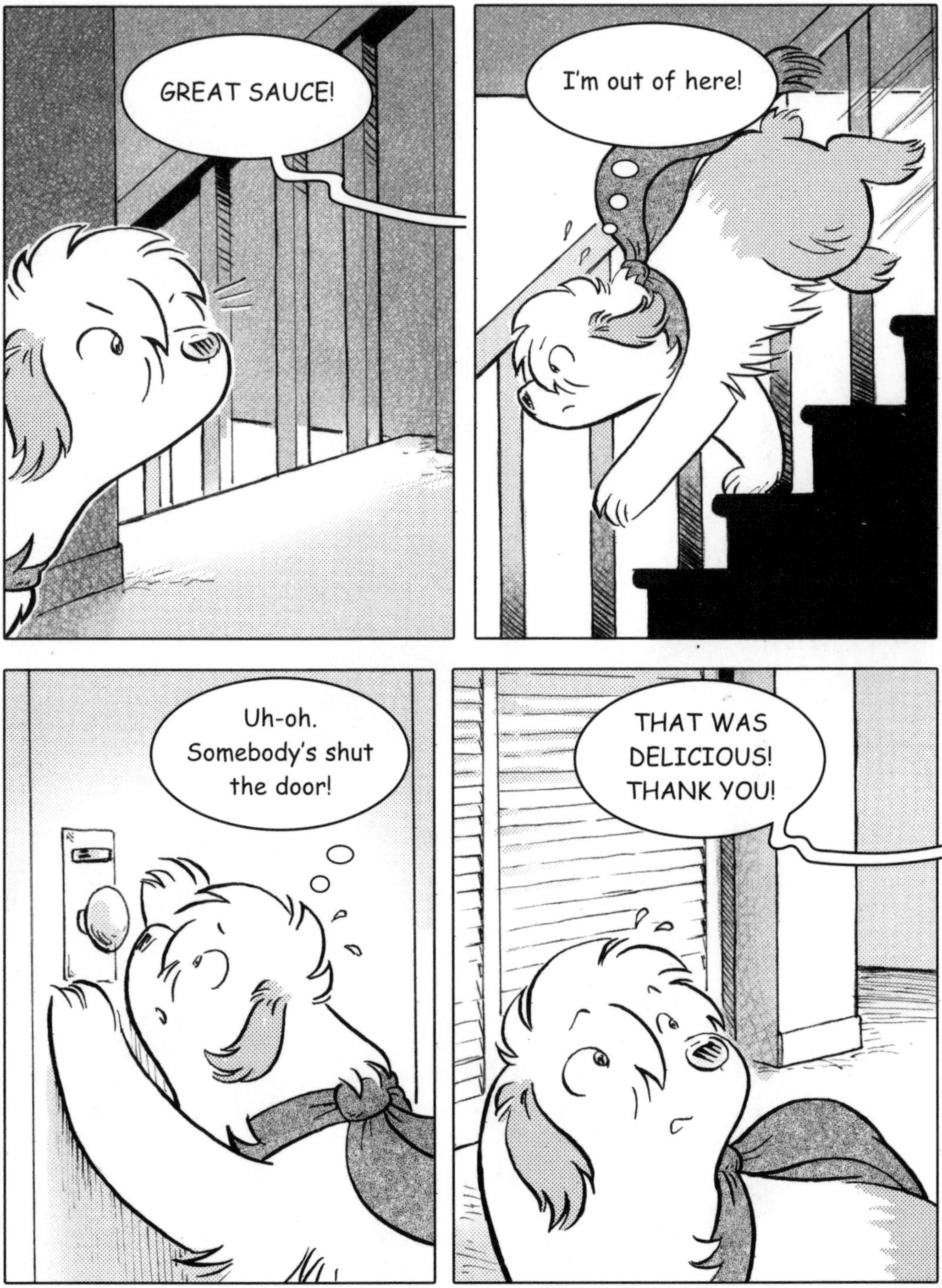
GREAT SAUCE!
I'm out of here!
Uh-oh. Somebody's shut the door!
THAT WAS DELICIOUS! THANK YOU!

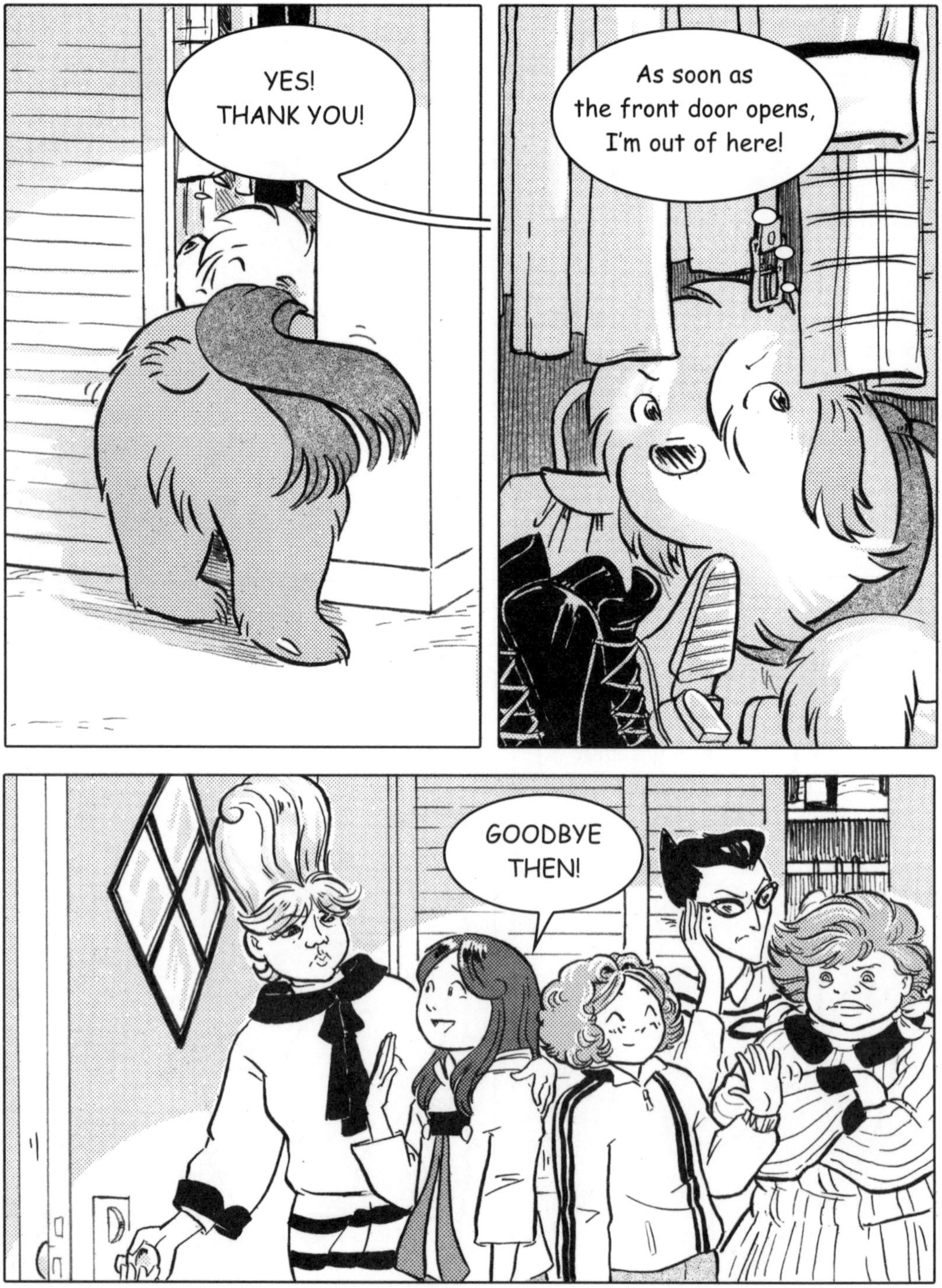
YES! THANK YOU!
As soon as the front door opens, I'm out of here!
GOODBYE THEN!

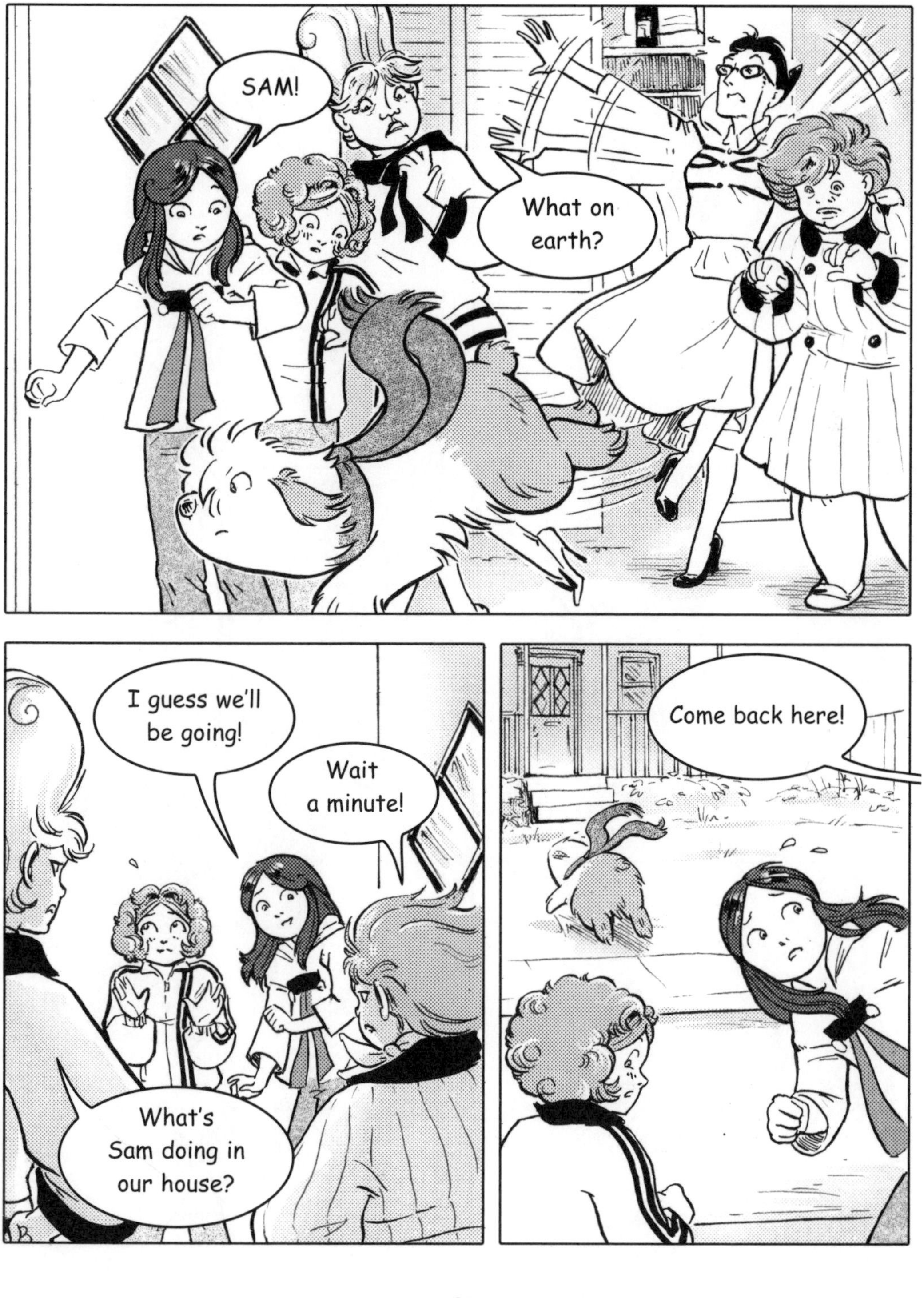
SAM!
What on earth?
I guess we'll be going!
Wait a minute!
What's Sam doing in our house?
Come back here!

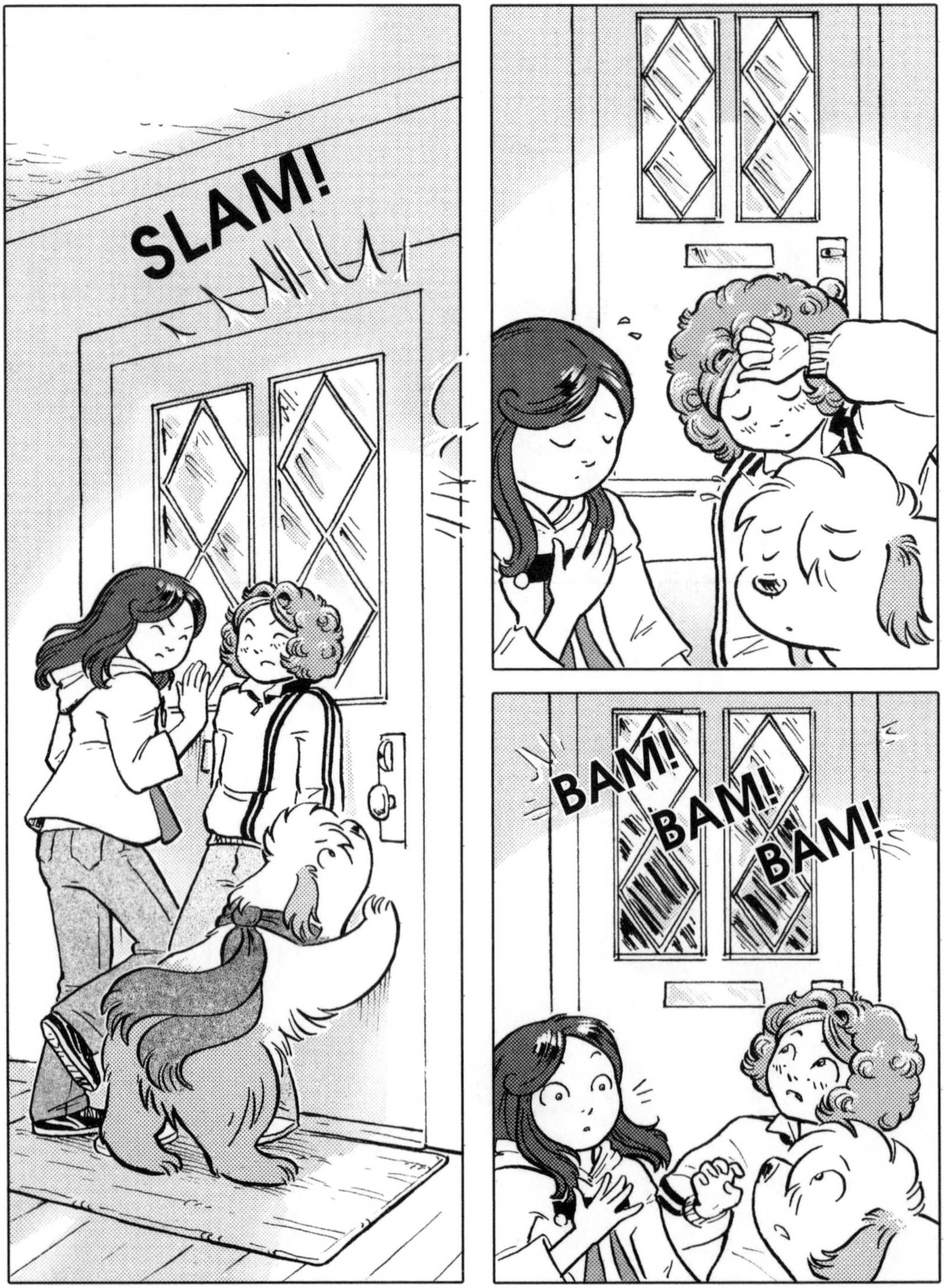
SLAM!
BAM!
BAM!
BAM!

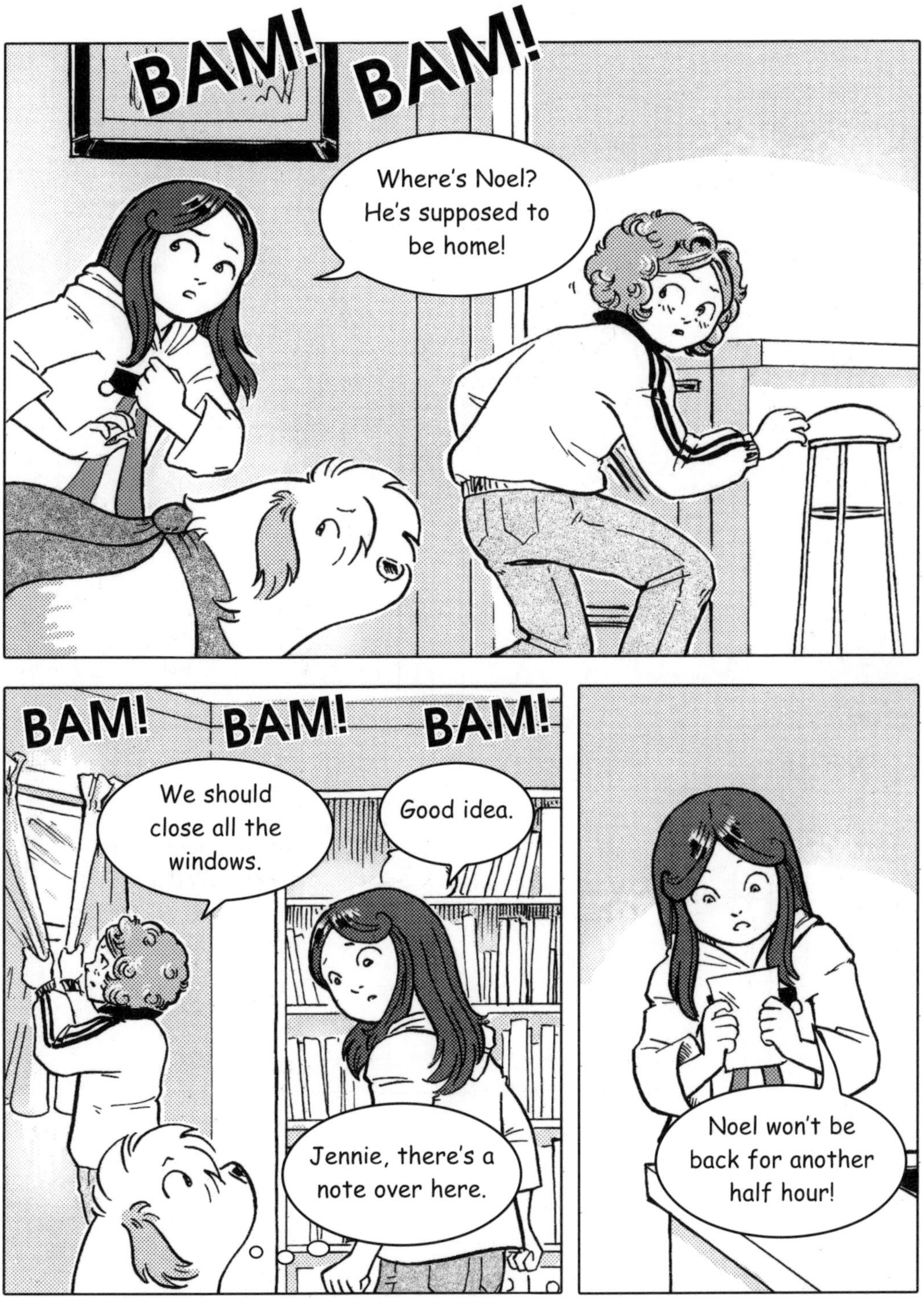
BAM! BAM!
Where's Noel? He's supposed to be home!
BAM! BAM! BAM!
We should close all the windows.
Good idea.
Jennie, there's a note over here.
Noel won't be back for another half hour!

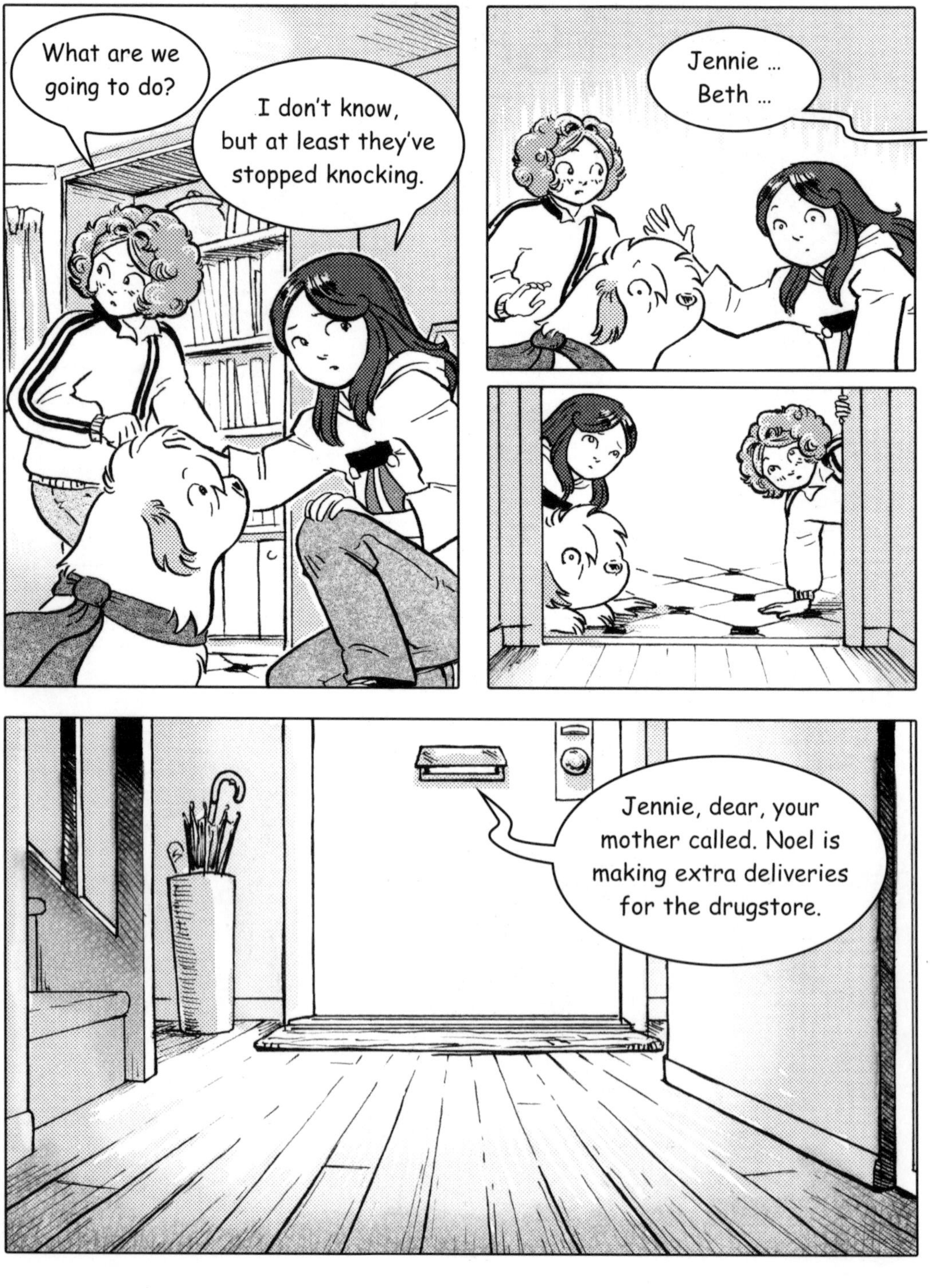
What are we going to do?
I don't know, but at least they've stopped knocking.
Jennie ... Beth ...
Jennie, dear, your mother called. Noel is making extra deliveries for the drugstore.

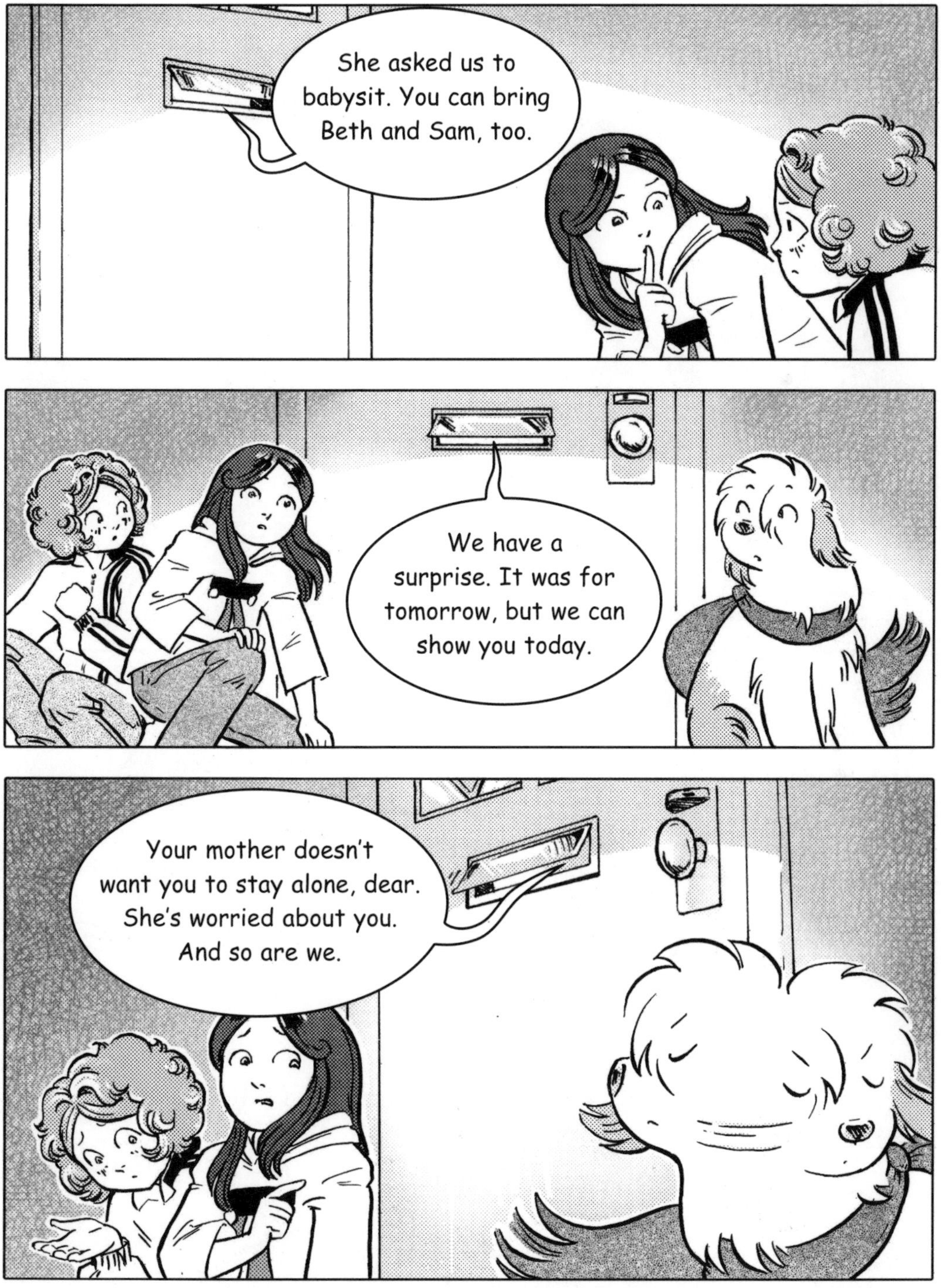
She asked us to babysit. You can bring Beth and Sam, too.
We have a surprise. It was for tomorrow, but we can show you today.
Your mother doesn't want you to stay alone, dear. She's worried about you. And so are we.

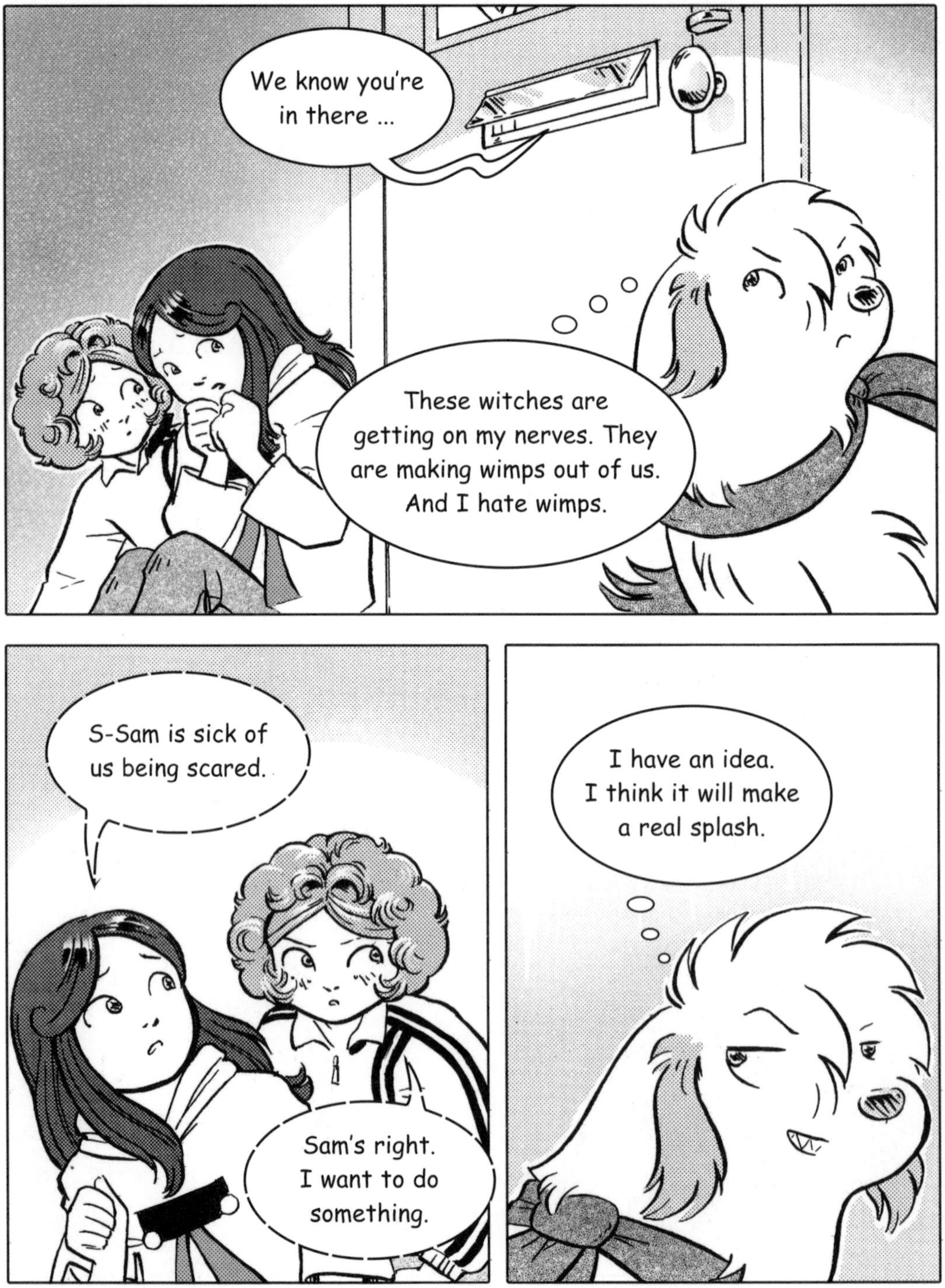
We know you're in there ...
These witches are getting on my nerves. They are making wimps out of us. And I hate wimps.
S-Sam is sick of us being scared.
Sam's right. I want to do something.
I have an idea. I think it will make a real splash.

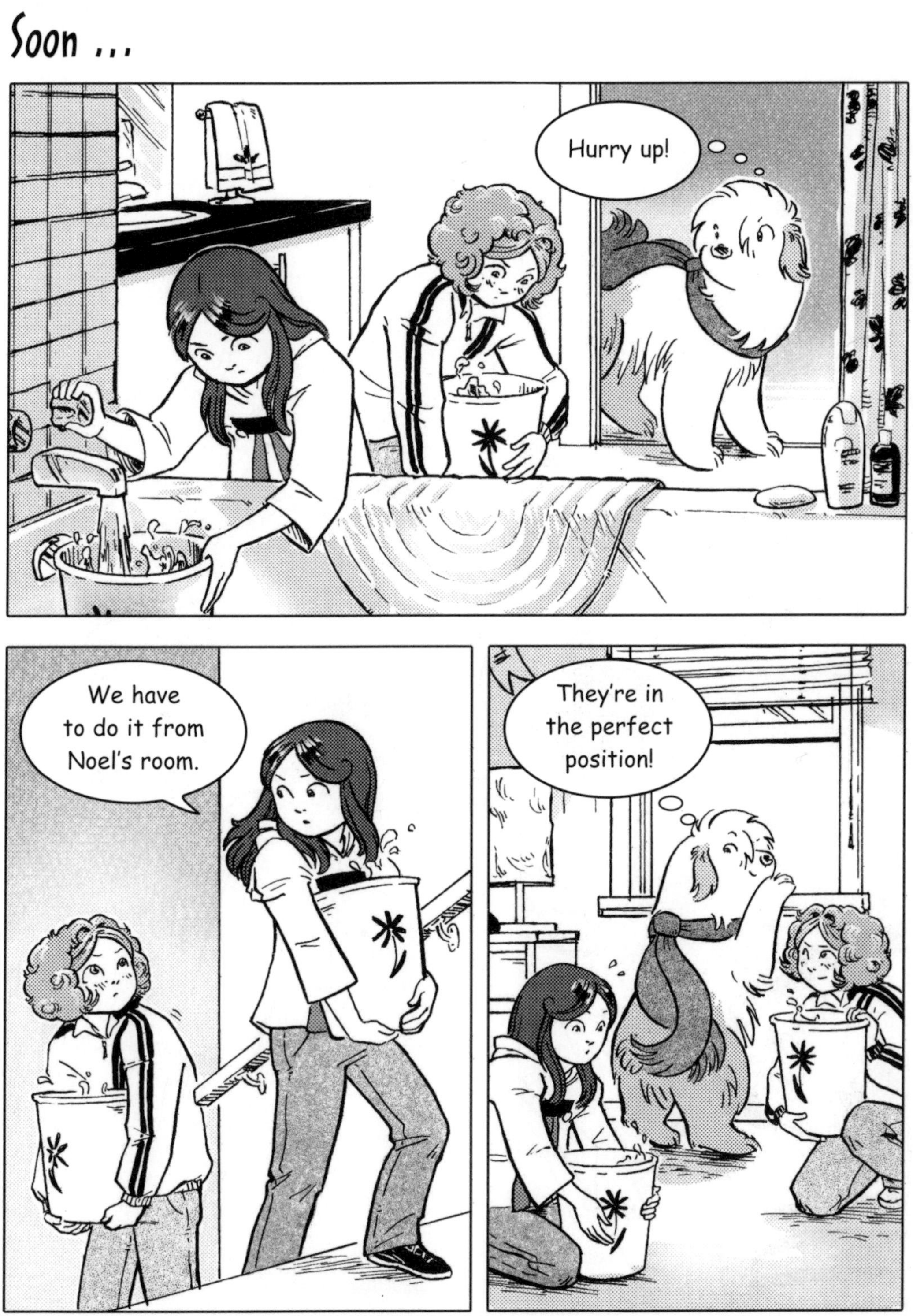
Soon ...
Hurry up!
We have to do it from Noel's room.
They're in the perfect position!

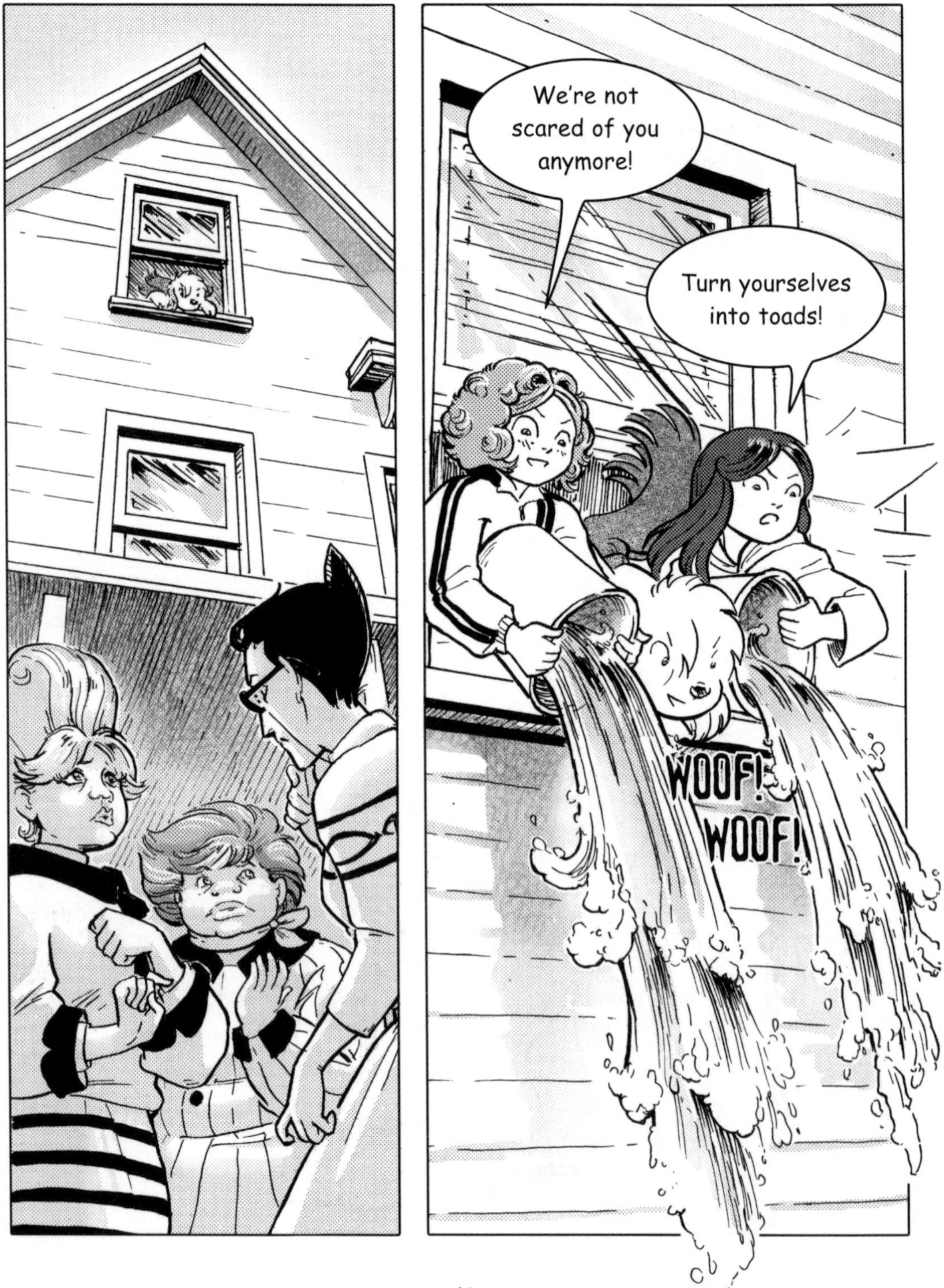

We're not scared of you anymore!
Turn yourselves into toads!
WOOF! WOOF!

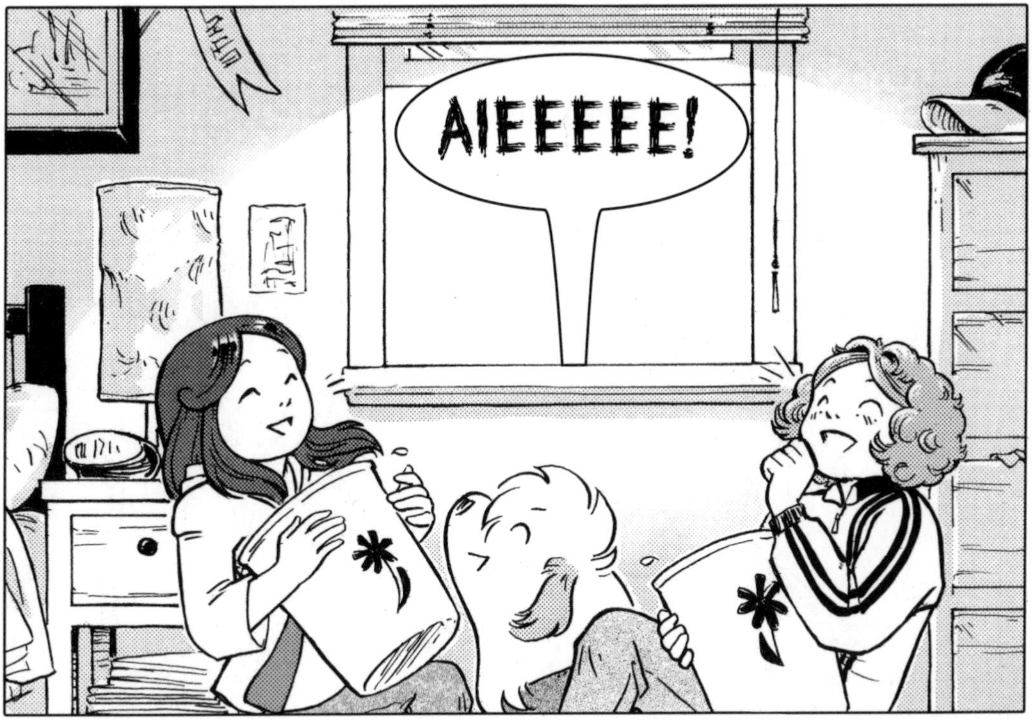
AIEEEEE!

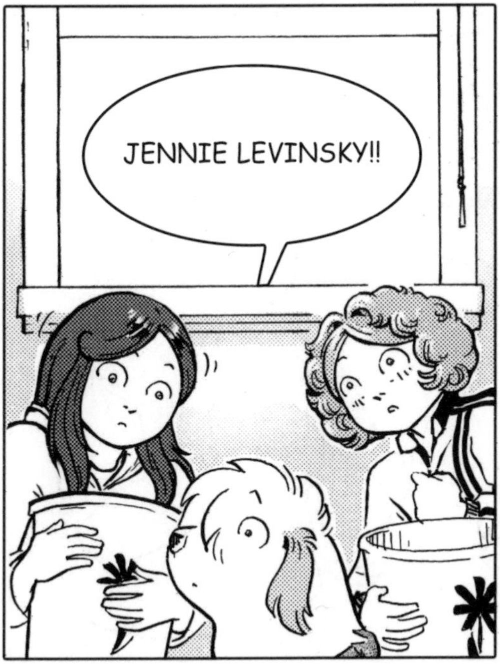
JENNIE LEVINSKY!!

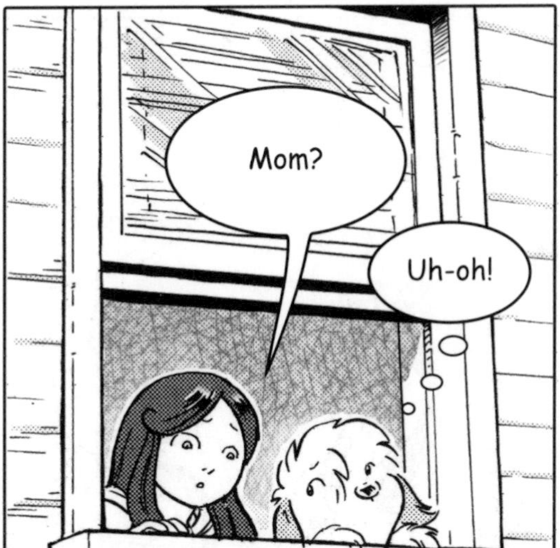
Mom?
Uh-oh!

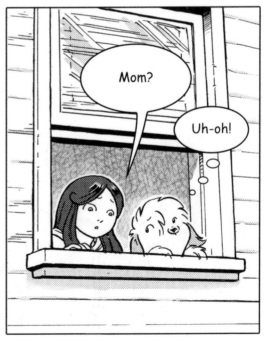

Soon ...

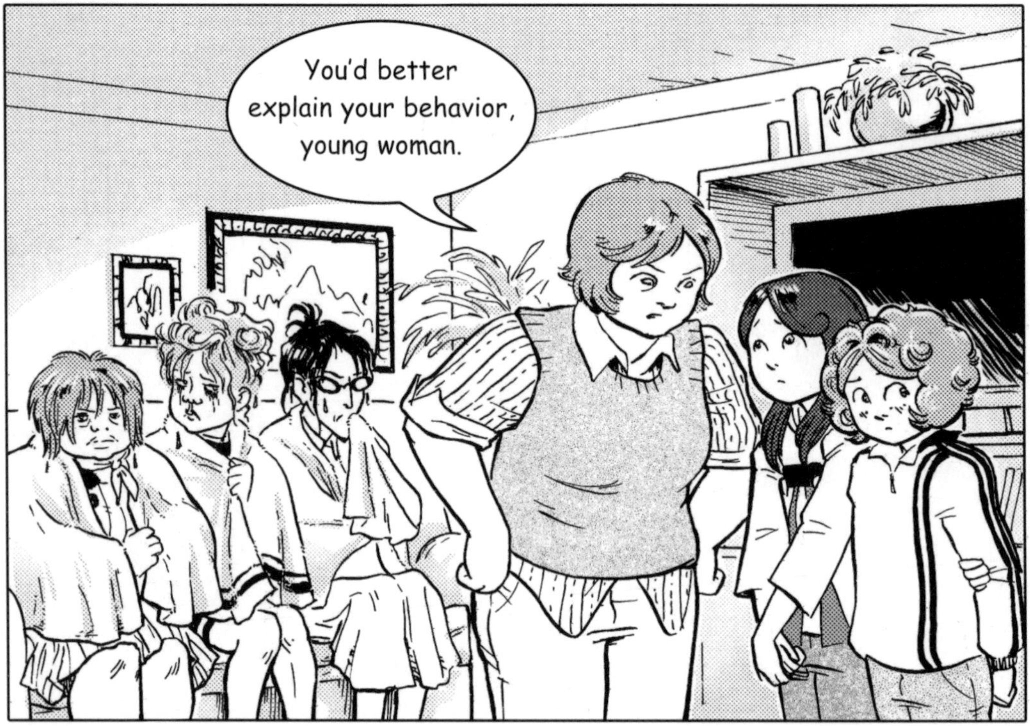
You'd better explain your behavior, young woman.

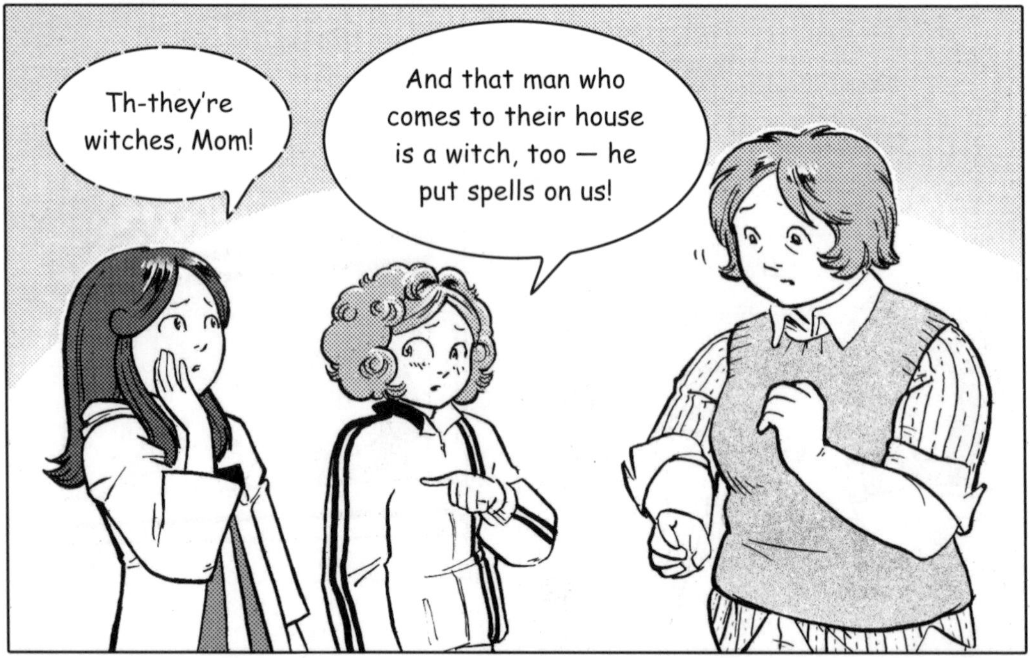
Th-they're witches, Mom!
And that man who comes to their house is a witch, too — he put spells on us!

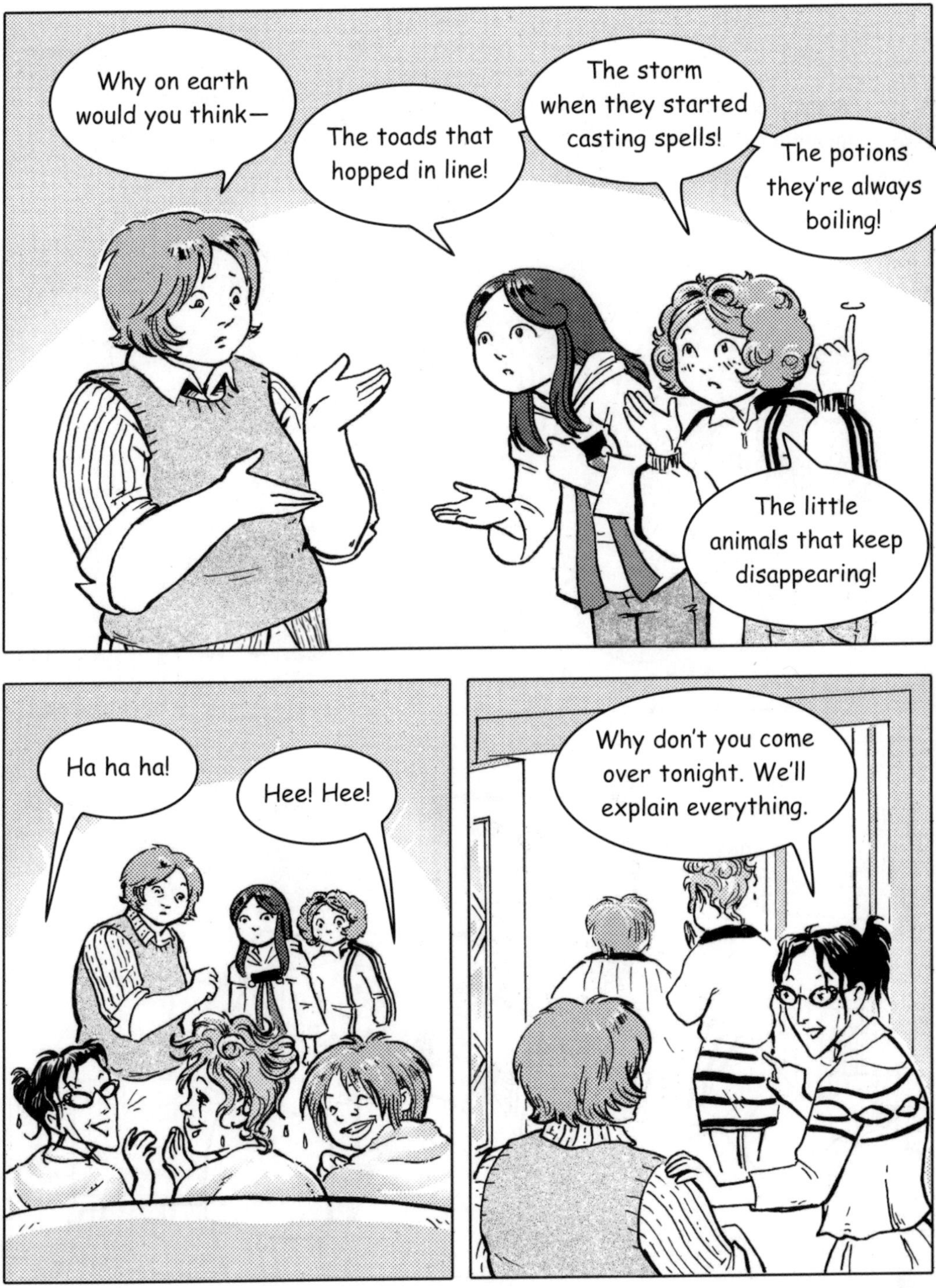
Why on earth would you think—
The toads that hopped in line!
The storm when they started casting spells!
The potions they're always boiling!
The little animals that keep disappearing!
Ha ha ha!
Hee! Hee!
Why don't you come over tonight. We'll explain everything.

That evening ...

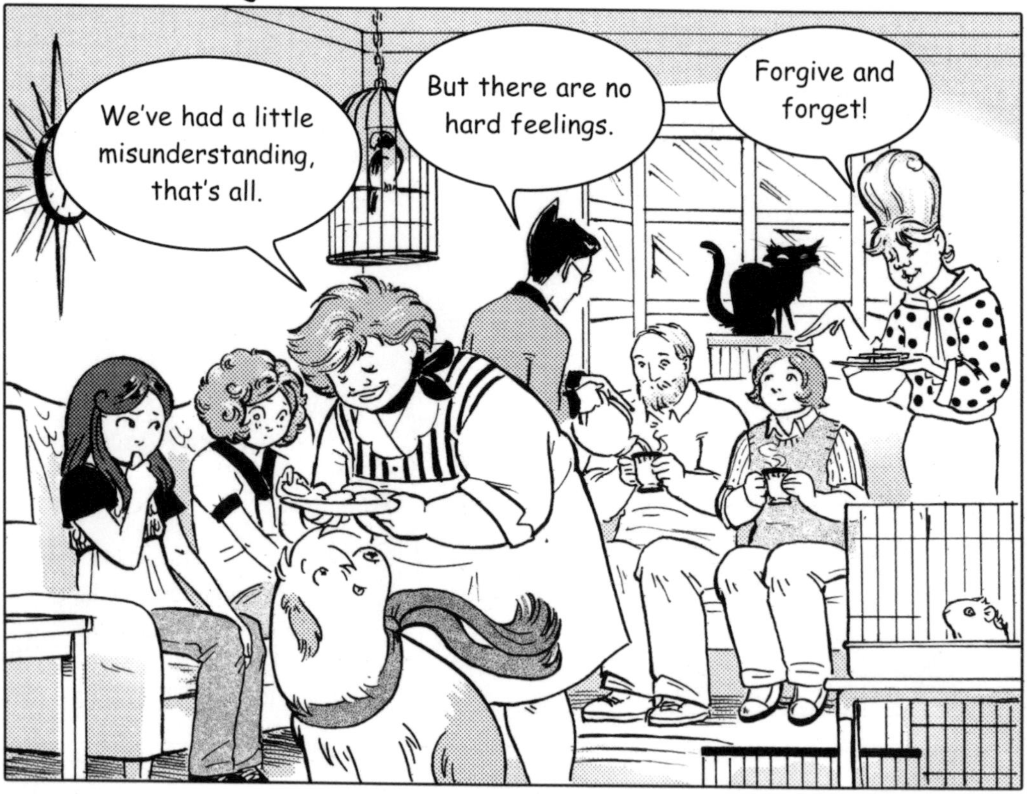
We've had a little misunderstanding, that's all.
But there are no hard feelings.
Forgive and forget!

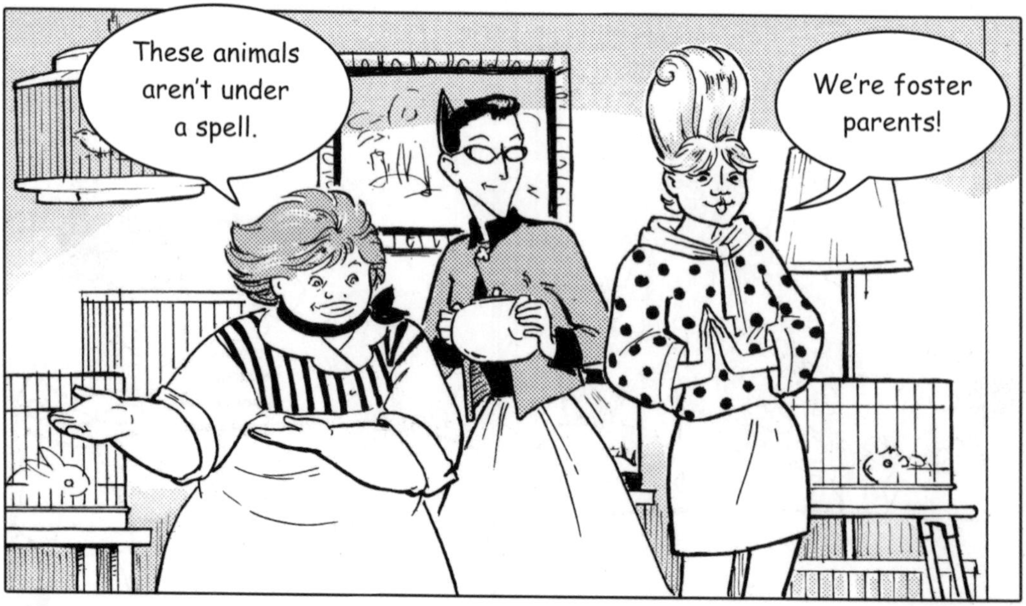
These animals aren't under a spell.
We're foster parents!

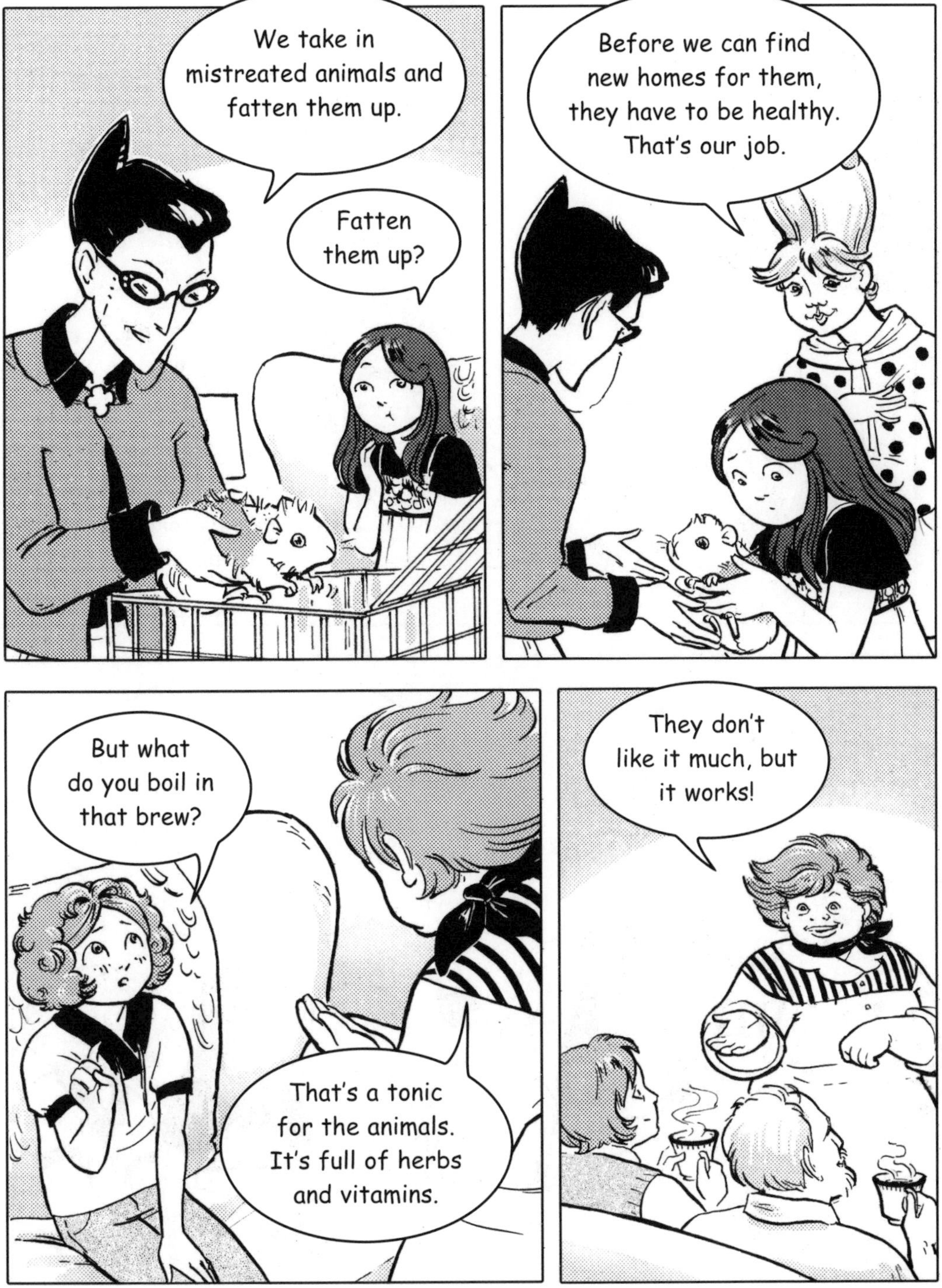

We take in mistreated animals and fatten them up.
Fatten them up?
Before we can find new homes for them, they have to be healthy. That's our job.
But what do you boil in that brew?
That's a tonic for the animals. It's full of herbs and vitamins.
They don't like it much, but it works!

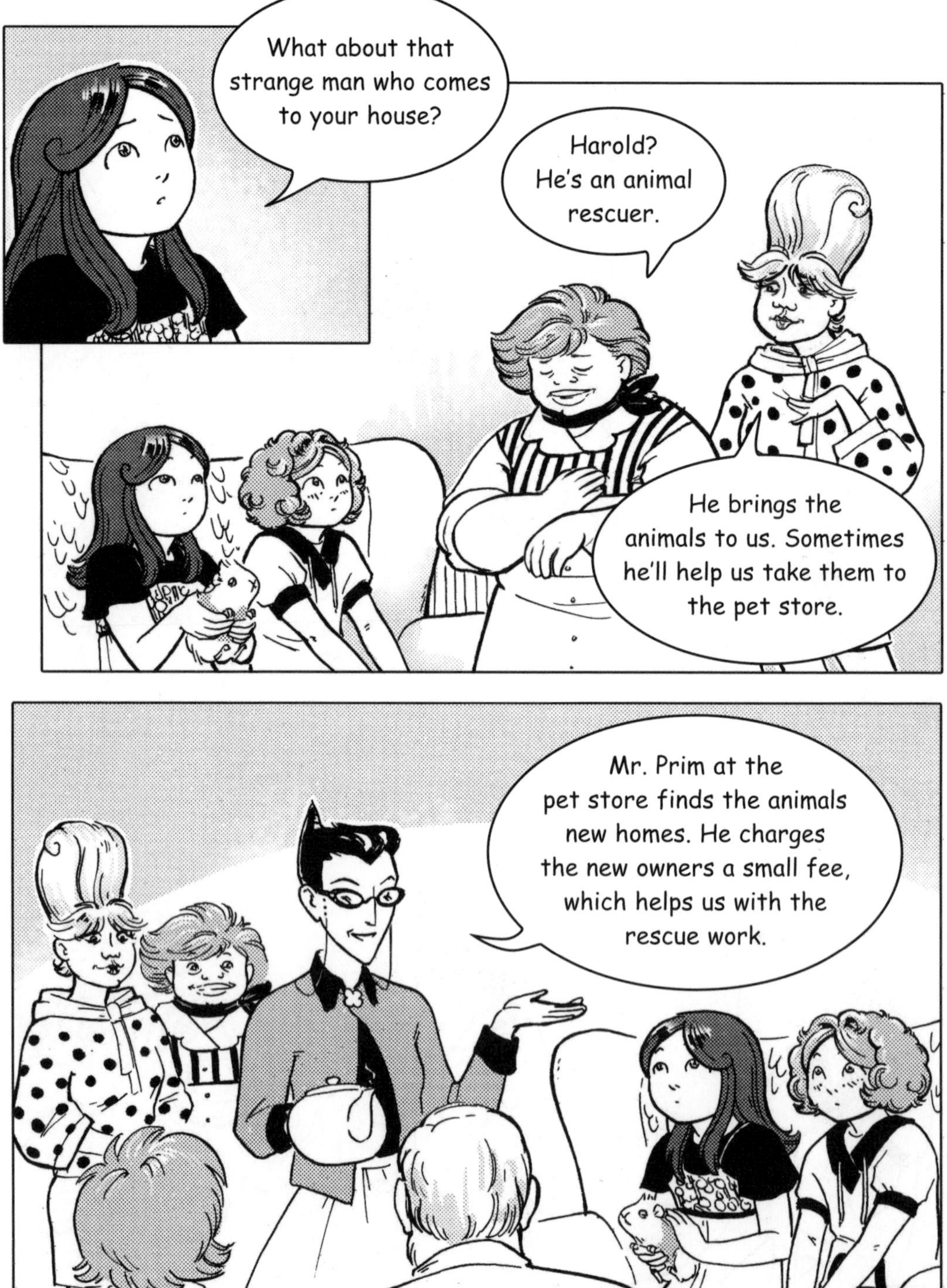
What about that strange man who comes to your house?
Harold? He's an animal rescuer.
He brings the animals to us. Sometimes he'll help us take them to the pet store.
Mr. Prim at the pet store finds the animals new homes. He charges the new owners a small fee, which helps us with the rescue work.

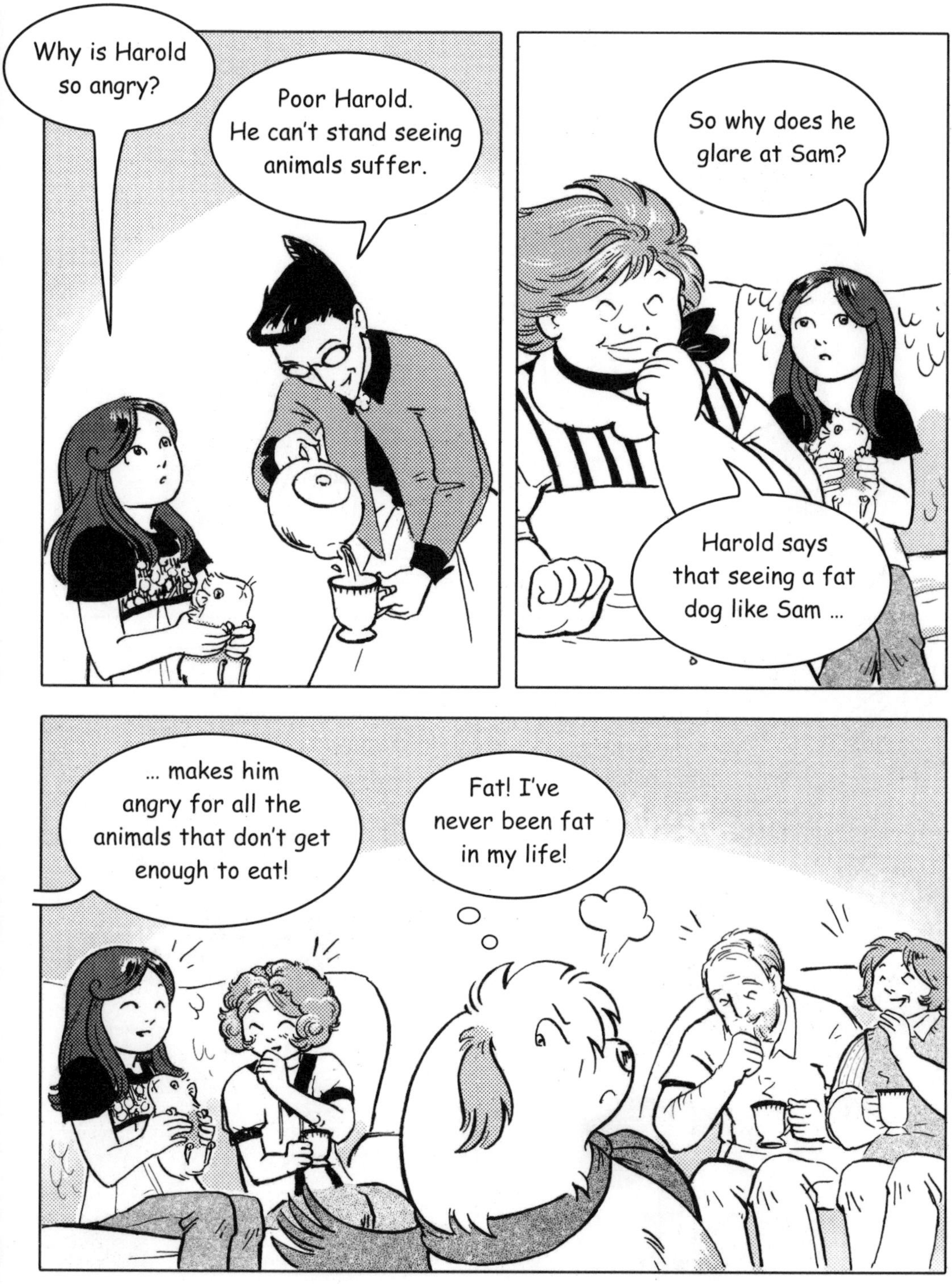
Why is Harold so angry?
Poor Harold. He can't stand seeing animals suffer.
So why does he glare at Sam?
Harold says that seeing a fat dog like Sam ...
... makes him angry for all the animals that don't get enough to eat!
Fat! I've never been fat in my life!

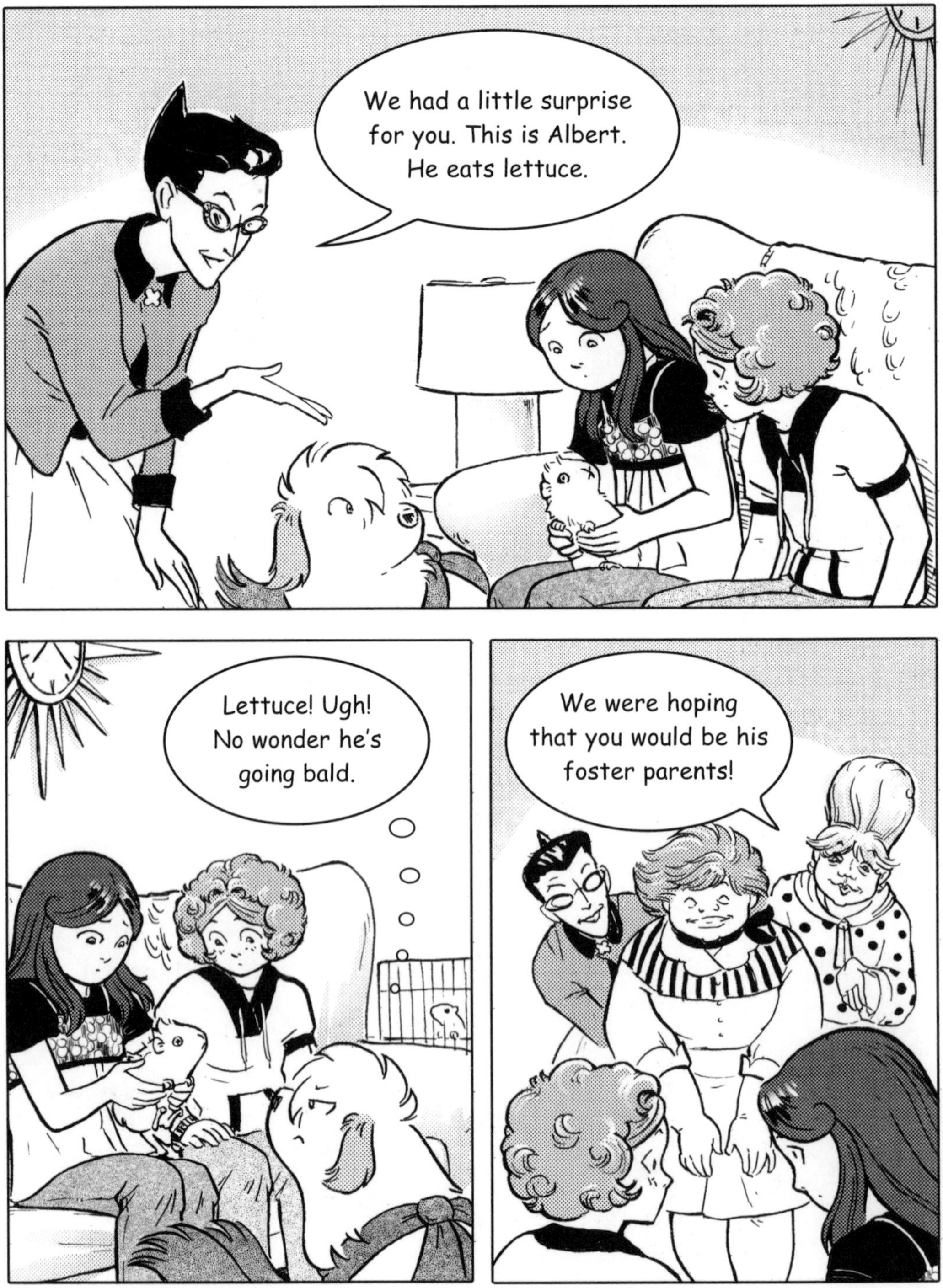
We had a little surprise for you. This is Albert. He eats lettuce.
Lettuce! Ugh! No wonder he's going bald.
We were hoping that you would be his foster parents!

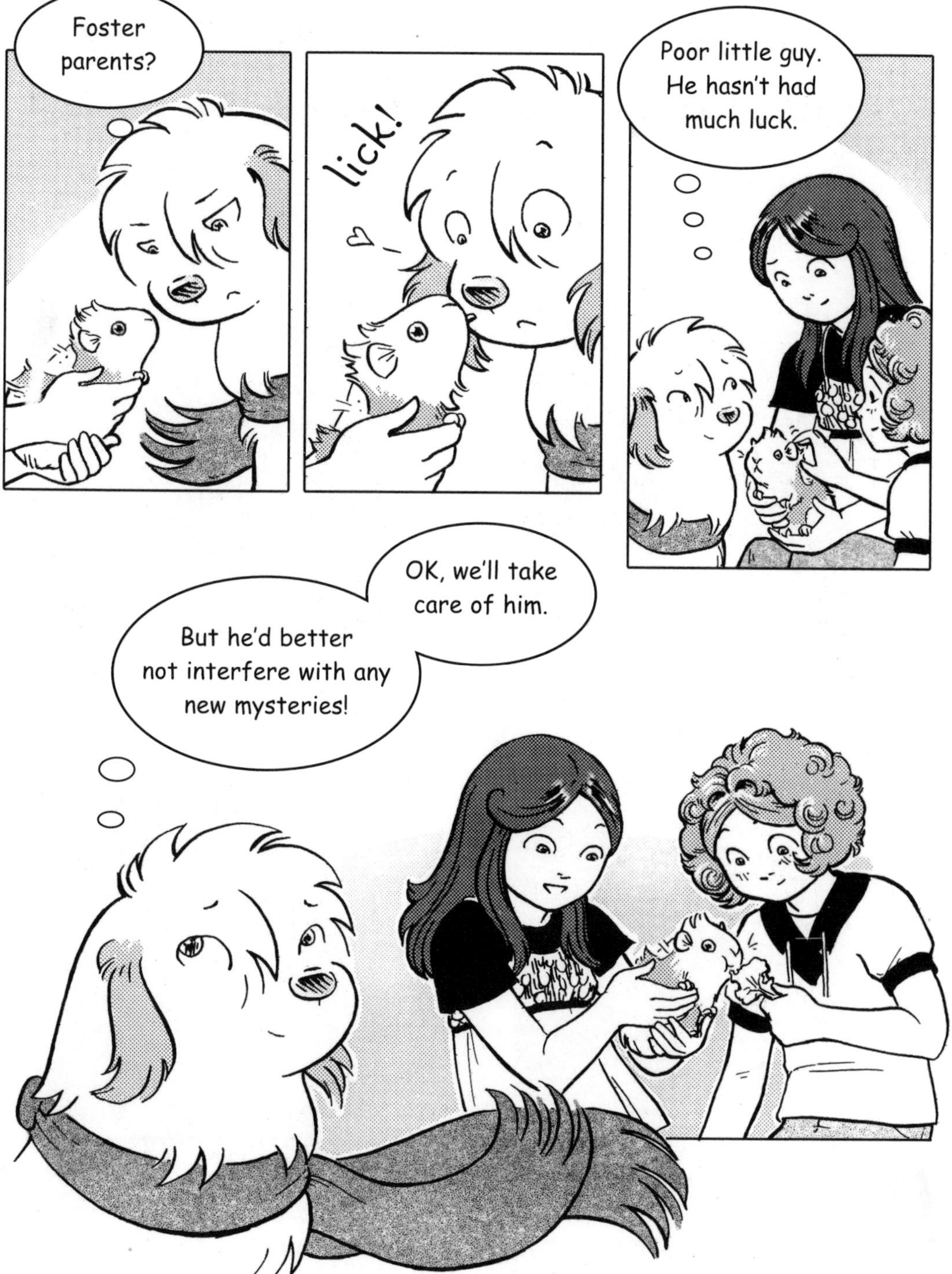
Foster parents?
lick!
Poor little guy. He hasn't had much luck.
OK, we'll take care of him.
But he'd better not interfere with any new mysteries!

The Best Things in Life Are Spooky

Collect all four Sam & Friends Mysteries!

Book One
Dracula Madness
A Sam & Friends Mystery
Mary Labatt • Jo Rioux

Hardcover 978-1-55453-418-0
Paperback 978-1-55337-303-2

Book Two
Lake Monster Mix-Up
A Sam & Friends Mystery
Mary Labatt • Jo Rioux

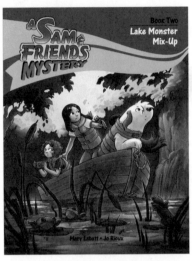

Hardcover 978-1-55337-822-8
Paperback 978-1-55337-302-5

Mummy Mayhem
A Sam & Friends Mystery
Mary Labatt

Hardcover 978-1-55453-470-8
Paperback 978-1-55453-471-5

Witches' Brew
A Sam & Friends Mystery
Mary Labatt • Jo Rioux

Hardcover 978-1-55453-472-2
Paperback 978-1-55453-473-9